The Gold Masters

Norman Russell

ROBERT HALE · LONDON

ISBN-10: 0-7090-8020-4
ISBN-13: 978-0-7090-8020-6

Robert Hale Limited
Clerkenwell House
Clerkenwell Green
London EC1R 0HT

2 4 6 8 10 9 7 5 3 1

Typeset in 11/15pt Sabon
by Derek Doyle & Associates, Shaw Heath.
Printed in Great Britain by St Edmundsbury Press,
Bury St Edmunds, Suffolk.
Bound by Woolnough Bookbinding Ltd.

Contents

1

After the Exhumations

Detective Inspector Arnold Box, walking with a young constable along the cobbled length of Aberdeen Lane, caught sight of his own reflection in the mirrored door of The Grapes public house, and winced. It wasn't right for a Scotland Yard officer to look so jaded and disreputable. His tightly buttoned fawn overcoat was smart enough, and his brown bowler was tilted fashionably forward over his forehead, but his shirt collar was grimy, and his cheeks showed unmistakable signs of needing a shave.

He and young PC Lane had been on duty from midnight, when the oil flares had been lit in the backyard of 14 Back Peter Street, Soho, and the navvies had begun to hack up the brick surface in front of the outside privy. What followed had been very trying, to say the least.

They passed the police stables, where one or two of the ostlers looked up from their work to greet them. As they rounded the corner into King James's Rents, a neighbouring clock struck half past seven.

Arnold Box looked at his silent companion with concern. When the last of the bodies had come to light, a three-foot-long bundle wrapped in sacking and secured with rotting clothesline, PC Lane had swayed on his feet, and blundered out into the dark alley behind the squalid house. There had been four bodies in all, but only the last of them, dragged from the dark pit excavated beneath the yard, had affected the young man so badly. How old was he? Twenty-two, twenty-three. Not old, by any means, but old enough to have seen some of the shocking sights that formed part of a policeman's lot.

The cobbled expanse of King James's Rents lay quiet and deserted in the early morning July sun. On the far side of the square lay the entrance to Whitehall Place, where the old buildings of Scotland Yard were still occupied, though the main body of the force had moved, two years earlier, to Norman Shaw's magnificent new headquarters on the Embankment – New Scotland Yard, as they called it.

Young PC Lane belonged over there, in Whitehall Place, because he was an officer in 'A' Division. Normally in uniform, he had been borrowed from 'A' at short notice for Box's plain-clothes detail, as they'd been short handed yesterday at the Rents.

Lane had told him that he had been attached for the last three years to the special detail raised to guard bank premises whenever bullion was to be moved. He had not been accustomed to the kind of vileness that they had unearthed that night just past in Back Peter Street.

There was something wrong with Lane, and Box wanted to know what that 'something' was. He looked up at the soot-stained irregular pile of buildings that constituted Number 4 King James's Rents, then turned to the young constable.

'You'd better come into the Rents for a bite of breakfast, Constable Lane,' he said. 'You can finish writing your report in my office, and then get back across the cobbles to Inspector French.' He quickly mounted the worn steps that would take the two men into the gloomy warren of offices and passageways known as the Rents.

*

Inspector Box sat in his favourite chair at the cluttered table in his office, a long, dismal room reached through swing doors from the vestibule, and watched PC Lane as he finished his report on the exhumations in Soho. He was left-handed, and the quill pen squeaked in protest as it scratched its way across the official buff form. He'd asked Box the date, which he should have known, and Box had told him: Monday, 10 July.

Lane had a round face, that would have looked cheerful if it wasn't for the droopy straggling moustache that he favoured. Box's own adornment was of the clipped variety, eminently suitable for a man of thirty-five with a growing reputation as one of the Yard's cleverest young inspectors.

PC Lane was nearly six feet tall, and strongly made into the bargain. But height, Box thought, wasn't everything. Box wouldn't have called himself small. Average stature, that was the expression. Of medium height, with fair, well-brushed hair and dark eyes. Not everyone in this world could be a giant.

The swing doors opened, and an elderly man in shirt sleeves and waistcoat edged into the office, carrying a tray containing tea things, and a plate of bacon sandwiches.

'There you are, Mr Box,' he said, as the inspector hastily made a space among the books and papers, 'that bacon's hot from the frying-pan, so eat up them sandwiches straight away. I've put a can of boiling-hot water for you in the ablutions, together with a bit of soap and a cut-throat. Don't leave it to go cold! Will that be all, Mr Box? I'm off at eight.'

'That's all, Charlie, and thanks very much for this breakfast. You're a shining ornament, if I may say so.'

The man called Charlie chuckled as he turned away towards the door. Mr Box came out with some funny expressions.

'And you likewise, sir,' he said. 'Don't let that water go cold. If you do, you'll have to go upstairs all cut and bleeding when Superintendent Mackharness calls down for you.'

'Mr Mackharness is away in Birmingham today, Charlie,' Box

replied. 'So I'll not be disturbed this morning. Not by him, anyway. But thanks for the hot water.'

When Charlie left the room, Box bit into his thick bacon sandwich, balanced what was left of it delicately over the edge of the table, and poured out two cups of strong tea from a brown enamel teapot. PC Lane pushed aside his completed report, and immediately attacked his breakfast with gusto. For some minutes the only sounds in the room were those of two hungry men breaking the fast of what had been a terrible night. Box glanced at the long railway clock on the wall beside the fireplace. Ten past eight.

'So what's the matter, PC Lane?' he asked, wiping his fingers delicately on a piece of ink-stained rag. 'What was it that made you stagger a bit back there in Soho? It wasn't just the exhumations, was it?'

PC Lane licked his fingers, and wiped them absent-mindedly on his coat. He gulped down a mouthful of tea, and sat back in his chair.

'No, sir, it wasn't the exhumations as such. It was the last bundle that did for me. It was a little girl. . . .'

The constable's voice faltered, and he brushed away a tear with his coat sleeve.

'Emily Elizabeth Foy, aged two and a half,' said Box, glancing at a paper in front of him on the table.

'Yes, that's right. Well, just over two weeks ago the wife and I lost a little girl of that age. Two and a half. She could walk when she was twelve months old, but was slow to speak. She'd just started to say a few words when she died. Diphtheria. She was a funny little thing. Catherine, her name was. Catherine Mary Lane. Catherine because we liked the name, and Mary after her mother.'

The two men sat in silence for a while, listening to the settling of coal in the small fire burning in the grate, and the hissing of the rackety gas mantle suspended from the grimy ceiling. Whatever the season, it was chilly and dark in Box's office. Box thought: What can you say when a man tells you tragic things of that nature? Best just to listen, and say nothing. He took a cigar case from his pocket, opened it, and offered it to PC Lane.

'For me, sir? Thanks. Thanks very much. So that's why I was a bit upset back there last night, Mr Box. That bundle made me think of little Catherine Mary, struggling for life in her little cot.'

Box lit a thin cheroot, and passed his box of wax vestas across the table.

'Where do you live, Constable Lane?'

'Batt's Lane, sir, just off Bevis Marks. Do you know it?'

'Yes, I do. It's almost across from the Baltic Exchange. How's your wife bearing up to it?'

'Well, sir, we've three other children, two boys and a girl, so she's got her work cut out. But it's cruel hard for her. She started to visit a medium – a spiritualist. I don't hold with it myself, and not just for religious reasons, as you'll appreciate, sir. There's a lot of fraud and deception going on in that particular world.'

PC Lane suddenly smiled, and his morose face lit up, revealing the man that he would have liked to be. He drew on his cigar, blowing perfect smoke rings up to the ceiling.

'The woman Mary goes to see is called Mrs Pennymint. Would you credit it, sir? I've been to hear her, and it was just a lot of silly rot. I told Mary that I'd not stop her going, but that I wouldn't go there myself any more.'

Inspector Box wrote the name 'Pennymint' on the cover of an exercise book. The constable's eyes seemed to hold an expression of unassuaged desire for certainty.

'Did any money pass, Constable?'

'Oh, no, sir. But then, they'd have known that I was a policeman. There was a collecting plate, though, on a table near the door. That's legal enough. It wasn't a private house. It was a kind of whitewashed meeting-hall with a platform, and gas laid on. It's called the Temple of Light, and it's in a little back crack off Leyland Street in Spitalfields.'

'Quite a drag from where you live, then. Do you *want* to go again? You looked quite wistful when you said you'd never darken its doorstep again!'

'Well, Mr Box, to be honest, I *would* like to give this Mrs Pennymint another chance. There may be something. . . . Two and a half, that's all my little girl was. She's in Putney Vale Cemetery.'

Arnold Box stood up. It was nearly half past eight, time to send PC Lane back across the cobbles to 'A' Division. He'd just have time to shave before Jack Knollys, his sergeant, came in from Syria Wharf.

'Well, Constable,' he said, 'if you really want to go back to that place, I'll go with you. You needn't tell your wife. We'll make it a kind of unofficial visit. Just let me know when you want to go, and I'll make myself available.'

PC Lane brushed a few crumbs from his overcoat, and picked up his hat from the table.

'You've been very decent to me, sir, what with breakfast and all, and I'll take you up on that offer, if I may. Good morning, sir.'

PC Lane drew himself briefly to attention, and hurried through the swing doors of Box's office.

Box rummaged round in the desk drawer until he found a spare white starched collar. Holding it in his hand, he left his office through the swing doors, turned abruptly right, and clattered along a bare-boarded passage that took him out into the enclosed yard at the back of the Rents. It was a roughly triangular area, wedged between tall black buildings. Superintendent Mackharness, a veteran of the Crimean War, liked to call it the exercise yard.

Box entered the ablutions, little more than a chilly stone passageway half open to the sky, and found his can of water still usefully lukewarm. A cut-throat razor and a piece of yellow soap lay ready on a square of towelling. He poured water into the brownstone sink, and began to shave himself, squinting into the fragment of mirror propped up on the ledge above the sink.

Poor young PC Lane. . . . To lose his little girl was bad enough, but having to witness the exhumation of a murdered infant must have been the last straw. Yes, he'd go with him to visit this Mrs Pennymint. Women like that were vampires, preying on people's grief. They could be had up under the Vagrancy Act.

As for the Back Peter Street murder, it was now a closed case. Joseph Foy, costermonger, aged thirty-two, and his wife Thora, thirty, had been taken up on suspicion, following an information laid against them with the magistrates at Bow Street by a suspicious neighbour. Joseph Foy, terrified by a ranting preacher doing the rounds of the Bridewell, had suddenly confessed all.

Foy and his wife had smothered their three children, aged two and a half, four, and six, and for good measure had strangled their wretched maid, Ada Mason, aged fourteen, on the principle that dead maids told no tales. All the victims had been made up into neat parcels, and buried in quicklime beneath the backyard privy. It was rumoured that Ada Mason was another of Joseph Foy's children, conceived out of wedlock. The lives of each of the four victims had been insured for five pounds. Joseph Foy and Thora Foy would both hang.

Box swilled the razor under the hissing brass cold-water tap that hung over the sink, then released the plunger, sending his shaving water gurgling down the waste pipe into the grated gully in the yard. He patted his face delicately on his handkerchief, then spent a grim minute or so fixing his newly starched collar to the front and back studs of his shirt. Smartness was a necessity for a man who was often in the public eye. A final look in the mirror? Why not? No one could say that he was a dandy.

Medici House, the town mansion of the international financier Sir Hamo Strange, stood in Blomfield Place, a secluded enclave of ancient houses sandwiched between Lothbury and King's Arms Yard. It had survived the Great Fire of London, and rose in all its Renaissance splendour behind high brick walls enclosing a small but attractive garden. Here, on the morning of 10 July, 1893, while Inspector Box and PC Lane were eating their bacon sandwiches, the great financier was preparing for his journey into the City.

Sir Hamo Strange was a man so thin that his many enemies – and some of his friends – called him 'the articulated skeleton', and assumed that he must live in constant ill health. But as soon as Strange spoke, his listeners heard how his voice sprang with unexpected power and resonance from his attenuated body. One expected his lungs to be sere and dry, so that his ringing tones always came as a shock.

Certainly, Sir Hamo Strange appeared fragile, but beneath the apparently delicate exterior, there beat a heart of steel and an adamantine will, the heart and will of a man ruthless in the pursuit of wealth, and of what wealth could bring. Hamo Strange knew well enough that he was numbered among the great ones of the world, as the world measured greatness, and that his wants would be satisfied without question.

From his study on the first floor of Medici House, Sir Hamo could see the towering edifice of the Bank of England's rear elevation on Lothbury. It was to the Bank that he had been summoned by a special messenger, who had presented himself at Medici House late on Saturday evening.

It was just after eight o'clock, and Sir Hamo, having taken an early breakfast, was sitting at the desk in his book-lined study. He was dressed very formally, in clothes so cunningly tailored that his skeletal thinness was all but obscured. His pale face, its skin like ancient parchment, was unlined, and his great luminous eyes shone bright from their dark pigmented rings.

'Is all ready, Curteis?'

A handsome man in his early forties, who looked as distinguished as his famous master, Curteis had long ago attuned his ears to the demands lying behind his employer's powerful and domineering voice. Strange, he knew, expected an affirmative answer to that particular question. Any prevarication would have led to an unthinkably unpleasant scene. The secretary's voice was deferential but firm, and a glance at the man would reveal that he, like his master, had hidden strength and power held deliberately in reserve.

'Everything is in order, Sir Hamo. Your provisional list of consortium members is in your leather document case, together with your estimates of their possible contributions. I venture to suggest, sir, that the Governor will be startled to see that you've read his mind!'

Sir Hamo laughed, and his confidential secretary recalled that his master was never averse to a well-turned compliment.

'I expect you're right about that, Curteis,' Sir Hamo said. 'But that's the rule in this kind of business: be at least two steps ahead of the others. That's why I went to Stockholm immediately after my visit to Austria. I beat the Governor of the Bank of England – and his Chief Cashier – at his own game.'

'Another brilliant coup.'

'Yes, I suppose so. But it's small beer, you know, Curteis, compared to – well, compared to other business in hand. Business to do with the Foreign Office and the India Office. You know what I mean.'

'Ah, that, sir! Yes. There could be a peerage for you in that business, if all goes well.'

Sir Hamo smiled, and in that smile there was a warning to Curteis to say no more. Curteis was the only man whom Sir Hamo trusted. He was a man content to hear half-truths, and accept them as gospel, as in the impending business with the Foreign Office. But Strange had permitted him to know every detail of his labours over the Swedish Loan.

'Talking of Austria, sir,' Curteis continued, astutely changing the subject, 'have you had time to examine your purchase? The ancient book you bought from Herr Sudermann? I should imagine that it will be most interesting.'

'I've glanced at it, Curteis, no more than that. By any criterion it's a beautiful work. Magnificently produced, you know, and in six volumes, but with a special secret of its own that makes this particular set unique. It's through there, in the sanctum, reposing in the safe. But there, the City awaits my coming. Tell Johnson that I'm ready to be dressed for the street. See that the brougham is brought round to the side gate.'

When Curteis had gone, Sir Hamo sat in thought for a while, thinking of his recent visit to Austria. There, in the remote hill town of Regenstein, nestling in the dense forests of the Duchy of Styria, he had fulfilled an appointment with Herr Aaron Sudermann, the renowned dealer in antiquities. A ponderous, stooping man with shrewd grey eyes, Sudermann was an acknowledged genius at procuring the unprocurable for collectors of every kind. Sudermann was as much a genius in his line as Sir Hamo was in the world of international money-dealing, and he had employed that genius to secure for Strange one of the rarest books in the world: the unique 1519 edition of the Complutensian Polyglot Bible. It had stood discreetly parcelled in green baize on Sudermann's dining-room table, six quarto volumes bound in ancient embossed calf.

Sudermann had prised this unique set of volumes from the hands of the reclusive Spanish nobleman, Count Fuentes de la Frontera. On his own admission, he had almost been too late. A learned Scotsman, an emissary from Strange's hated rival Lord Jocelyn Peto, second son of the Marquess of Millchester had arrived on the same morning. Sudermann had won the day, and Count Fuentes had accepted £5000 in sovereigns. Without demur, Sir Hamo had reimbursed him by means of a personal cheque drawn on Hoare & Company of London.

'The carriage is at the door, sir.'

'What? Thank you, Curteis. I will be down directly.'

The Polyglot Bible. . . . He had arranged for a young scholar from Cambridge to come up to Town and verify the provenance and authenticity of the work. Perhaps he should invite Lord Jocelyn Peto to view it? That would be an amusing revenge for Peto's attempt to thwart him in Spain. Peto's collection of old books and antiquities was of considerable worth, but he was not going to have the satisfaction of crowning its fame with the 1519 Bible.

Sir Hamo recalled himself to the present, and hurried down to the side entrance, where Johnson, his valet, was waiting to attire him for the short journey to the Bank of England.

'It's very good of you, Sir Hamo, to come down here to Threadneedle Street this morning. I know that you have many calls upon your time.'

The Governor of the Bank of England looked at Sir Hamo Strange, and thought: even a light breeze could blow him away. It's a wonder his bones don't creak as he walks. And yet, this man can sway the destinies of millions. . . .

'Not at all, Governor. As you know, I am always at your disposal.'

Despite his international reputation as 'the moneylender to kings and princes', Sir Hamo Strange always felt a special glow of satisfaction when summoned to Sir John Soan's imposing Roman-Corinthian edifice from which, to a great extent, all the commercial affairs of England were regulated. It comprised a vast complex of over 200 offices, covering, so he'd been told, an area of 124,000 square feet.

The Bank was staffed by over a thousand gentlemen clerks, and it was a bevy of these frock-coated denizens who had conducted Sir Hamo to the board room, where the Governor, Deputy-Governor, the Chief Cashier, and all twenty-four directors, had assembled to greet him.

'The crux of the matter, Sir Hamo,' the Governor was saying, 'is this. The Swedish Government, or rather their finance minister, has an urgent need this year to strengthen the holdings of the Royal Scandinavian Bank, consequent on the fall in value of the krona, and, of course, because of the loan that they were obliged under treaty to grant in January to the Polish Land Federation.'

Sir Hamo permitted himself a thin smile. They were telling him things he already knew.

'So the Royal Scandinavian Bank's vaults are empty, are they? How much do they want, Governor?'

'They want four million pounds in gold. If we won't give it to them, they'll ask the Bank of France—'

'No, no! That will never do, as you well know. The Government would look very sourly on any attempt to sit back and let the French forge an alliance of obligation with any of the Nordic countries. If you did that, Germany would want to know why. They'd interpret it as a signal to France and Denmark that they could do as they wished over the matter of Schleswig-Holstein – come, gentlemen, you know all this without my having to lecture you. So why have you sent for me?'

The powerful, almost hectoring voice carried to every corner of the palatial chamber. The directors were all attention. It did not do to miss a single word of the sere and paper-thin financier sitting in front of them.

The Governor sighed. What was the point of playing the fool with this man?

'We are, of course, talking about the immediate transfer of bullion, Sir Hamo,' he said. 'There's no question of promissory notes and Treasury mandates here. And if not bullion, then gold coins. Four million pounds. Now, we – the Bank of England – don't want to part with that much gold. Not this year. So we've asked you to help us out of our difficulty. Can you establish a consortium of private bankers who are still licensed to keep stores of bullion? Or who can lay their hands on gold from other sources? You obliged us before, you'll remember, in 1886, and again in 1890, at the time of the Baring Crisis.'

Sir Hamo Strange chuckled, and undid the straps of his document case.

'By pure coincidence, gentlemen,' he said, 'I was in Stockholm this last week. Indeed, I only returned to London this Saturday gone. While in Sweden I met – purely by chance – the deputy finance minister, Count Olafsson. He hinted that something like this was in the wind, so I came prepared today. Gentlemen, I have already pencilled in on this sheet of paper the potential members of such a consortium. I can undertake to guarantee their co-operation.'

'We are much obliged to you, Sir Hamo—'

'Four million in gold is a lot of money at short notice, but I will myself put in one million, currently lodged in my vaults at Carmelite Pavement – no, don't thank me; it's a matter of duty as well as a source of ultimate profit when the loan falls in! I have suggested another five names, all of whom will be familiar to you. I will approach each of them personally and ask for six hundred thousand. N.M. Rothschild is one, of course, and so is Abraham Goldsmith – I know for certain that those two will oblige.'

There was a sage nodding of heads and murmurs of approbation from the assembled directors.

'And finally, I would suggest three very thriving concerns which I need only to ask: Brown's of Lothbury, Thomas Weinstock & Sons, and Peto's Bank. Their contributions would be in uncirculated sovereigns, which they hold as guarantee against their paper. Give me your sanction, gentlemen, and you shall have your four million pounds in gold before the week is out!'

There was a further low sound of approval from the assembled directors. Really, thought the Governor, this man Strange is truly a giant of commerce. What brilliant foresight he had shown in anticipating their needs, and what generosity in immediately supplying them! But then, he, and the likes of Lord Jocelyn Peto, had daily access to vast quantities of gold – it was the familiar stuff of their daily commerce. Men like Deloitte, the accountant, or for that matter the Bank of England's own Chief Cashier, handled unimaginable sums of money daily; but they were sums imagined on paper, and manipulated with the aid of all the abstract skills of accountancy. But Sir Hamo Strange and his like dealt in real gold coin and real gold bullion: they were the Gold Masters. . . .

'I'm sure I speak for the Deputy Governor as well as for myself,' said the Governor, 'when I offer you my sincere thanks for your agreeing so readily to our request for help. We will not need to move the gold physically until the twenty-eighth of this month, which will give you ample time to convene the members of your consortium, and for us to put in place the necessary security measures.'

'It is my pleasure, as always, Governor,' said Sir Hamo Strange, 'to be of service to the Bank of England. I will put the process in train immediately, by walking down to St Swithin's Lane and calling on the Rothschilds at New Court.'

'Sergeant Knollys,' said Inspector Box, 'are you listening to me? Or is your great mind preoccupied with higher things?'

He looked with amusement at the yellow-haired giant of a man sitting opposite him across the office table. It was less than a year ago that the two of them had met in dramatic and desperate circumstances in a jeweller's shop down near the river in Garlickhythe. Since then, they had worked together on many cases, some of them of national importance. Box had originally been resentful of Knollys' appointment; now, he couldn't imagine working without him.

'Sir? I was listening intently. You were telling me about the new traffic regulations for Oxford Street — or did you say Regent Street? They intend to redirect the flow along, er, whatever street it was you said, from north to south, was it? No, east to west. . . .'

Jack Knollys' voice trailed away in awkward embarrassment. The livid scar snaking its way across his face showed white behind his blush.

'Well, sir,' he said, 'I'll have to admit that my mind *was* elsewhere. I was thinking about something I heard about you from a sergeant in "A". He and I were having a glass of light ale in The Grapes. . . .'

Sergeant Knollys gave vent to what he imagined was a delicate cough. Box jumped in alarm.

'Sir,' said Knollys, 'is it true what this chap said, that you've become a convert to spiritualism? Table-rapping and all that?'

'Who *is* this informant of yours?' asked Box, in mock indignation. 'You mustn't believe everything you're told, Sergeant. It'll get you into trouble, if you do.'

'He said that you're going to attend a seance with their PC Lane. It doesn't seem like you, somehow, sir, if I may say so.'

'You may, Sergeant. It certainly isn't my normal leisure activity. So let me tell you all about it.'

Sergeant Knollys sat in silence while Box told him about PC Lane, his bereavement, and his experiences at Back Peter Street in Soho.

'I'm very sorry to hear all that, sir,' said Knollys, when Box had finished his tale. 'So you're going to this seance to help PC Lane come to terms with his loss?'

'I'm going, Sergeant, because I don't like the sound of it at all. It's a plant of some sort, I'm convinced of it, but this Mrs Pennymint will have to get up very early to put one over yours truly. She'll find out, Jack, that Arnold Box wasn't born yesterday.'

2

Seance in Spitalfields

The evening of the 14 July was oppressively warm, a fitting close to a day that had threatened thunder, but had produced not a drop of rain. It was still light when Inspector Box and PC Lane turned out of Leyland Street, Spitalfields, into the narrow alley where the Temple of Light was situated.

Leyland Street had been alive with people lounging aimlessly on the pavements in front of a row of pawnbrokers and slop shops, while barefoot boys larked about on the granite setts of the carriageway. The alley – it seemed not to have a name – was quieter, flanked by the premises of a furniture factory and a whole-sale boot manufacturer, both closed and shuttered.

The Temple of Light stood at the end of the alley. It boasted a small classical porch, and its frontage was adorned with faded white stucco, though the sides of the building revealed the rough brick of which it was constructed. Box decided that at one time it must have been a Dissenting chapel.

A number of decent-looking men and women were mounting the steps of the temple, the door of which had been thrown open. To the left of the steps, behind railings, a placard pasted to a board announced the evening's attractions.

THERE IS NO DEATH!
See and hear the PROOF of IMMORTALITY tonight,
at 7 o'clock.
Resident Psychic: MRS PENNYMINT
Guest Medium: MADAM SYLVESTRIS, Belsize Park.
Retiring collection.
Arthur Portman, Chairman and Secretary

As Box and Lane joined the other enquirers, a single protester, a young woman in Salvation Army uniform, handed them leaflets, upon which was printed, *Brethren, Do Not Consort with Demons*. Most people took a leaflet without comment, though one or two reacted angrily, snatching them from the girl's hand and throwing them down on to the pavement.

By ten to seven, over twenty people had assembled in the temple. As Lane had mentioned, the interior was whitewashed, and flickering gaslights threw long shadows across the walls. The central space was filled with pews, presumably left in the building when its original owners had vacated it. Box and Lane slid unobtrusively into a back pew near the door.

The front of the temple was occupied by a raised platform, backed by heavy red plush curtains. A very well-dressed, rather prim man in his early forties sat at a table, looking appraisingly at the audience. His silk hat and walking-cane rested on the table, giving the impression that he had just dropped in to the temple for a few moments. In answer to a whispered question from Box, a woman sitting in the next pew informed him that this was Mr Portman, the chairman and secretary of the temple's governing committee.

Mr Portman slid a watch from the fob pocket of his evening waistcoat, glanced at it, and then rang a small hand-bell. The audience, who had been talking in low voices, fell silent.

'Welcome, dear brothers and sisters,' said Portman, in a quiet but clear voice that carried to every corner of the temple. 'We are assembled here, as always, to pull aside the veil dividing this dark and fallen world of ours from the Empire of Light, where death is no more, and evening shadows never fall. Tonight's service will commence with a demonstration of clairaudience and clairvoyance by our beloved resident medium, Mrs Pennymint.'

He half-turned as the plush curtains parted to admit a short, plump lady in a red velvet dress adorned with a massive corsage of thornless yellow roses. Her fair hair was pulled back from her forehead, and secured behind by a velvet bow. Mrs Pennymint's face was round, with a tendency to a double chin. Her blue eyes seemed quite guileless, and her face bore little lines of good nature around her mouth.

As the medium crossed the platform to sit down on an ornate upright chair facing the audience, two or three people moved around the temple, turning down the gaslights to a glimmer. Mr Portman lit a single candle on the table, and quietly joined the audience in the front pew.

Mrs Pennymint sat quietly, gently rocking forward and backward, a little smile on her face. Despite himself, Arnold Box felt a little shudder of apprehension. The woman was ridiculously over-dressed, as though she were trying to ape a young woman of twenty when it was obvious that she was well settled into middle age. But something about that steady rocking held Box in the grip of fascination. Nobody made a sound. The gaslights hissed gently along the walls. The hair began to rise at the nape of Box's neck.

Suddenly, there came a terrific report, as though a great weight had been dropped on the wooden floor. The medium did not flinch, and Box saw that her eyes had now closed. An echoing sound, that may have been a voice, seemed to articulate the name 'Benvolio' from somewhere near the back of the platform. The rocking of Mrs Pennymint's body ceased. She spoke, and it was the kind of pleasant, friendly voice that Box had imagined.

'Benvolio is here. . . . He was once an usher at the Court of Henry the Eighth, and he was burned for heresy in the days of

24

Bloody Mary. Benvolio is my spirit guide. He says I was once a princess at a royal court. We pass through many reincarnations on our voyage to enlightenment.'

For Arnold Box the spell had been broken. This woman was spouting the usual tosh that was the stock in trade of such people. Everybody had been a princess, or a courtier, never a simple hewer of wood or drawer of water. He glanced at PC Lane, sitting beside him in the gloom, and saw the look of vexed disappointment and disgust on the young man's face.

'I have a John here,' said Mrs Pennymint. 'Will anyone own a John? He passed over quite recently.'

'I know a John,' said a man in the audience.

'Don't we all,' muttered Box, and PC Lane's face broke into an involuntary smile.

'Well, this John has a message for Betsy. She is to keep smiling, he says. He's going now. . . . Benvolio is showing me a dog, a black and tan, that belonged to someone called Michael. Does anyone know them?'

'I knew a Michael,' volunteered another man, 'and he had a dog that was run over. But it was a golden retriever.'

'That's right,' said Mrs Pennymint cheerfully, 'such a dear doggie. Michael had a message for us all. Spend your life doing good. He tries to help from the Other Side. He's gone. They're called away quickly, you know, when higher service demands.'

'And we'll go quickly, as soon as is decent,' Box whispered, and Lane nodded his agreement.

'And now I have a Toby,' Mrs Pennymint continued, 'still in this life. Benvolio is showing him to me in a cloud, which tells me that he's still living. Toby has a message for his son, Arthur . . . Albert? No, Arnold.'

'Strewth,' cried Arnold Box, and someone nearby bade him 'Hush!'

'Toby wants Arnold to know that his Uncle Cuthbert has just passed over.'

Box sighed with relief. His old Pa, Toby Box, was still recuperating at Esher from the amputation of his leg early in January. It had been a lucky guess by Mrs P., but he, Arnold Box, had no Uncle Cuthbert, of that he was quite certain.

Mrs Pennymint had not waited for an answer, but had gone on to mention other spirits who had swum into her ken, introduced by the indefatigable Tudor courtier, Benvolio. There was a Gerald, a Mary, a Peter, and a few others with conveniently simple names, so that a few more members of the audience responded with delighted recognition of their departed friends and relatives.

Then it was over. Mrs Pennymint's eyes suddenly opened, and she moved stiffly on the chair, as though sensing for the first time how uncomfortable it was. She treated the audience to a friendly, unaffected smile, executed a rather theatrical curtsy, and left the platform to polite, subdued applause.

Mr Portman immediately resumed his place at the table. He was a narrow-faced man, with sparse black whiskers adorning his cheeks and meeting, in rather an old-fashioned way, beneath his chin. Box couldn't quite place him socially. Was he a gentleman – he dressed like one – or a prosperous tradesman? He certainly spoke well.

They were very privileged, Mr Portman was saying, to have the distinguished clairvoyant and physical medium Madam Almena Sylvestris with them that evening. He would remind the assembly that Madam sometime spoke in the direct voice, and that phantasms occasionally materialized, both of which phenomena could be distressing for those new to spiritualism. There was, he assured them, never anything to fear. Trust was essential, trust and faith.

Mr Portman lit a fresh candle on the desk, left the platform and took his seat once more in the front pew. The gaslights ranged along the temple walls remained low. The heavy curtains parted, and Madam Sylvestris appeared.

Here, thought Box, was someone decidedly different from the rotund, mundane Mrs Pennymint. Whereas Mrs Pennymint had appeared natural and homely, the impressive woman who now walked slowly to the seat at the front of the stage was very clearly a lady. She wore a well-cut dove-grey evening dress, adorned on the right shoulder with a diamond clasp. Her dark hair was elegantly cut and shaped in such a way as to leave her handsome face clear. She was, Box judged, in her early forties, but that fact could not have been gleaned from her flawless complexion. When she spoke, her voice was that of a cultured lady.

'Dear friends,' she began, 'I very much hope that I will be able to bring comfort to the bereaved tonight, and at the same time demonstrate to any newcomers among us that our loved ones do indeed live and progress after they have left their envelopes of clay. As you know, I cannot predict what forms the spirit beings will take, but I exhort you all to have no fear.'

Madam Sylvestris folded her hands in her lap, and stared ahead of her across the entranced audience. Box watched her closely, and saw her eyes begin to close. For a single moment they caught his across the intervening space of the hall, and her lids quivered as though she was for the moment alarmed. Then her eyes closed, and her head fell gently on to her chest.

The candle on the table guttered and went out, and a sibilant murmur passed through the audience. At the same time, a shower of bright red sparks hissed and flickered around the medium's head, then vanished. Madam Sylvestris groaned. Nothing happened for over a minute. Someone suppressed a cough. Suddenly, Madam Sylvestris spoke.

'Is there an Alexander present? Alexander P . . . I can't hear the last name. P, or B. Tom is here. Is there an Alexander?'

A young man in one of the middle pews stood up. He was dressed in a dark, work-worn suit, and there was a mourning band on his right arm.

'My name's Alexander,' he said, his voice quavering, 'Alexander Prentice. Tom was my brother. He died in Africa of fever. On the Gold Coast—'

'Well, he's here, now, and wants to tell you that all's well. He felt nothing at the end. He sends his love to Beth—' The medium's voice suddenly dropped to a whisper, and she turned sharply to her left. 'What? Are you sure? Very well.'

Madam Sylvestris groaned more deeply, and covered her face with her hands. The gaslights along the walls seemed to turn themselves lower. They could all hear the medium's stertorous breathing. Presently, a column of smoke-like substance began to build up beside her, partly obscuring her body. It glowed very faintly, and seemed to pulsate in sympathy with the medium's breathing. As they watched, the figure of a young man appeared to step forward from the darkness into the glowing smoke.

'Tom!' The young man called Alexander Prentice sprang forward as though to run on to the platform, but he was stopped when a man's voice called strongly to him from the psychic mist.

'Stay put, will you, Alexander! I wanted you to see me, and now you can. And you can hear me, too, thanks to this lady, who's got the knack of living in two worlds at once! Tell Helen that I still love her, and would have married her, if the fever hadn't taken me away from your world to this one. Tell your friends that—'

Suddenly, both spirit-form and phantom voice were swallowed up in the smoke, which dissipated like an early mist. The lights turned themselves up as if by magic. Madam Sylvestris took a number of deep breaths, and then smiled.

'I do not go into deep trance at these demonstrations, my friends,' she said. 'I simply feel a heightened awareness of the two worlds impinging on each other, and then, quite suddenly, the two worlds are one. Did I bring you any comfort, Mr Prentice?'

'You did, ma'am, you did,' cried the young man with the mourning band. 'Now I know that spiritualism is true, and that there is no death. How can I ever thank you?'

The audience broke out into a spontaneous burst of clapping, and Madam Sylvestris held up a hand to quell it. She looked pleased, and rather amused.

'Wonderful!' said Box. 'A wonderful performance. That's what they call the "direct voice", you know. It's supposed to be the actual voice of the dead person speaking through the medium. In fact, it's a man secreted somewhere with a long, flexible speaking tube. I expect that man Alexander Prentice is an accomplice.'

Madam Sylvestris placed her hands once more in her lap, and her head fell on to her chest. A steady breeze seemed to cross the platform, ruffling the medium's hair. She gasped, and writhed in her chair. The breeze stopped abruptly. The candle on the table spontaneously rekindled, and burned with a steady flame.

A sound came from the medium's mouth, an unpleasant, rasping noise, like the steady pulsation of incoming waves beating upon a shore. Then, from the centre of the noise, a single piping word emerged.

'Dada.'

With an oath PC Lane sprang to his feet, throwing off Box's restraining hand. The baby voice continued to make itself heard over the hideous rasping sound issuing from the woman on the platform.

'Dada. Cathy didn't want to go. You gave me Polly to come with me. A nice lady came for me. Dora. Theo. Dada, when will you and Mammy come?'

'That's my little girl, Catherine Mary!'

PC Lane had struggled out of the pew, and was making his way rapidly to the front of the temple. His face was as white as chalk, and his frantic voice showed that he had thrown off all prudence. One or two men in the audience sprang up, and physically restrained him from climbing on to the platform.

'That's my little girl, I tell you! That's what she called me: Dada. Polly was the name of her little doll. We put it in with her . . . And she's with her great-grandmother, Theodora. She can't say it properly, she's not three yet. Let me talk to her!'

The woman on the platform stared at PC Lane with no apparent sign of recognition. She sagged in her chair, and for a moment it looked as though she would faint. Mrs Pennymint suddenly appeared from behind the rear curtain, and began whispering rapidly in her ear, while gently stroking her forehead. Madam Sylvestris sighed, and sat up straight.

'Thank you, Minnie,' she said, 'I'm all right now. Poor man,' she continued, looking now at PC Lane, 'your outburst closed the door between the two worlds, and left your little girl's question unanswered! I am so sorry for you. Perhaps you would like to come to my home in Belsize Park for a private sitting?'

'A sitting, ma'am?' PC Lane's voice had steadied. There would be no further outburst from him.

'Yes. It's just another word for a seance. I am quite sure that Catherine Mary will come through if you are there, and perhaps you will see her materialize. I'm sorry that the direct voice upset you so. But it is a great wonder, a great miracle, for which we should be thankful. See Mr Portman at the end of the service. He will give you my address. Oh, and there will be no fee. Your assent to the teachings of spiritualism will be all the payment I shall need.'

In a private dining-room of one of the sumptuous gentlemen's clubs in Pall Mall, a convivial luncheon was reaching its conclusion. The dessert plates had been removed, and a very old, fine claret had been produced, its appearance heralding a tattoo from appreciative fingers on the round table. There followed a scraping of matches, and the lighting of cigars.

The host was a fine-looking, hearty man in his mid-fifties, a man with a ready smile and a penchant for sudden bursts of loud laughter. He boasted a fine head of black curls, which made him look younger than his years. He was dressed formally, in clothes that suggested 'banker', but there was a certain jauntiness about him, and about the brilliant red rose in his button-hole, that denoted a man who was something more than a mere toiler in the City.

Lord Jocelyn Peto drew on his cigar, and glanced round the table. His guests were all busy talking to each other, their tongues loosened by the magic of superb food and the choicest wines. That was all to the good, for these gentlemen had been invited to lunch for the purpose of striking bargains with each other. Why do business in a poky office when you could do it in style, in Pall Mall?

Old Forbes there was discussing the details of a loan to young Everett. How the old devil smiled, and how the young rake misread that smile for disinterested kindness! Oh, well, all was fair in business. Tom Weinstock was whispering earnestly to Sir Abraham Goldsmith, who was pretending to listen. Tom wanted Goldsmith to amalgamate their two banks; this was a pleasant way of getting Tom to realize that Goldsmith wasn't interested!

They were all welcome, here, at his club, or out at his home in Croydon. Some of these men had been friends of his from school-days at Eton, others were the comrades of a lifetime in business as principal of Peto's Bank in the Strand.

A slight frown crossed Lord Jocelyn Peto's brow as he thought of the man waiting patiently to see him downstairs in the smoking-room. Damn the fellow, couldn't he have called at the bank, or, failing that, summoned him, Peto, to that rarefied Renaissance palace of his in Blomfield Place? No; he was content to wait, like an errand boy, downstairs, until this jolly lunch was over! A typical mean manoeuvre by Sir Hamo Strange to make him feel guilty and gauche. Well, he could wait until all this claret had been consumed, and the good company dispersed.

As Peto's mind dwelt further on his old business rival, he suddenly smiled, and then laughed out loud. Dear me! Poor old Strange! Not everything was going to fall effortlessly into the lap of the man they called 'moneylender to kings and princes'. Sometimes, the best laid plans of mice, men, and international financiers, went awry. Oh, well, he'd better go downstairs and see what the fellow wanted.

*

'My dear Sir Hamo!' cried Lord Jocelyn. 'How good of you to call on me here at the club! You had only to say the word, and I would have presented myself at Medici House.'

Sir Hamo Strange smiled, and it seemed to Lord Jocelyn that his smile was like a cloud passing over the sun. He had bade his guests conclude their lunch at leisure, and had hurried down to the all but deserted smoking-room.

'It's no trouble, I assure you, Lord Jocelyn,' said Sir Hamo Strange. 'I only called, really, to ask whether you'd send me written confirmation of your willingness to oblige the Bank of England with six hundred thousand sovereigns. The Governor will want paper guarantees, as I know you'll appreciate.'

Lord Jocelyn Peto carefully moistened his lips. It would not do to let this walking skeleton see that his mouth had gone dry.

'Certainly. I'll have my secretary type out a guarantee, and a messenger will take it round to Threadneedle Street later this after-noon. Six hundred thousand . . . For how long, did you say?'

'I didn't. And neither did they — the Bank of England, I mean. But I suppose it'll be the usual six months. These government loans usually run to that.'

Each man watched the other. Neither gave anything away. Old enemies, they had long ago taken each other's measure, and acted accordingly.

'I suppose it hasn't got to be all sovereigns? I mean, I have a hundred thousand in Austrian schillings still crated and between lead foil. That's my only holding in foreign gold. Everything else under the Strand is coin of the realm.'

'Schillings will do very well, I'm sure, Peto. None of your gold is going to be unpacked. It will just lie in the vaults of the Royal Scandinavian Bank until such times as the Swedish Government feel confident enough to return it. Well, you know that without my telling you.'

Sir Hamo Strange picked up his silk hat and cane from the floor as though to take his leave, but then apparently thought better of it. He leaned forward confidentially.

'There's something else I want to tell you, Peto. You and I have been friendly rivals as collectors of rare and unusual things for many years now. Well, I know you'll be pleased to hear that I have just acquired the Ferdinand and Isabella Polyglot Bible. The only one of its kind. Congratulate me, Lord Jocelyn!'

Sir Hamo Strange closed his eyes, savouring the deliciousness of the moment. Peto had been after that book for longer than *he* had. According to Sudermann, he had sent an emissary hotfoot to Count Fuentes, but he'd got there too late. Yes, he'd pipped Peto to the post this time. He opened his eyes. Lord Jocelyn Peto was still smiling.

'My dear Strange, I'm so glad!' he cried. 'We both coveted that book, so I'm happy to know that one of us, at any rate, has secured possession of it. I expect you employed Aaron Sudermann?'

'Yes, yes, I did. I must say, Peto, that I'm pleased at your response. I thought you'd be vexed.'

'Not at all. I sent a man of my own, you know, a man who'd also tracked the Bible to its hiding place in Spain. But there: I was too late. Perhaps you'd let me call some time at Medici House to inspect the volumes? I suppose you'll have them authenticated?'

'Yes, indeed. I've a man coming down from Cambridge to look at them. He's bringing an epigraphist with him. Perhaps I'll arrange a little reception . . . I'll send you an invitation.'

'Thank you. An epigraphist, hey?' Lord Jocelyn laughed, and shook his glossy curls merrily. 'Well, I look forward to seeing your latest treasure. As for the Swedish loan business, I'll send that note round to the Bank this afternoon. Meanwhile, I must say farewell to my guests. Goodbye.'

Sir Hamo Strange sat alone in the smoking-room of Peto's club, wondering what lay behind his rival's assumed careless indifference. For it *must* be assumed. Peto had toiled for years trying to track down that unique edition of the Polyglot Bible. But then, he'd had plenty of time to prepare his response, as his man would have dashed post haste from Spain to tell him of his failure.

That was it. Peto was pretending indifference simply to annoy him. That would be typical. A shallow buffoon of a man, struggling to understand the subtleties of the financial markets from his vantage point on the heights of the aristocracy. His palatial bank in the Strand, his reputedly vast wealth — all had been inherited. He was an amateur in business, and a dilettante in the serious vocation of collecting. Well, over the matter of the Polyglot Bible he'd met his match.

3

Mackharness's Master Plan

'Williams,' said Lord Jocelyn Peto to his coachman when he eventually left his club, 'I shan't go back to the bank this afternoon. I've some private business to transact. Take the carriage back to the Strand coach house.'

Lord Jocelyn watched his carriage until it had disappeared from sight round the corner from Pall Mall into St James's Street, and then hailed a cab.

'Belsize Park, cabbie,' he said. 'Put me down at the corner of Melbourne Avenue and Prince Albert Road.'

He settled back on the musty upholstery, and closed his eyes. It was a long haul from St James's to the prosperous suburb of Belsize Park, but it was decidedly worth the journey. Madam Sylvestris always made him welcome. . . .

What a fascinating woman she was! No one knew much about her history, apart from the fact that she was a young widow — well, youngish — and that her late husband had been a scion of the Romanian Royal Family. That's what *she* claimed, anyway. Not that it mattered a fig. Nor did her claim to be a spiritualist medium. What mattered was that Madam Sylvestris knew how to soothe away the cares of jaded businessmen like himself.

Lord Jocelyn Peto fell into a light doze, from which he was

jerked awake by the cab's lurching as it passed out of York Gate and into Regent's Park. They'd be there, soon. He wondered whether she had appreciated the gleaming new brougham that he had purchased for her, together with a fine black horse to match its sable smartness. She had nagged him for over a month about her need for a small, smart carriage, and her conduct towards him had made it a good bargain as far as he was concerned. Almena Sylvestris was an expensive hobby – very expensive, if the truth be known. One of these days he'd have to talk to her about the need to make economies. But not yet. No, not yet.

Lord Jocelyn left Madam Sylvestris's elegant house in Melbourne Avenue at just after four o'clock. The road was deserted, except for a tall, distinguished man with a waxed beard and moustaches, who was peering through tinted spectacles at the noticeboard of a redbrick Methodist church. He was wearing a rusty-looking frock coat, and wore a silk hat that had seen better days.

Lord Jocelyn walked to the cab rank in Eton Road, climbed sedately into the first cab, and told the driver to take him across the river to London Bridge Station. It was time to go home to Croydon. As soon as the cab had left the rank, the man with the waxed beard, who had been sauntering nonchalantly behind Lord Jocelyn, jumped into the next waiting cab, which moved out into the road, and kept close to the noble banker until he arrived at London Bridge.

At London Bridge Station, Lord Jocelyn, who was a director of the Brighton and South Coast Railway, showed his gold badge, and was ushered to a first-class carriage on the waiting train to Croydon. As they began their journey through the drab manufacturing district of Bermondsey, Lord Jocelyn closed his eyes and lapsed into a gentle doze. He'd stay like that until they came to Forest Hill, with its pleasant prospect of neat villas reposing in gentle countryside.

Poor, wretched Hamo Strange! What a rude shock he was in

for! He'd been tempted to tell him the truth, but it would be much more amusing to leave him in complacent ignorance until he found out the reality of the business himself. Strange was as rich as Croesus, but what a common fellow he was at heart! Everything in that vulgar house of his was new, or bought second-hand from sale rooms. The man had no pedigree.

Lord Jocelyn missed Forest Hill, but his eyes opened as they were passing the magnificent Crystal Palace, towering on its eminence at Sydenham, 200 feet above the track to the right.

Confound the Royal Scandinavian Bank! Why should it have chosen to panic in July, of all months? It had been reassuring to be approached by Strange to make up the consortium, but it was going to be a near thing – a very near thing. He could have declined in perfect safety, but Strange would not have forgotten. Well, there was no real cause for concern – but it would be a near thing, a very near thing.

At Norwood, the train gathered speed, and Lord Jocelyn, dismissing the articulated skeleton and his doings from his mind, let his thoughts dwell on the comforts of Duppas Park House, his elegant mansion in Croydon, on his wife, dull, worthy Lady Marion, and on his flighty daughter, Clemency.

Marion was incorrigible, long given over, body and soul, to good works of the most depressing kind. It was lucky that she'd never been of a jealous temperament, otherwise she might have put spies on him to see where he went when he claimed, several times a month, to be kept all night at his offices in the Strand. It would not do, for poor, plodding Marion to find out about visits to the fascinating and magical widow out at Belsize Park.

Clemency, still only twenty, was supposedly 'finishing' in Paris, but he suspected that she was, in fact, enjoying herself hugely in the fast set surrounding the young Marquis de Montfort. Well, let her. She was her father's daughter, and he was amused, rather than angry, at her constant pleas for sustaining cheques. He had a shrewd feeling, born of his natural affinity with his daughter's temperament, that she would choose to remain in Paris for good.

As for Strange – well, let him go to the Devil, together with his money-grubbing cronies! There was more to life than rooting round in the corners of bank vaults, looking for spare crates of coin.

Confound the Royal Scandinavian Bank! It was going to be a near thing on Friday the twenty-eighth – yes, a very near thing.

'Up here, Box, if you please. I shan't keep you more than ten minutes.'

Box had hurried into the vestibule of 4 King James's Rents just after eight o'clock on the morning of Tuesday, 18 July, to find Superintendent Mackharness waiting for him on the landing at the top of the stairs. He must have seen him from the window of his dark front office on the upper floor of the Rents, as he'd crossed the cobbles from Whitehall Place.

'Sit down there, will you, Box, while I glance through these letters. Then I'll tell you what I want you to do.'

Box regarded his superior officer with a judicious mixture of affection and apprehension. Mackharness was well over sixty, and afflicted by occasional bouts of sciatica, which had given him a more or less permanent limp. His yellowish face was adorned with neatly trimmed mutton chop whiskers. He was a neat man, dressed in a black civilian frock coat, which made him look rather like an elderly clerk in a counting-house. Box thought that he deserved better accommodation than the gloomy, lopsided chamber, smelling of stale gas and mildew, that he was obliged to occupy.

'Now, Box,' said Mackharness, putting aside the last of his letters, and fixing his subordinate with a steely eye, 'I've called you up here to tell you that, in ten days' time, there's to be a movement of bullion from a number of City banks; to be precise, a consign-ment of specie worth four million pounds—'

'Strewth! Four million? Specie, did you call it, sir?'

'Yes, Box. Specie means current coin of the realm. Bullion's too vague a word, though to most people it means gold and silver bars. My grandfather once saw a wagon laden with silver bars in the forecourt of Rothschild's bank in St Swithin's Lane. But this is specie – gold sovereigns, you know.'

Mackharness tapped the scuffed leather surface of his massive old desk with a large, spatulate finger, while regarding Box with an almost abstract air of speculation. Arnold Box said nothing. He looked at the superintendent's cluttered mantelpiece, and then at the massive rectangle of vacant space above it, where a top-heavy full-length portrait of Sir Robert Peel had hung until recently. He wondered what had become of it.

'So that's it, Box,' Mackharness resumed, 'yes, indeed. But what was it I wanted to say? Oh, yes. "Strewth". I've said before that you should try to find some more elegant epithets to use when you feel compelled to utter an exclamation. To the fishwife, or the costermonger, such infelicities are no doubt commonplace: they sit ill upon the person of one of Her Majesty's police inspectors.'

'Sir—'

'Well, just bear what I say in mind. There's no need to apologize. You'd better come with me now to Room 6, where I've set out my plans for this operation on the twenty-eighth. Scotland Yard will only be at the periphery, as the actual movements will be supervised by the City of London police, a couple of special officers from "A", and the dock people. But where we are concerned in the matter, Box, the Governor of the Bank, and the Commissioner, will look for efficiency, discretion, and success.'

Superintendent Mackharness heaved himself up from his desk, and lumbered out into a narrow, echoing passage to the right of the landing. Box followed him.

Room 6 resembled a company board room, with long, baize-covered tables arranged in a horseshoe. The walls were hung with flyblown portraits of previous commissioners of the Metropolitan Police. The missing Sir Robert Peel was propped up against the wall in a dark corner.

The tables were covered with a massive map of London, a huge canvas affair, its surface yellow with varnish. It served as a kind of table cloth for Mackharness's beautifully drawn route maps, to which were attached instructions and comments in his bold copperplate writing. Rulers and magnifying glasses lay where the superintendent had left them on finishing his task. Box sat down at one of the tables, and listened while Mackharness explained the details of the coming operation.

'This four million pounds in gold, Box, is required by the Royal Scandinavian Bank to bolster their holdings. For various reasons, the Bank of England doesn't want to transfer its own specie, and has called in Sir Hamo Strange to raise a private loan. He did this in the space of five days, calling in five prominent bankers to assist him. Sir Hamo Strange is advancing one million pounds of his own gold. This will be moved from his private bullion vaults at Carmelite Pavement, which is on our side of Blackfriars Bridge. One of the two men from "A" – in fact, Constable Lane, who assisted you at that business in Back Peter Street – will be on duty at Sir Hamo Strange's vaults, where he is well known.'

The fat finger pointed to a spot on one of the hand-drawn maps. Box saw the double dotted lines that indicated the tunnel passing under the Embankment to Carmelite Pier, Sir Hamo Strange's private landing-stage.

'All the other consignments will be moved in secure vans hired from Chaplin's, the carriers at Victoria. Each van will have a City of London policeman up on the box with the regular driver. The vans will proceed to five separate destinations along the river, where steam launches will be waiting. A launch will also be standing with steam up at Sir Hamo's private landing stage.'

'So there will be six steam launches, sir? Won't that be a strain on the River Police?'

'They'll be private launches, Box, hired for the occasion from Moltman & Sons, who have a fleet of specially strengthened vessels used for conveying very heavy cargoes at speed along the river. These special craft will be provided at the expense of the consortium.

'Now, very briefly, I'll take you through the details of the other five bankers in the consortium, insofar as they affect our policing on the twenty-eighth. Each of them is putting up six hundred thousand pounds. The first is N.M. Rothschild, at New Court, in St Swithin's Lane. You'll see my proposed route on that plan over there – Cannon Street, across Upper Thames Street, into Swan Lane, and so to Swan Lane Pier.

'The second banker is Sir Abraham Goldsmith, at Old Change Court, south of St Paul's, just off Carter Lane.' Mackharness described the short but tortuous route that would take Sir Abraham's gold sovereigns down to Queenhythe Steps, close to the Middlesex end of Southwark Bridge.

'I wondered what to do about the next bank, Brown's of Lothbury. I was tempted to combine their consignment with that of Rothschild's, as the two banks are virtually neighbours. But it's better to be safe than sorry. So Brown's van will go out of Lothbury, into Old Jewry, then Cheapside, and along New Change Lane, skirting St Paul's. It will then cross Upper Thames Street, and end up at White Lion Stairs, on the City side of Blackfriars Bridge.

'The two remaining banks are simpler propositions. Thomas Weinstock & Sons are in Fenchurch Street, so it's a fairly straight route for their van to take them out beyond London Bridge at Grant's Quay. Peto's Bank is in the Strand, which means that their consignment can simply proceed down Surrey Street to Temple Pier.'

Superintendent Mackharness sat back in his chair, and permitted himself a little smile of self-congratulation. Box pulled the various plans towards him, and studied them in silence for a while. Really, he thought, the guvnor's first rate at this kind of work. There were six separate hand-drawn plans, one for each of the journeys, and a seventh, which depicted a great arc of the

Thames stretching from their own stamping-ground at Whitehall Stairs to Tower Bridge. The river had been tinted a pale blue, and the six moorings where the special steam launches would be waiting were clearly marked in red.

'Take those drawings away, will you, Box, and make yourself familiar with them. I don't anticipate any trouble, but it's as well to ensure that we understand fully what will be happening on the twenty-eighth.'

'I suppose this will be mainly a task for the City of London Police, sir?' asked Box. He was beginning to wonder why he had been made privy to Mackharness's clever scheme, but knew better than to ask. A subtle approach always worked well with Old Growler.

'Oh, yes, Box, it's a matter for City, as it was when something similar was done in '90. That, as I recall, was another of Sir Hamo Strange's financial manoeuvrings. But, as I said, the Home Secretary and the Commissioner both feel that Scotland Yard should be involved in matters involving a foreign power.'

'And the six launches—'

'The six launches, Box, each with its cargo of treasure, will leave their respective berths at a time predetermined by me, and will all arrive over a period of half an hour at a spot opposite Globe Stairs Pier, from whence they will proceed into the West India Import Dock. Their cargoes will be offloaded into a tender, with armed guards on board, found by the London Rifle Brigade. The tender will convey the whole consignment to the Swedish merchant steamer *Gustavus Vasa*, lying at anchor in Limehouse Reach.'

'Excellent, sir,' said Box. 'And do you see a role for me in this exercise?'

'What? Well, yes, Box, otherwise I shouldn't have asked you to come up here. Had you waited for me to finish, instead of inter-rupting, I'd have told you what I want you to do.

'During the course of this week, you are to survey the six routes that I've delineated on these plans, and report to me any possible snags that you notice. Road works, and things of that nature. Then, on the twenty-eighth, at fifteen minutes before eight o'clock in the morning, I want you to station yourself with field-glasses on Morgan's Lane Pier, on the Surrey side, and watch all six launches sail under Tower Bridge. All six will have white funnels, with a red band, and a letter and numeral in black beneath the band. So there you are, Box: the details of what I hope will prove to be an efficient operation. Take those plans downstairs with you, and commit them to memory. I think that's all. Good morning.'

Clutching Mackharness's set of plans to his chest, Box shouldered his way through the doors of his office, which swung to behind him with a series of reverberating thuds. Sergeant Knollys had come in from his lodgings at Syria Wharf, and was sitting on his side of the table, his notebook open in front of him. Box took a cardboard wallet from a drawer, slid the plans into it, and tied its faded red draw-tapes.

'Well, Sergeant?' he asked. Jack Knollys turned over a page of his book.

'Sir, Mrs Pennymint lives in a house at Brookwood, Woking. Twenty-four Charnelhouse Lane. Her husband's a market gardener. Mr Alfred Pennymint, and Mrs Wilhelmina Pennymint. They've been on the rate books there for twenty-eight years.'

'Mrs Pennymint's a cheeky lady, Sergeant. Fancy suggesting that I had an uncle called Cuthbert! What a liberty! So she's not a native of Spitalfields?'

'No, sir. When she comes up to town for her seances, she stays with the secretary of the Temple of Light, a Mr Arthur Portman. He lives in one of those nice little houses in Henrietta Terrace, near the Strand.'

'And what did you find out about Mr Portman? He looked almost like a toff, but I don't think he was. Very respectable, at least in the outward parts. For the inner man, of course, I can say nothing.'

Sergeant Knollys smiled.

'Mr Arthur Portman, sir, is chief counter clerk at Peto's Bank in the Strand. Very convenient for him, living in Henrietta Terrace. He and his wife have lived there for seventeen years. They rent the house from the Bedford Estate.'

Peto's Bank. . . . Their £600,000 in gold was to be moved by van down Surrey Street to Temple Pier. And Mr Arthur Portman was chief counter clerk. Box shifted uneasily in his chair. From somewhere beyond the darkness of surmise, an idea was rising, but it had not yet come into the light. And Woking. . . .

'You know, Sergeant Knollys,' said Box, 'the very mention of Woking gives me the pip. All those thousands of people, and most of them dead! That necropolis at Brookwood is one of the biggest cemeteries in the country. And to make matters worse, they've got one of those great smoking crematoriums—'

'Crematoria.'

'Yes, that's what I said. And then there's the lunatic asylum. . . . Woking! I wouldn't live there, Sergeant, if you was to pay me. Mrs Pennymint, though, will feel quite at home, and so will her spirit guide, Benvolio, I expect.'

'Yes, sir. And now we come to Mrs Almena Sylvestris. She lives in a very nice house in Melbourne Avenue, Belsize Park. Discreet enquiry among the neighbourhood grooms and maid-servants elicited the information that she is a genuine lady, and highly regarded by all—'

'Why all these long words, Sergeant? "Elicited", and so on? You sound like a policeman. There's only me here, you know. So she's a lady – well, I could have told you that, having seen her in the flesh, if that's not too indelicate an expression. And anywhere in Belsize Park is a good address. Single, is she?'

'She gives herself out to be a widow, and I think she probably is. I saw her alighting from her carriage, and that's how she struck me. The local residents know that she's a medium, but for all that – or maybe because of that – she's highly respected.'

Jack Knollys stopped speaking, and gazed thoughtfully into the small fire burning in the grate. Whatever the time of year, it was always cold in Box's office. Box looked at him. What an asset he'd proved to be! When he'd told him to make enquiries about the two mediums, Knollys had done so without asking any potentially embarrassing questions. Strictly speaking, Mrs Pennymint and Madam Sylvestris were no concern of Box's.

'There's more, isn't there?' asked Box. 'There's something you don't want to tell me.'

'I don't like rumours where a lady's concerned, sir, but you'd better hear this one. There's talk in Belsize Park that Madam Sylvestris was installed in that house – number eight, Melbourne Avenue – by a rich admirer, who still maintains her there in style. It's just rumour, but it may be true.'

Arnold Box said nothing. He removed from the table drawer the folder containing Superintendent Mackharness's plans for the bullion movement on the twenty-eighth, and handed it to his sergeant.

'Take that through into the drill hall, Sergeant,' he said. 'Sit quietly there among the trestle tables for an hour, and see if you can soak up its contents. You'll see what it's all about when you open it. Thanks for looking into those mediums. They're up to something nasty. Mark my words.'

'Don't you like spiritualists, sir?'

'No, I don't, Sergeant. They're vultures, battening on to people's grief to get money out of them. And these particular vultures have got their talons into a Metropolitan Police officer, the kind of man they'd normally run a mile to get away from. I'm going out to Finchley tomorrow afternoon to have a word with Louise – Miss Whittaker – about them. About mediums and suchlike. She knows a lot of clever folk at London University, and I've heard that some of them take all this ghost business seriously. I'm going out now to see Mr Shale in Beak Street. By the time I come back, I expect you to have learnt the contents of that folder off by heart!'

Sergeant Knollys laughed, stooped his great frame under the arch, and made his way to what Superintendent Mackharness called the drill hall.

As Box struggled into his overcoat, he thought of PC Lane. Was he losing his sense of proportion? His niggling concern for the bereaved young man was in danger of becoming an obsession. Lane was no direct concern of his, and there were others in Whitehall Place who would minister to his needs if necessary. Nevertheless, he'd been right to get Jack Knollys to investigate the background of those two mediums.

Most clairvoyants, tarot-readers and suchlike, were poor, ignorant folk, eking out a hand-to-mouth existence by accepting coppers for dubious predictions; but Mrs Pennymint lived in comfort down at Woking, and Madam Sylvestris in affluence in Belsize Park. What lay behind their interest in PC Lane? Box intended to find out.

4

Voices from Another World

Sir Charles Napier, Her Majesty's Permanent Under-Secretary of State for Foreign Affairs, looked at the two men whom he had invited to visit him in his spacious office overlooking St James's Park. Colonel Augustus Temperley he knew well: a veteran of the Afghan War, he had long been strategic adviser to the China Desk at the India Office.

'You'll understand, Sir Hamo,' said Temperley to Napier's second guest, 'that Her Majesty's Government is anxious that all our dealings with you should be entirely confidential. No one – not even your closest confidants – must have the slightest inkling of what we have asked you to do.'

A distinguished man with greying hair and moustaches, Colonel Temperley wore his civilian clothes as though they were a uniform, and sat bolt upright on his chair.

'Sir Hamo knows all about that, Colonel,' Sir Charles Napier interposed. 'He and I met at the Rapprochement Banquet in the Goldsmiths' Hall last May. I talked to him then about the possibility of a special loan. Now that he has worked his usual wizardry in the money markets on our behalf, I feel that he must be apprised fully of the situation on the Sino-Indian border.'

'I'm very much obliged to you, Sir Charles,' said Sir Hamo

Strange. What a tremendous *thrill* it was to be summoned to these exalted places! This distinguished diplomat was a household name in England, a man who could prevent wars by the power of words and the exercise of a brilliant and informed mind. Such men, close to the Sovereign and to the great Ministers of State, had the potential to become invaluable allies. But enough of this daydreaming! Listen to what Colonel Temperley was saying.

'You will be aware of the dangerous tensions that built up when Russia turned her greedy eyes towards Afghanistan, a British dependency, in the '80s. They violated the Afghan border in 1885, and we were obliged to frighten them away. I recall that Mr Gladstone persuaded Parliament to grant him eleven million pounds for the project.'

Napier smiled behind his hand. Colonel Temperley was a staunch Conservative.

'Now, one outcome of that dangerous moment,' the colonel continued, 'was the Tsar's quite sudden conviction that any ventures into Afghanistan would be interpreted by Britain as an aggressive move towards the Indian border—'

'India and its borders, Sir Hamo,' Napier interrupted, 'being utterly inviolable, and their integrity non-negotiable. She is protected by vast oceans lapping her boundless shores, by great and virtually impassable mountain ranges to the north, and by the British Raj. Pray continue, Colonel Temperley.'

'As I say, the Tsar began to see sense, and turned his attention to China. He needed to expand *somewhere*, you see, and unlike the other European powers, Russia had paid no attention to Africa until it was too late.'

'Thank God for that,' muttered Sir Charles Napier, and it was Temperley's turn to give vent to a wry smile.

'Expansion, Sir Hamo, is made along railway lines, and the Tsar realized that other possible areas of expansion, such as the vast deserts of Persia, and the mountains of north-west India, were closed to him. So, China it was, and last year the Tsar began his so-called Trans-Siberian Railway—'

'Why "so-called", Colonel Temperley?' asked Sir Hamo Strange.

'Because the railway is simply a modern means of invading China. Russia hopes that it will very quickly subdue the crumbling Chinese Empire by sending its troops to every corner of that vast land.' Despite himself, Colonel Temperley laughed. 'I expect he dreams of building onion domes on top of the Buddhist temples, and converting all those Taoists to Orthodoxy.'

'What Temperley means, Sir Hamo,' said Napier smoothly, 'is that Russia will fail in its project. It has accused China of being effete. It needs to look nearer home.'

'The Trans-Siberian Railway was funded by France, but when the possibility of a secret alliance in consequence of that funding began to fade at the beginning of this year, France began to find it difficult to continue the massive payments required.'

'There's more to it than that, Sir Hamo,' said Napier. 'There's a lot of secret diplomacy involved, which we cannot talk about here. Suffice it to say, that, while we don't want to discourage Russia's turning towards France (it turns her away from Germany, you see) we don't want her losing interest in China, and turning her attention once more to India. So the British Government secretly determined to offer the Tsar a massive loan, at one per cent, on the condition that he maintains absolute secrecy. And that was why we called you in, Sir Hamo, to raise an international loan, from private sources, of thirty million pounds. And to our amazement and delight, you never even asked what the money was to be used for.'

'That is how one should treat a client, Sir Charles, be he a little shopkeeper or the legislature of a great nation. When you say the British Government—'

'I mean *us*, Sir Hamo. The Foreign Office and the India Office together. The Tsar must continue his imperial progress through the celestial empire, and no one must know that his funding has come

49

from Britain. That knowledge would lead to a violent rupture with France, among other things. Even Parliament doesn't know. There, I've put all my cards on the table.'

Sir Hamo Strange sat back in his chair, and looked with open admiration at the two experts in foreign policy. What brilliant men they were! Well, he'd done what they'd asked. It would now be his exquisite pleasure to tell them about it. He leaned forward in his gilded chair.

'I have raised the whole of this loan, gentlemen, from private financial institutions in Austria, Romania, Germany and Italy. I fought shy of the London markets, and of the national banks, although, of course, I'm welcome in all the capitals of Europe. I also decided not to approach the Rothschilds, because word of any such approach would have reached France.'

'Well done, Sir Hamo! That was very clever of you.' Sir Charles Napier's voice held genuine admiration for the famous financier's acumen.

'Thank you, sir. You are most kind. In all cases I have used inter-mediaries, who have approached the various banks ostensibly on behalf of different manufacturing companies and timber concerns, all of which are under strong obligations to me. There is one ques-tion, however, to which I need an immediate answer. Is the Tsar acting with the consent of his parliament in this matter, or is his railway venture a private concern?'

'The Russian parliament — the Duma — does exactly what the Tsar tells it to do. The Tsar rules the Russian Empire directly, as autocrat. In the matter of the Trans-Siberian Railway, the Tsar is acting on his own initiative. What he does, the Duma will endorse. The Duma knows nothing of the French finance that was origi-nally behind the project. Or says it doesn't,' Sir Charles added drily.

'Very well. The thirty million pounds – which is in promissory paper and specially purchased German and Italian government loan stock — is lodged entire with the Obolensky Private Bank for

Nobility in St Petersburg. It is there for the Tsar to use as he wishes.'

Sir Hamo Strange found himself blushing with pleasure as both high-ranking public servants broke into spontaneous applause. All in all, it was proving a heady day! There followed a certain amount of bowing and hand-shaking, and after a few fulsome compliments had been paid, the great financier was ushered out of the Foreign Office by a bevy of secretaries.

Sir Charles Napier handed Colonel Temperley a glass of whisky, to which he had added a minute quantity of water. He stood at the window, looking out across the summer languor of St James's Park. He sipped his own glass appreciatively.

'You know, Napier,' said Temperley, 'that fellow's one of the most remarkable people I've ever met. That loan – I never imagined he could arrange it so brilliantly. There's nothing to show that we are concerned at all. Britain, I mean.'

'Oh, yes, Temperley, Sir Hamo Strange is a national treasure. He's not an expert in foreign policy – why should he be? – but he's got a feel for it, a sense of what's going on, what is serious business, and what is mere charade. In these stirring times I don't think we could do without Hamo Strange.'

Colonel Temperley drained his glass and stood up.

'I must get back to the India Office. I've left Lubbock manning the China Desk, but I want to be there when a certain report comes in from Tsinan-fu. It's coming in Latin script, of course, but Lubbock's Chinese is pretty rudimentary.'

'What do you think will happen to the Tsar's foray into China? Speaking as a China expert.'

'Well, I think he'll find he's made a big mistake venturing into that part of Asia at all. I think he's embarked on the road to ruin.'

'You think China has hidden strengths?'

Colonel Temperley laughed, and shook his head.

'China's falling apart. It's an empire only in name. No, it's not China I'm thinking about. You see, if the Tsar ventures further enough east, he'll find himself up against Japan. And Japan, by all accounts, is a sleeping giant that's about to wake up. It's Japan, Napier, that one of these days could turn out to be Russia's nemesis.'

PC Lane was admitted to Madam Sylvestris's attractive modem villa in Melbourne Avenue, Belsize Park, by a woman in her early thirties, wearing the cap and apron of a house parlour-maid. She spoke good English, but with a foreign accent. Lane thought that she might have been French. He had just a brief moment to admire the bright Turkey carpets and the gleaming brass-work of the entrance hall before he found himself following the maid up a wide staircase, past a stained-glass window, and on to a bright, sunlit landing. Part of him was impressed by Madam Sylvestris's beautifully appointed residence; another part of him was possessed by superstitious fear.

The maid opened a door, and ushered Lane into a spacious drawing-room. It was somewhat over-furnished, and heavily panelled in oak, but there was nothing sinister to disturb a nervous visitor. Standing in front of a marble fireplace was Mr Arthur Portman, Chairman and Secretary of the Spitalfields Temple of Light.

'Mr Lane, sir,' said the maid, glancing swiftly at Portman and then lowering her eyes.

'Thank you, Céline, that will be all. Come in, Mr Lane!' Portman advanced to meet him, offering a welcoming hand. 'Sit down in this chair. That's right.'

Two upholstered upright chairs had been placed facing a curtained recess to the left of one of two tall, sash windows looking out on to a pleasant and well-tended summer garden. Lane did as he was bid, and Portman sat down near him on the second chair.

'You're nervous, aren't you, Mr Lane?' he said, in his quiet, confiding tones. 'Well, that's understandable. But there is nothing to fear, and much to hope for. Today, Madam Sylvestris will recall your little girl from the world beyond the grave, and once again, if we are lucky, Catherine Mary will materialize. But—'

Portman wagged an admonitory finger at Lane, and his face assumed an expression of sudden sternness. 'But there must be no outbursts, either of words, or sudden violent actiosn, like the ones you produced at the Temple of Light last Friday. Is that understood?'

'Yes, sir.'

Mr Portman relaxed in his chair, and the welcoming smile returned to his narrow face.

'Now, Mr Lane,' he said, 'let me briefly explain what happens to a materializing medium during a seance. The manifestations, when they appear, are composed of the substance of the medium's body, which is gradually built up in a ribbon-like extrusion from the medium's mouth, a substance that we call ectoplasm. The medium's body loses weight, and she becomes very weak. Sometimes, the materialization remains attached to the medium by a rope of ectoplasm, but at other times, it becomes detached, and for a while assumes the form of a sepa-rate entity.'

As Portman spoke, Lewis Lane began to feel a rising, choking panic. Was any of this loathsome mumbo jumbo true? He glanced around the pleasant room, glimpsed the blue summer sky from the window, and then looked at the mysterious curtained alcove in the corner of the room. Arthur Portman was still speaking.

'If you yield to temptation, and touch the half-materialized spirit figure, you will inflict severe injuries on the medium's body. It you touch the fully materialized figure, the medium will die. . . .'

Arthur Portman rose from his chair, and drew aside the curtains covering the alcove. It was something of a shock to PC Lane to see Madam Sylvestris sitting there, apparently in a deep sleep. She was elegantly dressed in a green silk morning gown, and her hands, folded in her lap, held a small ebony crucifix. The noise of the curtains as they were pulled back on their brass rail failed to disturb her. As though answering Lewis's unspoken question, Portman told him that the medium was not asleep, but in a light trance.

'I'm going to close the window shutters, now,' said Portman, 'and then I'll light that small red-shaded oil lamp which is standing on the table near the door. After that, I will place a cylinder on the phonograph, and we shall hear an organ rendition of Bach's "Jesu, Joy of Man's Desiring". Music of the right sort assists in opening the gate of perception in the psychic barrier. After the music has ceased, the seance will begin.'

As PC Lane's eyes accustomed themselves to the darkness, he was aware of the faint red light cast by the shaded oil lamp. He saw that the alcove curtains had been partly drawn, but Madam Sylvestris was still clearly visible, sitting entranced on her chair. The soothing notes of Bach's music filled the room for a while, and then came to a halt.

Madam Sylvestris gave a choking cry, and shifted in her chair. At the same time, the tinkling of a hand-bell was heard. Something fell to the floor near where PC Lane was sitting. He glanced down at the carpet, and saw that it was a child's rattle.

A luminous mist was developing in the alcove and, as Lewis Lane watched, a ribbon of white substance began to stream from the medium's mouth. It seemed to slither down the front of her dress like a somnolent snake. Then a figure began to form in the mist beside Madam Sylvestris. As Lane and Portman watched, the figure stepped out of the mist, through the parted curtains, and into the room.

The man standing before them was middle-aged, with an elfish, good-humoured face. Although he was illuminated only by the dim red light near the door, Lane could see that he had blue eyes, greying side-whiskers, and a fleshy, expressive mouth. A white light flickered briefly above his head, and then disappeared.

'That light,' Portman whispered, 'shows that this is a true discarnate spirit from the other side. A physical manifestation has no such light.'

The spirit's lips began to move, but the words that he uttered came not from him, but from the entranced medium in the chair.

'Lewis,' said the spirit, in a friendly, rich voice, 'you'll not recognize me, I expect?'

'No.' Lewis wondered where he had summoned the courage to speak to this creature. What was it? He longed to fling open the shutters, and reveal the whole damnable business to the light of day. But he was held in thrall by the urge to see his baby daughter again.

'I am Roger Wilcox, your wife's uncle on her mother's side. I was the black sheep of the family, you know—'

'Roger Wilcox!' cried PC Lane. 'Yes, I remember her telling me about you once, long ago, before ever we were married. You did a stretch – I beg your pardon, sir – you went to prison for a year's penal servitude for larceny. It was before either of us was born. There's – wait! We have a photograph of you on our mantelpiece, an old, faded photograph. . . .'

'Yes, you have. And you were right about me being in prison. I was sent out to the Malay Straits, where I died of fever in 1865. But I'm not here, Lewis, to talk about myself. I want to tell you about little Catherine Mary. She's been with me a lot since she passed over, and has tried to tell me what happened. She says she was playing in Wellclose Lane, near the railway bridge when she felt bad.'

'Yes!'

PC Lane listened as the spirit of his wife's uncle told him about Dr Morland, who had attended the case, of the sympathetic sister in the hospital, who had wept when Catherine Mary had died. He, Roger Wilcox, had been present at the little girl's funeral, and had tried to comfort them both, but to no avail.

'And now, Lewis, I must tell you that Catherine Mary is wanted in the Garden of Innocence, where she will be taught to grow and advance. It is a wonderful place, and you must steel yourself to let her go there. I think you will see her today, and then on one more occasion, when she will be able to speak more fully to you. They are teaching her already, you see. Goodbye, Lewis. Trust! All these things that I have told you are true.'

The spirit of Roger Wilcox turned, and walked slowly back into the cabinet, where it was absorbed in the swirling luminous mist. Madam Sylvestris, still entranced, sat upright in her chair. The stream of ectoplasm trailed from her mouth, and PC Lane saw how it disappeared into a denser cloud of mist behind the medium's chair. Madam Sylvestris began the stertorous breathing that Lane had heard at the Spitalfields seance, and presently the mist parted, to reveal a little girl standing uncertainly in the centre of the cabinet. Lane half rose, but Portman pushed him back almost roughly into his chair.

Lane could not see very clearly, but the little girl was the image of his dead child, and she was wearing her favourite pink flounced dress — the dress in which she had been laid to rest in Putney Vale Cemetery.

'Dada!' The lisping voice came not from the child, but from the medium. 'Dada! Nora Maitland is here. She's been playing with me. She only came yesterday. Tell Mammy not to cry. Next time you come, I'll not need to speak through the lady.'

'Catherine Mary! You're to be a good girl, and do what they tell you up there. Dada will come to see you again—'

Suddenly, the spirit disappeared, and the medium uttered a long, heavy sigh, and opened her eyes. Mr Portman quickly rose, unfastened the shutters, and rang a bell at the side of the fireplace. The bright morning sunlight flooded into the room. There was nothing to be seen but the empty corner with Madam Sylvestris sitting in her chair. The seance was over.

The door opened, and the foreign maid came into the room, carrying a tray on which stood three glasses of sherry. She placed them on a table, curtsied to her mistress, and went out, closing the door behind her.

'How did it go?' asked Madam Sylvestris. She looked drawn and tired, and to Lane's amazement seemed to know nothing of the events of the last hour. 'I do hope the dear child came through. I saw her in the spirit yesterday, but only as a thought-form.'

'It was a triumphant success, madam,' said Alfred Portman. He handed her a glass of sherry, and motioned to PC Lane to take a glass himself.

'It was wonderful, ma'am,' said Lewis Lane. 'It was my baby, right enough. She mentioned poor little Nora Maitland, a neighbour's child who was run over and killed by a runaway horse and cart only yesterday. I don't know how you do it, ma'am, but it's a miracle!'

The handsome woman smiled, and sipped her sherry.

'I don't "do" anything, Mr Lane, I'm simply a medium, a channel, if you like, through which the so-called dead can communicate. Did you see a man called Roger Wilcox?'

'I did, ma'am, and he told me that I'd see Catherine Mary only once more, before she went off to the – what was the place called?'

'The Garden of Innocence,' said Portman gravely, though Lane thought he saw a spasm of amusement cross the man's face.

'That's quite true, Mr Lane,' said Madam Sylvestris. 'And on that last occasion Catherine Mary will appear as a detached entity, who will be able to speak independent of my voice-box, and come close to you, with all the semblance of a child still living in the flesh. By then, too, she will have mastered the art of speech quite dramatically, and she will be able to take a loving farewell of you in more understandable language. Please come here, to my house, at eight o'clock on the morning of Friday, the twenty-eighth of this month.'

'The twenty-eighth? But, ma'am, my work—'

'I know your work is terribly important, Mr Lane,' said Madam Sylvestris sharply, 'but surely you can find a substitute for that morning? It cannot be any other time but that which the spirits have decreed. It is the last time that you will see the fully evolved spirit of your child on this side of the grave.'

'Yes. . . . Yes, ma'am, you're right, and I'm sorry if I appeared ungrateful. I thank you for your goodness and kindness to me from the bottom of my heart, and I shall be here without fail on the morning of the twenty-eighth.'

'Curteis,' asked Sir Hamo Strange, as his confidential secretary came into the study after dinner that evening, 'is there anyone waiting for me downstairs? I fancy I heard the front-door bell ringing a minute ago.'

'There's a gentleman newly arrived, sir, who said that he was expected. He wouldn't give his name, and I humoured him by not pressing the point. I've settled him in the writing-room.'

Curteis made no attempt to suppress a rather contemptuous smile.

'Narrow-faced man? Black whiskers?' asked Strange. 'Very well. Bring him up here, will you, Curteis. You know who he is, I expect?'

'Yes, sir, but I thought it advisable to pretend that I didn't recognize him. That kind of silly pretence seems to satisfy the fellow's vanity.'

'Yes, well, never you mind about his vanity. He's a man with many uses. Bring him up here, now, and then make yourself scarce.'

When Curteis returned with the visitor, he ushered him into Sir Hamo's study, closed the door silently, and went downstairs. Strange told the visitor rather curtly to sit down.

'Now, Portman,' said the great financier, 'have you carried out the little commission I entrusted to you? Or did you have scruples in the matter? Maybe it's of no significance, but it's as well to cover all eventualities. Whatever the outcome, you won't lose by it.'

'I have undertaken the commission, sir,' Arthur Portman replied, 'and I've come here this evening to tell you the result. Our vault at Peto's Bank in the Strand contains just over half a million pounds in gold. When the Swedish consignment leaves there on the twenty-eighth, there will remain nine hundred pounds in sovereigns, sufficient to stock the tills, but nothing else.'

'Hm . . . You do appreciate, do you not, that when you come to work for me, you will receive double at least what Peto pays you as chief counter clerk? Good, I see you do. All I ask in return is discretion. And the Temple of Light – all went well there, I trust?'

Mr Arthur Portman smiled, and his smile was met by that of Sir Hamo Strange.

'Oh, yes, sir. All went well in that direction. If I may say so without disrespect, the spirits have been very much on our side this month.'

Sir Hamo Strange motioned towards a fat envelope placed on the edge of his desk. Portman picked it up, put it without comment into the pocket of his well-cut morning coat, and walked softly from the room.

'*Sir*', Box read in a note that had been brought across to him from Whitehall Place, '*it was all true. I saw the spirit of my wife's uncle, who talked about things known only to our family. And then Catherine Mary appeared, looking just as she did in life. She was wearing the dress in which we buried her. I saw her lips moving, but the words came from the mouth of Madam Sylvestris. It's all true, Mr Box. I've been promised that at the next seance Baby will speak in her own little voice!*'

Arnold Box put away PC Lane's hastily scribbled note in the desk drawer. It was after nine, and the usual evening calm had settled over 4 King James's Rents. Box sat in thought, watching the flames leaping in the fireplace. Could it be true? No . . . These people had all kinds of subtle and not so subtle ways of parading their deceit. Lane was an "A" Division man, no concern of his;

nevertheless, he'd keep a careful eye on the police constable who had witnessed the apparitions of folk who were supposed to be dead.

5

Sir Hamo Strange Discomfited

Lady Marion Peto was still distinguished enough to find her portrait reproduced in the better society magazines, but since turning fifty she had begun, so her sister declared indignantly, to 'let herself go'. Her fashionable clothes had yielded to a wardrobe of plain greys and browns, and her hair, once tended by a celebrated London coiffeuse, was now pulled back sternly from her forehead, and tied in a bun.

'Lord Jocelyn came home at an odd hour this afternoon, Marion,' said Lady Marion's sister, Lady Riverdale, putting down her tea cup on its saucer. It sounded like a statement, but it was, in fact, a question.

'Lord Jocelyn keeps bankers' hours, or so he tells me, Cornelia,' said Lady Marion drily. 'Far be it from me to inhibit his freedom. But then, Jocelyn has always done just as he liked. He decided long ago that I was a credulous fool, and it suits me at present to let him go on thinking that.'

She glanced at her younger sister, and thought: she looks more like my daughter, beautifully dressed, *soignée*, what their father used to call 'an ornament of society'. That's because Lord Riverdale dotes on her. She's no need to run charities and sit on committees, as I do, to mask my sense of worthlessness.

'Well, my dear,' said Lady Riverdale, 'I still wish that you'd come to stay with us at Rivermead Place for a few weeks. Alfred would be delighted to have you, so think about it. I'm your only sister, and I'd like to see more of you.'

'Well, Cornelia, I'll think over what you've said. It's very kind of you both, but I have many projects on hand at the moment that can't be left. I'll write and let you know.'

When her sister had made her farewells, Lady Marion sat in thought. What was to become of her? She was fading visibly, and very soon whatever slender bond still existed between her and her husband would be broken. He knew that, too, and had already made the necessary arrangements. . . .

She knew nothing for certain, but she would not be long in that state of ignorance. To judge from his air of smug contentment, his latest abandoned female was someone more distinguished than his usual flower-shop girls and minor actresses. He thought she was a fool. Did he also think that she was harmless? Did he—?

The door of her sitting-room opened, and a young housemaid appeared.

'Shall I clear away, your ladyship?' she asked.

'Yes, Alice, you can clear, now. Have the ladies from the Dorcas Society arrived yet?'

'Yes, madam. They're ready in the drawing-room.'

Lady Marion watched the housemaid as she left the room carrying the tea things on a silver tray. Alice despised her, of course, for failing to please her lord and master. They all despised her for abdicating her role as gracious companion of a distinguished public figure, and chatelaine of Duppas Park House. Well, she didn't blame them. Her own sister despised her, and Clemency, who was her father's daughter in every respect, treated her with a mixture of pity and impatience. But then, she despised herself.

Rising from the table, she went downstairs to meet the dull and worthy women of the Dorcas Society.

*

Arnold Box stepped down from the omnibus that had brought him out to Finchley, and made his way along pleasant roads of red brick houses adjoining a number of playing fields and small public gardens. Turning into a brand-new avenue of modern villas, he knocked at the door of the third house on the right-hand side, and waited for Ethel, Miss Louise Whittaker's trim little maid, to admit him to the house.

Over the two years since Box had encountered Louise Whittaker, the London University scholar and he had become firm friends. It was his habit – and his great pleasure – to go out to Finchley to consult her, whenever he wanted a female slant on some aspect of a case.

The door opened, and little Ethel, as neat as ever in cap and apron, stepped out into the front garden. She put a finger to her lips, and setting convention aside, drew Box by the sleeve into the shade of one of the laurel bushes flanking the path.

'Oh, Mr Box,' she whispered, 'Missus has got a young gentleman with her this morning. Do you still want to come in? Or will you leave your card?'

'A young gentleman?' asked Box truculently. 'What kind of a young gentleman? What are you talking about, Ethel?'

He was conscious of how ridiculous his jealous resentment must have sounded to the 14-year-old girl who was still clutching his sleeve, and viewing him with an infuriating air of compassion. Ethel giggled.

'You'd better come in, Mr Box,' she said. 'This young gentleman is another scholar, come to talk about books and suchlike. They're having morning coffee and biscuits in the study, so I'll fetch another cup. Mr James, he's called, this young gentleman. Mr M.R. James, it said on his card.'

Box followed the little maid into the house, where he was conducted without ceremony to Louise Whittaker's study, which occupied the spacious front room of the house. Serenely beautiful as ever, the lady of the house rose to greet him. She had been sitting at the round tea table near the fireplace, upon which stood a silver tray bearing a tall coffee pot, cream jug, sugar bowl, and two china cups and saucers.

'Why, Mr Box!' cried Louise. 'How kind of you to call.' Her voice, amused, musical and educated, carried its own subtle authority. She fixed Box with what seemed to be a limpidly innocent smile, a technique of hers that never failed to make him feel awkward and foolish.

'May I introduce Mr M.R. James, of King's College, Cambridge?' she said. 'Mr James, this is my friend Detective Inspector Box, of Scotland Yard.'

A fair-haired young man in a dark suit half rose from a chair by way of greeting, and there was something nervously awkward about the gesture that told Box that he was not in the presence of a rival for Miss Louise Whittaker's affections.

'Box?' said James. Are you *the* Inspector Box? The man who exposed that confounded rogue Gideon Raikes, and solved the 25-year-old murder of Henry Colbourne? My dear sir, I'm honoured to meet you.'

M.R. James sprang to his feet, and shook Box heartily by the hand. At that moment Ethel entered the room bearing an extra cup and saucer, which she placed on the table. She contrived to ignore Box, as though she had never seen him before in her life.

'Sit down, Mr Box,' said Louise, 'and I'll pour you some coffee. What dramatic police business brings you out to Finchley?'

'I'm engaged on an investigation that's taking me into the murky realms of spiritualism, Miss Whittaker,' Box replied. 'I don't mean the usual knavish tricks, like spirit writing, or table turning. They're all in a day's work, so to speak. And spirit photography, likewise – all those little faces cut out from magazines, and stuck on cotton wool. I could do those myself.'

'This is something more serious, isn't it, Mr Box?' asked Louise, setting his coffee cup beside him, 'Something sinister, I shouldn't wonder.'

'It is, Miss Whittaker. The medium I'm investigating has produced the spirit of a dead child, who spoke to her father in such a way that he was convinced that the manifestation was real. I was there myself, and witnessed it. The father has since attended a second seance, and once again the child appeared, and spoke to him through the medium. He sent me a note to tell me all about it. What I want to know, is whether such things are possible.'

All three were suddenly quiet, as though some unseen presence had joined them. A horse and cart trundled slowly along the road, the sound of hoofs muffled by the heavy velvet curtains half-drawn against the strong sunlight. The silence was broken by M.R. James.

'Spiritualism, Mr Box,' he said, gravely, 'came to England from America, bringing with it a whole baggage of crudity and vulgarity. From the start, it's been shot through with chicanery and fraud. For that reason most educated people disdain to examine its phenomena. For the man of science, to do so would be to invite professional suicide. However, there are a number of courageous people at Cambridge and elsewhere who are determined to examine the phenomena of spiritualism in the cold light of reason. Professor and Mrs Sidgwick spring to mind, and Professor Barrett, of course.'

'Do *you* think there's any truth in it, Mr James?' asked Box.

'I think there must be some truth lurking behind all the fraud and deceit. One does hear of the strangest things happening at seances.'

While James was speaking, Box caught Louise's eye, and read there a plea that he would change the subject. He suddenly realized that she was uneasy with, and perhaps a little frightened by, spiritualism. An innocuous question was in order.

'Do you live in London, Mr James?' he asked.

'No, indeed. I'm a Fellow of King's College, in Cambridge, but I've come up to London at the behest of Sir Hamo Strange, the famous bibliophile. I'm by way of being an expert on the provenance of ancient books and manuscripts.'

'Sir Hamo Strange? It's odd that you should know him, sir. I'm engaged on some very important police work for him this very week. Work to do with his banking interests. I didn't know that he was a collector.'

'Oh, yes, Inspector, he's very well known in that sphere of activity, and he recently acquired a set of volumes that were lost to sight for nearly two hundred years. They began their wanderings again earlier this month, after a long and secret rest in Spain. I heard on the rumour mill late last year that its owner, Count Fuentes de la Frontera, was about to part with it, and that Sir Hamo Strange, and his great rival, Lord Jocelyn Peto, were both determined to acquire it—'

'Lord Jocelyn Peto is another of my customers, sir, if I may put it like that.'

'Indeed? Coincidence is a curious thing, Inspector. But let me tell you about this celebrated book. The six volumes comprise a unique copy of the Complutensian Polyglot Bible, which was printed in six volumes in 1520. "Polyglot", of course, means simply "many languages", and this Bible was printed in Latin, Hebrew, Chaldaean and Greek, arranged in parallel columns. It was printed in the Spanish town of Alcala de Henares, the Roman name for which was Complutum. And thus the work is called the Complutensian Polyglot Bible.'

'And Sir Hamo Strange was the successful bidder?' asked Box.

'He was, and he wants me to verify that the volumes that he had acquired are genuine. You see, it's a unique and very special copy of the Polyglot Bible. It was pulled from the press in 1519, a year before the general publication, and set into the front board of the first volume there is a pouch or pocket, containing a document actually written in the Chaldaean script, and printed with the same fount of type as that used in the Bible itself—'

'The Chaldaean Cipher!' cried Louise. 'Of course, I've heard about that, but I thought it was just a legend.'

'No, Miss Whittaker, it's real enough, and Sir Hamo Strange

now has it in his possession. This secret document – no one knows who composed it – reveals many personal and secret details about the life of Charles the Fifth of Castile, and also private and intimate facts relating to Queen Isabella. It surfaced briefly in France in the early 1700s and then was lost to sight again until quite recently.'

'A rare treasure, then, sir,' said Box. 'And you say it had gone on its travels from Spain? How were you able to track its movements? I'm interested in the detective side of things, as you'll appreciate.'

'Well, Mr Box, there's a man called Aaron Sudermann, who's known as "the shop-keeper of princes". It was he who obtained the lost Leonardo from the Sultan of Turkey last year, at the request of the King of Italy. Now, I happen to know that Aaron Sudermann was in Vienna at the end of June, where my friend Professor von Metz saw him setting out for the hill town of Regensburg on the Styrian coach. Styria is where Sudermann likes to meet his more reclusive clients. It was there that he handed over a bundle of rare Greek manuscripts to Sir Hamo Strange in the autumn of 1890.'

'And how does all this fit in with this Count Fuentes and his Polyglot Bible?'

'As to that, Mr Box, Aaron Sudermann was in Andalusia for most of June, and Andalusia is where Count Fuentes lives. All interesting parts of a minor puzzle!'

'I find it very difficult to fathom people like Strange,' observed Louise. 'To see a book merely as a collectable object is very alien to my habit of mind. Books to me are sources of knowledge. I can see no virtue – or pleasure, even – in merely owning them.'

M.R. James laughed.

'That's because you're not a dedicated book collector, Miss Whittaker. There are two varieties, you know. One is the bookseller, a man who loves all the books that he acquires, and knows all about them, their contents, their history, and the history of their various owners over the centuries. When a client picks up one of his treasures, he longs to cry, "No! Please, sir, put it back on the shelf. I love that book. It is part of me." But then, the voice of commerce prevails, and he immediately urges his customer to buy. And so he parts with what he loves.'

'And the other variety?' asked Louise.

'The other variety is the man who wishes to acquire a volume in order never to part with it. Its value to him lies in its rarity, its uniqueness, and its monetary value. It is virtually certain that he will never read it! I call such men bibliomanes, because they are afflicted with the disease of bibliomania. Such a man is Sir Hamo Strange, and, to a lesser extent, his dreaded rival Lord Jocelyn Peto. Like all obsessions, bibliomania can de dangerous.'

When it was time for Arnold Box to leave, Louise Whittaker preceded him into the narrow hallway of her house, closing the study door behind her. Little Ethel was evidently engaged elsewhere, and it was Louise who handed Box his hat. She opened the front door, and walked with him down the garden path to the gate. The road was deserted, and the strong summer sun made the white shale of the carriageway glow, so that Box's eyes were dazzled.

'After you've solved this case, you must come to tea, Mr Box,' said Louise. 'Tea for two, with a special chocolate cake from Fortnum and Mason. Ethel can act as duenna.'

'I'll look forward to that, Miss Whittaker,' said Box. 'Had you been alone this morning, I'd have told you much more about this seance business that's worrying me. Something's going to happen, but I don't know what it is.'

Louise laid a hand on his arm.

'Arnold,' she said, and it was one of the very rare instances of her using his Christian name, 'I don't like this spiritualism business. You've heard of the darkness of ignorance? Well, these seances encourage the ignorance of darkness. Their ghosts and wraiths can't abide the light! Devotees may be content to whisper to shadows of the dead in a darkened room, but I'd rather remember them with gratitude here, beneath the honest brightness of the summer sky.'

In the grand reception room of Medici House in Blomfield Place, Sir Hamo Strange awaited his visitors. 'Guests' would have been too intimate a term to use for his fellow banker and deadly enemy, Lord Jocelyn Peto, and the two scholarly experts whom he had retained to help him gloat over Peto's failure to secure the great prize.

Strange turned from the window, from which he had been contemplating his favourite view of the Bank of England's Lothbury elevation, and crossed the sumptuous room to a long table placed below a great mirror, which had come from the palace of a seventeenth century Duke of Florence.

He caught sight of his face, with its sallow skin stretched like parchment across his prominent cheekbones, and smiled. It was the smile of a spectre in a haunted ruin, but it pleased him, for all that. He was certainly not as handsome as Lord Jocelyn Peto, but he was assuredly more powerful, and, to all appearances, infinitely richer. For a moment his mind reverted to his interview with Sir Charles Napier and Colonel Temperley. How intoxicating it had been to talk familiarly and as an accepted equal with such high-placed gentlemen!

He dropped his gaze to the table where, upon a long green baize cloth, the six quarto volumes of the Complutensian Polyglot Bible had been carefully laid out for inspection. He had appreciated their fine bindings, and the quite beautiful array of typefaces in which they had been printed, but what he appreciated most of all was that they were *his*.

Two young maidservants entered the room, curtsied, and positioned themselves behind a small buffet in a corner near the window. A tempting selection of sandwiches lay on porcelain plates under glass domes, together with an array of decanters and sparkling wine glasses. Sir Hamo Strange opened his watch. Half past two. There was nearly an hour before the visitors would arrive.

'Scholes,' he said to one of the two maids, 'I may as well sustain myself before the visitors arrive. It was a mistake to have skipped luncheon. Bring me a plate of cinnamon toast and a pot of Earl Grey tea. Lemon, and no sugar. Temple, go with her.'

The two maids curtsied again, and hurried from the salon.

'Curteis!' Sir Hamo called out for his secretary, and the man appeared instantly from the adjacent study.

Sir Hamo chuckled, and rubbed his hands together in a kind of controlled glee.

'What do you think Peto's up to, Curteis? He accepted my invitation to view the Bible with suspiciously commendable speed. In fact, he sent up his reply from the Strand by messenger.'

'He may be trying to save face, sir. Pretend that he doesn't care, you know, just to vex you. But I wonder at times if he's as big a fool as we think he is. We'll find out soon enough, I expect.'

'Good, well perceived, Curteis. I wonder about him, too. He was all smiles the other day when I called on him at his club, and told him that I'd snatched the prize from under his nose. All smiles. . . . You'd better find Mahoney. He's dropped from sight since he and I returned from Austria. He's a brutal villain, by all accounts, but he makes an excellent bodyguard when I decide to visit the more lawless parts of Europe. Drag him out of the alehouse, bail him from prison: do what's necessary to get him ready for service – just in case. I expect you know what I mean.'

'My dear Strange,' said Lord Jocelyn Peto, 'once more, I congratulate you. A priceless acquisition. And now, duly fortified with those tasty sandwiches and excellent claret, your renowned experts can reveal the secrets of these unique volumes!'

Damn it, there was something wrong! The fellow had been laughing and smiling since he'd arrived, pretending that his vitals hadn't withered up with envy of what he had failed to acquire. The servants had deferred to him as though he were the master of Medici House, and he had shaken his abundant curls in their direction as a sign of his loathsome aristocratic condescension. Confound him! Why was he so confoundedly cheerful?

'You are very kind, Lord Jocelyn,' said Strange. 'As you see, I arranged a small reception, but limited the guests to yourself, and these two gentlemen. You will, of course, have heard of Mr M.R. James, who has agreed to authenticate the volumes. Neither of us will have met Dr Alois Krenz, specialist epigraphist from University College, London. Gentlemen, would you please now examine the volumes of the Complutensian Polyglot Bible?'

M.R. James began to conduct a careful examination of the precious volumes, while Dr Krenz, a taciturn, lightly bearded man in his thirties, sat down on a chair near the long table, and watched James at work. The two bankers kept their eyes fixed on M.R. James as he peered through a series of hand lenses at the bindings, and then at a selection of pages, evidently chosen to a pre-arranged scheme, turning the heavy, hand-made folios with a pair of ivory tweezers. Each volume received the same attention, and the process occupied nearly half an hour.

'Gentlemen,' said James, when he finally straightened up to face his audience of two, 'these volumes are all undoubtedly authentic, and part of a single impression. The bindings are contemporary with the paper, dating from about 1520, and ornamented in the restrained Castilian blind-stamped fashion of that time and locale. Without any doubt, this is one of the original editions of the Complutensian Bible.'

Sir Hamo Strange sat back in his chair with a little sigh of satisfaction. It was as well that all doubt on the matter of authenticity should be removed. He glanced at Lord Jocelyn Peto, sitting beside him. The man seemed subdued enough, but was that a gleam of suppressed merriment in his eye? Nonsense. The fellow was devastated.

'The title page,' James continued, 'is dated at the foot in the

Arabic numerals 1519, confirming that this is indeed the unique copy of the Bible, pulled from the press a whole year before its official issue in 1520. And here, in the special pocket let into the front board of the first volume, is the fabled document, written in the Chaldaean script, which is said to reveal the secret passages in the lives of Charles the Fifth and Isabella. Dr Krenz will now give the document his attention.'

Nobody spoke while the taciturn Krenz used James's ivory tweezers to remove the fragile sheets of paper inserted into their special pocket centuries earlier. He carefully smoothed out the pages on the green baize, and then selected a hand lens from James's little collection. They could see the curious ancient characters inscribed in bold black and red on the old document.

After a few moments, Dr Krenz put down the lens, and turned to M.R. James.

'Mr James,' he said in a low voice, 'would you care to examine the paper upon which these characters are written?'

James sat down near him at the table, and peered closely at the first sheet of paper. Then he carefully felt it between the thumb and forefinger of his right hand. Ignoring his audience, James strode towards the window, and held the sheet up against one of the panes.

'A watermark!' he exclaimed. 'It shows a bear holding a staff, with a star above its head. This paper is from the mill of Jacob Müller of Nuremburg. It's seventeenth century. There's something seriously amiss here, gentlemen.'

Dr Krenz stood up. He had thrown the remaining sheets down on the table in contempt.

'That confirms what I know to be the truth,' he said. 'These characters are Chaldaean, sure enough, but what they spell out is gibberish. It's a forgery, and not a very clever one. The ink – I'm sure the ink's modern—'

'But the volumes themselves are genuine,' said James, returning to the table. 'As for the date on the title page – ah, yes! I can see the true date now, 1520, partly scratched out with an etching knife, and the numerals 1519 substituted.'

'A forgery?' cried Sir Hamo Strange. He rose from his chair, and began quite literally to tear his hair in rage. One of the two maids began to cry. 'A forgery? They shall pay for this. They will be hunted down without remorse— A forgery? Scholes, Temple – take those rubbishy volumes away. Take them down to the base-ment, and throw them in the furnace!'

Both maids stood petrified with fear behind the buffet. Neither of them moved.

'Do you think it was Sudermann?' asked Peto. His voice held grave concern, but Strange could see that he was writhing with concealed glee.

'Sudermann? No, it's not Sudermann. He's honest enough. It's Fuentes who has engineered this. Count Fuentes de la Frontera. He contrived to sell Sudermann a fake, while the real Bible – well, he will have sold that, too. Oh, yes. He will have sold that, too. . . .'

With some effort, Sir Hamo Strange recovered his equanimity.

'Mr James,' he said, 'and you, Dr Krenz, I thank you for coming here today, and revealing this squalid sham. Lord Jocelyn, thank you for your commiseration and support. I am naturally a little upset, so I will bid you all good day.'

As soon as the last guest had departed, the imperturbable Curteis appeared from the study.

'Curteis,' said Sir Hamo, *'he's got it himself.* He beat me to the post, and has been laughing ever since. He came here today simply to gloat at my loss. But he'll not get away with it. The money is nothing to me. What is five thousand pounds? It's the shame, the sense of loss. . . . He's got my book – *my* book – out there in that gimcrack house of his at Croydon. Get out now, and find Mahoney. Tell him to sober up, and come to see me, here.'

'Do you think that's wise, sir? You have great projects in train, and in any case it's getting perilously near the twenty-eighth—'

'Damn it all, man, do you expect me to take this personal affront lying down? Do as I tell you. Get out there now, and find Mahoney!'

6

The Murder at Duppas Park

In the crowded public bar of The Recorder, a popular hostelry for clerks in a narrow lane near Barbican, Mr Arthur Portman took a delicate sip from his glass of port, and addressed a few words to the man sitting beside him.

'To be quite frank with you, Mr Beadle,' he confided, 'I've been considering a move for the last year. I've been very comfortable at Peto's Bank, as you know, but — well, the time's come for a change.'

Mr Beadle, a large man in a black three-piece suit, shifted his bowler hat further along the bar to make room for his elbow, and stared gloomily into his empty porter pot. Presently he turned his shrewd grey eyes on Portman, and regarded him with a look which held the fathomless wisdom of a man who had been secretary to a private banker in Gresham Street for over forty years.

'A change, hey? What do you want a change for? You look as gorgeous as Peto himself in that fancy rig of yours. I'd say you're not short of a few bob working for Lord Jocelyn Peto.'

Mr Beadle glanced round the crowded, stuffy bar, where the lunchtime noise level was rising to a crescendo. He liked his daily pie and porter in The Recorder, especially when there was any juicy item of City gossip to retail. When he spoke again, he lowered his voice to a conspiratorial whisper.

'Or are you hinting at something, Portman? A change, hey? Why, do you think there's something fishy in the wind? If that's the case, then for God's sake, man, guard your words. Any little hint that all's not well with Peto's and you'll have the crowds battering at your doors.'

He expected Arthur Portman to begin an indignant denial, but the chief counter clerk at Peto's Bank merely frowned, and said nothing. Presently, he bade his companion a rather stiff farewell, as though he regretted having said too much, and left the old secretary to finish his lunch at the crowded bar. A rather rusty-looking elderly man clutching a tankard of mild beer pulled him by the sleeve.

'What was all that about, Beadle? What's that insufferable hypocrite Portman been telling you? You look worried.'

'I think he was dropping me a hint. You know that our people are involved in joint guarantees with Peto's Bank? Portman was suggesting that all's not as well as it should be at Peto's. Rumour's a deadly thing, but I wonder whether I shouldn't drop a hint myself to my guvnor? If Peto's goes to the wall—'

'Hush, man: there's a hundred pairs of ears in here, all listening for tips and rumours, and bits of gossip. Still, it's odd . . . Peto's are one of the parties to the Scandinavian loan. It's hardly the moment, you'd think, for Portman to start hinting at closure, unless there were something in it. If I were you, I'd tell your guvnor what you think. As a matter of fact, I think I'll drop a word in the right direction at *my* place. . . .'

The handsome and urbane Mr Curteis, private secretary to Sir Hamo Strange, leaned against a wall near the narrow opening to an alley in a poor quarter of Stepney, and watched an impoverished ragged man perform a lively tap dance on the pavement. He was accompanied by another man who was beating a complex and regular time by using a pair of china dinner plates, which he rattled together, then banged on his knees and elbows in a very effective and cleverly patterned percussion.

Really, thought Curteis, it was a very creditable performance, lively and entertaining. Both men were highly skilled in the exercise of their lowly arts. The tap dancer's eyes showed only bleak despair, though his companion, a younger man, still retained some natural jauntiness. They were performing at the end of a near-derelict street, the open channel running its length choked with rubbish, and many of the mean houses shuttered and barred.

The dance came to an abrupt stop, and the small audience of working men and women managed a clap and a cheer. One or two of them threw a halfpenny in the dancer's ragged cap. They had all moved aside when Curteis, in tailored overcoat and silk hat, had alighted from a cab, and joined them on the pavement. Now they drifted away, and Curteis felt in his pocket for a half crown, which he threw into the cap. The poor man looked at it in disbelief, and then bowed clumsily to Curteis, uttering some grotesque sounds. The secretary realized that the man was dumb.

He turned aside, and made his way down the narrow alley. It smelt of garbage and decay, and not for the first time Curteis wondered how people could be content to live in such squalid places.

Suddenly, a menacing figure lurched out of a side-entry, and blocked his way. It was another poor man, but a man whose face was bloated with drink, and brutalized by a life of unremitting toil allied to vice. He smiled contemptuously at the gentleman whom he had waylaid.

'Free with your money, aren't you?' the man sneered. 'Well, you can give *me* some of it, unless you want me to break your arm for you. Come on, blast you! Don't keep me waiting or—'

Without the slightest warning, Curteis lunged forward, and his right arm shot out to seize the man's throat. His fingers seemed to find their own way to the vital spot on the man's neck that sent him crashing with a strangled shriek to the ground. He lay writhing and gasping, his eyes wide with fear. His would-be victim calmly extracted a penny from his purse and flung it in the man's contorted face.

At the same time, a heavy, brutal fellow appeared at the mouth of the alley. His massive face was pitted and disfigured by the legacy of smallpox, and he stood with his arms hanging loosely at his sides, fists clenched. There was more than a little of the simian about him, thought Curteis, but behind those fists was the power of an ox.

The brute glanced at Curteis, then turned his attention to the thug, who was still writhing on the ground. He delivered a savage kick to the man's back, and his whines turned to a yelp of pain. Summoning up what strength remained to him, the would-be robber rose to his feet and staggered away along the alley.

'It wasn't his lucky day, was it, Mahoney?' said Curteis with a smile.

'There'll be worse days for him, Mr Curteis, if he ever crosses my path again. You'd better come into the house. I suppose *he's* sent you?'

'He has. There's a job he wants you to do for him before the twenty-eighth.'

Curteis followed the big brute along the side-alley, and the two men entered a wretched hovel of a house through its rear yard.

'Now then, Mahoney,' said Curteis, when they had sat down at a rickety table in the back kitchen of the house, 'I want you to listen carefully to what I have to tell you. I'm just the mouthpiece, as you'll appreciate: all these instructions come directly from *him*. He wanted me to take you back with me to Medici House, but I persuaded him that you'd be happier talking to me.'

'That's a matter of opinion, Mr Curteis. Me and old Strange get along fine, but you're a dangerous kind of cove. Very fancy and gentlemanly you are, but I wouldn't care to turn my back on you!'

'You're hardly a beauty yourself, Mahoney,' Curteis replied with

78

a dangerous smile. 'That ugly face of yours would crack a mirror, always supposing you were foolish enough to look into one, and no one would describe your character as pure and unblemished. I could mention the names of three men now lying in their graves—'

With an oath, the brute lunged at the smiling secretary, but in a moment he found himself crashing from the table and flat on his back, with the other man standing over him. Mahoney suddenly laughed, and Curteis hauled him to his feet.

'You and your Japanese tricks,' the big man grumbled. 'I don't know why I put up with you, Mr Curteis. Anyway, you'd better tell me what he wants.'

'He wants you to go out to Duppas Park House, in Croydon, which is the residence of Lord Jocelyn Peto, and there indulge your genius for breaking and entering. Peto has a kind of sanctum on the third floor, where he displays some of the choicer items in his private collection. On the wall facing the window there hangs an old Tudor tapestry, representing Daphne and Apollo—'

'Who?'

'What a pity, Mahoney, that you're so ignorant and unlettered! Let's just say it's a tapestry hanging on the wall. You know what a tapestry is, don't you?'

'Yes. And if there's any more of your lip, Mr Curteis, I'll flatten you against that wall behind you, Strange or no Strange. I suppose there's a safe behind this tapestry?'

'How clever of you! Yes, there's a nice modern Milner safe, five bolts, two locks, and inside it there should be a parcel of six old books, wrapped in green baize and tied with string. You're to take those books, and deliver them to Sir Hamo Strange via the usual channels. Here's a little something to make the job easier for you.'

He passed Mahoney a small packet done up in brown paper, and secured with sealing-wax. The big brute smiled rather grimly, and slipped it into one of his pockets.

Curteis reached into an inner pocket of his overcoat, and

produced a sheaf of notes and diagrams, which he handed to Mahoney.

'These notes will give you the lie of the land. Duppas Park House is a new building,' he said, 'and there's an iron fire escape to one side of it, with access to all floors. Very convenient, in more ways than one. He wants the job done on this coming Monday, the twenty-fourth.'

'Monday? What's the matter with the old fool? Monday's too near the twenty-eighth for comfort. We're going to need to concentrate on the twenty-eighth. Incidentally, why has he gone to all these lengths to lure that PC Lane away from Carmelite Pavement on the day? I could have arranged an accident for Lane. It'd have been cheaper than calling in Spooky Portman to arrange all that rigmarole about ghosts.'

'Sir Hamo Strange has his reasons, Mahoney. PC Lane has done excellent work guarding his bank vaults for the last three years. He's a good man, hence all the rigmarole, as you call it. Well, he's already been told that another officer has volunteered to stand in for him next Friday, while he rushes off to the magical lady in Belsize Park. And as for Spooky Portman – well, he's doing valuable work stirring up doubts in the City about Peto's Bank. One way or the other, Sir Hamo means to cook Lord Jocelyn's goose.'

Curteis rose from his chair, and glanced around the kitchen. A heavy serge police uniform hung on a peg behind the door.

'I see you've got your togs for Friday,' he said. 'Really, Mahoney, I wonder that you don't blush to wear that suit. You're such an evil villain. So you'll do the job?'

'Well, of course I'll do the job. Milner's five-and-twos are child's play to me, though I'm grateful for the little packet you gave me, all the same. Am I to be paid? Or does he want me to chalk it up on the slate?'

'Here's a hundred pounds in Bank of England notes. You'll get twice that when you've delivered the goods. I've had enough of this vile den of yours, so I'll bid you good day.'

As Curteis walked towards the back door that would take him out once again into the alley, Mahoney made a sudden lunge, and pinned him, breathless, to the wall. His brawny right forearm straddled the secretary's throat, and his eyes, the eyes of an ungovernable savage, glared at the elegant secretary with a momentary hatred. Curteis only smiled.

'Did you want to tell me something?' he said. 'I wish you weren't so emphatic.'

He made a sudden hooking movement with his left foot, and the giant thug slid with a shout of anger to the dirty kitchen floor. He uttered a rueful laugh, and sat up, rubbing the back of his head with a ham-like hand. Curteis hauled him to his feet.

'This is becoming a habit,' Mahoney muttered. 'But it makes me think. If ever things go wrong for you and me, Mr Curteis, we could team up, and go into business on our own account. You'd provide the fancy front and the nimble brain, and I'd be the enforcer. Protection, that's what I have in mind.'

Curteis paused with his hand on the door latch, and looked appraisingly at the big, pockmarked brute still sitting on the floor.

'I'll think about it, Mahoney,' he said. 'It's an idea. Yes, decidedly, it's an idea'

At the ornate entrance to The Pen and Wig in Carter Lane, Mr Arthur Portman smiled to himself, then pushed open the swing doors, which afforded him entrance to yet another haunt of the hungry and thirsty denizens of the City at lunchtime.

'Portman!' cried a cheery voice from a crowded table in the corner. 'Come and join us. Have the spirits been giving you any further investment tips? Not that you need them, working at Peto's. You look very smart, today, if I may say so.'

'I may look smart on the *out*side, Joe,' said Portman, sitting down at the crowded table, 'but that doesn't mean I'm feeling smart inside. Don't judge a book by its cover! As a matter of fact,' he confided, 'I'm thinking of a change. . . .'

'You can take my word for it, Vickers,' said Dr George Freeman to the rector of St Jerome's, Duppas Park, in the leafy suburbs of Croydon, 'that what you're suffering from is dyspepsia, combined with the kind of sleeplessness that comes with advancing years. There's nothing wrong with your heart, so you needn't frighten yourself to death by imagining that every twinge is the onset of something fatal. Take those cachets I've given you as directed. I'll call round tomorrow morning, after ten, to see how you are.'

Doctor Freeman put back his stethoscope into his black case. As he picked up his hat and stick from the table of the rector's study, a clock somewhere in the room struck eleven.

'You should have more trust in Providence, Vickers,' said the doctor, an old friend who knew that his attempt at humour would not be taken amiss. 'Why, even your name shows that you were destined to become a clergyman, so try to behave like one! A very apt name – Vickers.'

The Reverend Edwin Vickers smiled with amused resignation. He was nearer seventy than sixty, and had listened for fifty years to countless people who had felt impelled to say that Vickers was an apt name for a clergyman.

'Yes, Freeman,' he said, 'so apt, indeed, that no one in the church's hierarchy ever thought fit to promote me out of a parish. Not that I'm complaining, of course. Croydon is a remarkably pleasant town, and Duppas Hill's a healthy situation. So, I'll submit myself to your strictures, take my medicine, and exercise due patience. Good night, and thank you for coming out at so unconscionable an hour.'

When the doctor had gone, Edwin Vickers settled himself into his big chair in the window of his study. It was a quiet, orderly room at the front of his yellow-brick rectory on the opposite side of the vast expanse of grass separating his parsonage from Duppas Park House, the imposing modern mansion of Lord Jocelyn Peto, rising in all its opulence above Jubilee Road.

Sleeplessness was a wretched condition. It would keep him in this chair, looking out across the dark scene towards the blazing lights of Duppas Park House, until dawn, though there would be bouts of fitful dozing and uncomfortable jerks into renewed wakefulness.

Odd, how one's eyes could play tricks. On Saturday, he'd seen a hulking brute of a man lurking in the narrow rear garden of Lord Jocelyn's house, and had felt at once that the man had been up to no good. The figure had reminded him strongly of a former parishioner, a giant of a young man who had joined the local Croydon police, and then had been poached, apparently, by Scotland Yard. But, of course, young Jack Knollys would never have skulked around in that fashion.

The man had appeared again on Sunday, towards dusk, but he had soon lost sight of him. Oh, well, he'd best close his eyes, and go through the motions of sleeping!

The Reverend Edwin Vickers dreamt that he was adrift on an ice floe, his right side pressed hard on the gunwale of the boat, which was adrift in the Arctic Ocean. Gradually, the majestic icebergs, and the dark sky, brilliant with freezing stars, dissolved into his silent study, where he had slumped against the hard side of his chair. The cold was real enough. How long had he sat, cramped and confined in his chair?

He sat up, felt for his matches, and lit the candle standing ready on a little table close at hand. The room leapt to life, and he let his eyes wander across the many shelves crammed with well-thumbed books, then over his desk, where his sermon notes from Sunday still lay among other papers, and finally to the staid grandfather clock near the door, which showed him that it was nearly three o'clock in the morning.

He levered himself out of his chair, and wandered rather aimlessly around the room. His old housekeeper, he knew, had retired hours ago. He caught sight of himself in a mirror, and paused to look critically at the large-boned frame of a man who had been formidably strong in his youth.

He smiled ruefully, and shook his head. Those heady days were long gone, when he had been one of the last hackers under the old rules at Rugby School. He'd gone on to win himself a place in the famous Oxford side which had thrashed the Light Blues at Blackheath in '61. Young Knollys had been a promising rugby player, one of those massively strong lads who made good lock forwards. . . .

Edwin Vickers crossed to the window, and pulled back the curtains. A strong summer moon was climbing down the sky, vying with the long line of gas lamps running along Park Road, the leafy thoroughfare skirting the park. Across the green, he could see Duppas Park House bathed in moonlight.

As he looked, the light of a lantern moved across one of the windows on the third floor. It disappeared, only to reappear in the next window to the right. Surely those were the windows of Lord Jocelyn Peto's gallery? Vickers seized a pair of binoculars from their place on the window sill, and trained them on the distant house. Like many clergymen, he was an amateur ornithologist; tonight, though, he was spying on a more deadly species than rare garden birds.

A figure suddenly appeared on the top level of the iron fire escape, a huge, burly man, carrying a heavy sack. The man's head turned slowly, surveying the scene, and then he disappeared once more into the house. A burglar! No doubt it was that brute whom he'd seen lurking about over the weekend.

Now fully awake, Edwin Vickers hurried out into the hallway, chose a heavy stick from the hall stand, and left the house, pulling the door to behind him. Lord Jocelyn was a decent, public-spirited man, entitled to keep what was his. As he strode along Park Road, he thought to himself, this impudent thief may find an insomniac former Rugby Blue rather more than a match for him!

He arrived, breathless, at the foot of the fire escape, and stood in the grass, which was damp with the night dew. Common sense suddenly prevailed. He was an old man, no match for a strong young villain. He would walk on to Hatchard Street, and knock up the constable.

He had just turned to make his way silently across the grass to Jubilee Road when the burglar, who had emerged on to the top platform of the fire escape, threw his sack of loot down to the ground. It caught Vickers squarely on the shoulders, and with a cry he fell down on to the grass. He could hear the remorseless clattering of the man's boots as he ran down the steps and, as he raised himself on one arm, his senses were assailed by the fellow's fierce, angry breathing. If he could get up in time, he would be able to run for it. If not, then he had his stick, and he would make a valiant effort to defend himself. Here he was, now!

'Inspector Box, and you, Sergeant Knollys,' said Superintendent Mackharness, 'I've called you up here because I have just received a note by special messenger from Inspector Price at Croydon. As you know, the Croydon force are quite separate from us, but they do co-operate in a very welcome fashion. Would that could be said of every provincial force! But there. This is not a perfect world.'

Superintendent Mackharness had summoned both men to his first-floor office at the Rents soon after nine o'clock on the morning of Tuesday, 25 July. He sat at his massive desk, immaculate as always, but with a worried expression in his normally fierce eyes. He kept glancing enigmatically at Knollys, as though something in the note that he had received applied specifically to him.

'Yes, indeed,' Mackharness continued. 'Yes. I – what was I saying, Box? That attentive look of yours, rather like an over-eager spaniel, makes me forget what I was going to say.'

'About Inspector Price's note, sir.'

'Yes. This is a very bad business, Box. Just after six o'clock this morning, in the grounds of Duppas Park House, Croydon, the dead body of the Reverend Edwin Vickers was found. He had been bludgeoned to death. Sergeant Knollys—'

'Yes, sir, I've known Mr Vickers all my life. I'm a Croydon man myself, as you know, and it was Mr Vickers who baptized me. He was a wonderful man, sir, a famous rugby player in his youth. Bludgeoned, you say. . . . Murdered?'

'Oh, yes, Sergeant, murdered without a doubt. I'm very sorry that you knew the victim personally, and I know you'll not take offence if I remind you that no personal considerations must interfere with the impartiality of your investigation. There, I have to say that, though I know it's quite unnecessary. I want you both to go straight away to Croydon, and associate yourselves with Inspector Price, if that is his desire.'

'Duppas Park House, sir,' said Box. 'That's the residence of Lord Jocelyn Peto—'

'It is, Box, and I share what is evidently your unease at that fact. On Friday of this week the bullion of the Swedish Loan is to be moved, and now one of the principal furnishers of that loan has a murder in his back garden. See if you can clear the matter up, will you? There was a robbery at the house – Price tells me in the note that it involved a successful assault on Lord Jocelyn's safe. I think it more than likely that the unfortunate clergyman was struck down in trying to prevent the robber's escape.'

The superintendent drummed on the desk with his stout fingers for a while, gazing rather mournfully into space.

'It might be one of the usual riffraff – Croaker Mullins, or Killer Tom Dacey. They're both out of prison at the moment. Or it might be— Get out there, will you, Box, before the trail goes cold. Try to clear it up if you can, or at least so far as to hand the business back completely to Croydon before you leave. I want a clear run, if possible, up to the twenty-eighth.'

They left Mackharness's office, and made their way downstairs. It was one of the rare moments when the entrance hall was deserted, and Box had time to notice the oblique rays of sunlight thrown across the bare wooden boards from the tall, barred window at the foot of the stairs.

'Croydon! It's a far cry, Sergeant Knollys,' he said, 'from the hub of the Empire, by which I mean the crowded canvas stretched between King's Reach and Pentonville Road. Still, it's your native place, and you'll be able to guide me through its complexities, and show me its many delights.'

Knollys smiled to himself. The guvnor, he knew, was trying to cheer him up. That was like him. Old Mr Vickers had been an integral part of Knollys' early years. He had never expected the man who had christened him, taught him in Sunday school, and later encouraged him on the rugby field, to meet a brutal end in the pleasant purlieus of his own parish.

Within a quarter of an hour Box and Knollys were sitting in a cab that would take them across the river to London Bridge Station, and the Croydon train.

7

A Thief in the Night

Box and Knollys walked swiftly along Croydon's narrow high street, and past the imposing town hall in its attractive gardens. Both men appreciated the Surrey town's provincial charms and open aspect, particularly as the streets were bathed in the strong morning sunlight.

'We'll cross here, sir,' said Knollys, 'and cut through Laud Street. That'll take us up Duppas Hill and into the park.'

They threaded their way through the traffic in the main street, and reached the narrow thoroughfare named in honour of the only Archbishop of Canterbury to be beheaded. A few minutes' brisk walk brought them on to the open prospect of Duppas Park, where a few tall houses of good quality rose behind painted railings on the edge of the green expanse.

'That's Duppas Park House, sir,' exclaimed Knollys, pointing to an imposing three-storey mansion clad in gleaming white stucco. A number of carriages stood in the road beyond the gardens, and a knot of curious bystanders had congregated on the pavement of the nearby Jubilee Road.

As they approached the house, a smartly dressed uniformed police inspector caught sight of them, and beckoned them to join him near the iron fire escape at the foot of which the Reverend

Edwin Vickers had met his violent death.

'That's Inspector Price,' said Knollys. 'I worked with him for a time when I was still in uniform. He must have recognized me.'

Inspector Price met them at the corner of the house. He had an eager, bronzed face, and small bright eyes that seemed to dart everywhere. There was something about him that reminded Box of a ferret.

'Hello, Knollys,' he said, in a lilting Welsh accent. 'Sergeant, now, isn't it? Congratulations. And you'll be Detective Inspector Box. We've never met, but I've seen your picture in the daily prints more than once. Let me show you both the scene of this damnable murder.'

He led them to the foot of the black-painted iron fire escape that rose through all three storeys, from each of which it was accessed through a metal-framed French window. Box looked up, and saw that the window on the third storey stood open. Inspector Price followed his glance.

'That's one of the windows of Lord Jocelyn's gallery, where he displays his old books and paintings. A robbery took place in that room, Mr Box, in the early hours of the morning, and the robber left with his loot through that window, and down this fire escape. He'd brought a dark lantern, which he left up there on the top platform.'

Price moved to a spot about a yard from the fire escape, and crouched down on the grass.

'On reaching the ground, I believe he encountered the late unfortunate Mr Vickers, Rector of St Jerome's church. He was an elderly man, but still hale and hearty. As Sergeant Knollys will tell you, he'd been a celebrated rugby player in his youth.'

'What was Mr Vickers doing out of doors at that hour of the morning?' asked Box.

'He was an insomniac. For some reason or other, he could never get to sleep at night. Dr Freeman had been to see him that very evening, and had left him some medicine in the form of cachets.

His housekeeper heard the front door slam, and knew that he'd gone out for one of his lonely night walks. She struck a match and looked at the clock. It was just on five past three.'

'What do you think happened then, Mr Price?'

'I believe that poor Mr Vickers grappled with the intruder in an attempt to save his neighbour's property. He'd left the rectory carrying a walking stick. It was with this stick, Mr Box, that the intruder battered Mr Vickers to death.'

The inspector pointed to a patch of bloodstained grass.

'His body was lying there, with the skull crushed in by a number of heavy blows. The stick was lying some feet away from where he was found. Our police surgeon's had a look at the body, and says that death occurred at some time between three o'clock and half past. Mr Vickers was discovered this morning by a gardener who had just come in from the town to work.'

Price hauled himself to his feet, and looked quizzically at Box, as though expecting him to ask a question.

'What do you want *me* to do, Mr Price?' asked Box. 'Do you want me to associate myself with this crime, or leave it to Croydon?'

'This is a straightforward case, Mr Box. A burglary took place, and the intruder committed murder – for murder it was – to prevent capture. We can handle this investigation well enough, though if we need help from Scotland Yard, then, of course, we'll call on you and ask for it.'

'But you think the robbery's a case for the Yard?'

'I do. There's something odd about the whole thing, if you ask me. Lord Jocelyn is the soul of courtesy and co-operation, but he's very ill at ease. I think he knows who was behind the robbery, and doesn't want to tell us who it was.'

'What was stolen? Something very valuable, I suppose.'

'Books, Mr Box. Some books, wrapped up in a green baize cloth.'

'Books? Well, well, I wonder. . . . You're right about this robbery,

Mr Price. If what I already suspect to be the case is true, then this is definitely a matter for Scotland Yard.'

Box and Knollys were admitted to the house by a middle-aged butler, who was striving manfully to remain calm and collected in a house that had been burgled only hours since, and in the grounds of which a brutal murder had been committed.

'If you will remain here a moment, sir,' said the butler, 'I will tell Lord Jocelyn that you are here.'

The hall was light and airy, with delicate white panelling, and a curving staircase of marble and brass in the art nouveau style. There was a magnificent stained-glass window on the first-floor landing, and a crystal chandelier hung down from a vaulted plaster ceiling.

The doors of the main reception rooms led off from the hall. One door, to their left, stood open, and they saw a lady in a mauve morning dress presiding over a group of rather homely women, all engaged in stitching and hemming. The lady in mauve glanced up briefly, caught Box's eye, and bowed stiffly in what he imagined was an attempt at gracious acknowledgement of his presence. He recognized the lady from her photograph in a recent number of *The Strand Magazine*. Lady Marion Peto, a renowned beauty in her youth, was now a rather commonplace, matronly figure, much given to charitable works.

Suddenly, Lord Jocelyn Peto erupted into the hail. He was followed by the butler, who stood stiffly a few feet away from his master.

'My dear Inspector Box!' Peto cried. 'How very good of you to come. I gather that the Commissioner spoke to your superior officer about this unfortunate business. Are you here for the murder, or the robbery?'

As he spoke, Lord Jocelyn darted towards the room where his wife was closeted with her friends, and drew the door closed.

'I'm here about the robbery, sir,' Box replied. 'And before you start telling me all about it, I'd like to survey the scene of the crime myself. I should like you to accompany us, if you will, Lord Jocelyn, and it would save some time if your butler would come, as well.'

'Certainly, Inspector. Come, Tanner, let us all go upstairs to the gallery.'

The long room on the third floor was adorned with pieces of antique statuary, old paintings, and glazed bookcases, the shelves of which were filled with ancient and valuable volumes. On a section of the wall facing the front windows of the gallery an old tapestry had been pulled aside to reveal a tall, green-painted safe set into a deep alcove. The heavy door stood open. Lord Jocelyn strode over to the safe, and made as if to speak, but Inspector Box had walked resolutely towards the end of the gallery, where the metal-framed French window gave access to the fire escape. Sergeant Knollys followed him.

While master and servant stood irresolutely near the rifled safe, Box knelt down in front of the window. He donned a pair of round, gold-framed spectacles, which made him look older than his years, pushed the window outwards on to the platform, and peered closely at the sill.

'Lord Jocelyn,' said Box, still kneeling beside the door, 'there are traces of felt fibre here, on the metal sill, and one or two little strands of the same material caught on the small splinters between these polished floor boards.'

'Is that of any significance, Inspector?'

'Yes, sir. It tells me that the intruder wore felt over-shoes, and that in turn suggests to me that he was a professional burglar. I rather think— Ah!'

Box had turned his attention to the window lock, and even from where he stood, Lord Jocelyn could see the sudden glint of excitement spring into the detective's eyes. Box stood up, automatically dusting the knees of his trousers.

'Mr Tanner,' he said to the butler, 'I noticed when I arrived here that all three windows giving access to the fire escape are of this type, French windows with metal frames, each furnished with a mortise lock. This one has a bolt at top and bottom. So what we have here, in effect, are three doors, each accessible from the outside, and facing away from the front of the house, and from Jubilee Road. A godsend for burglars, you might say. Were they always locked at night?'

'Yes, indeed, sir. I lock all three myself every night at eleven o'clock, after I've secured the front and back entrances of the house.'

'There is no key in this lock.'

'No, sir. I thought that it would be inviting trouble if keys were left in the locks during the night hours. It would be easy, you see, for an intruder to smash one of the small glass panes, reach his hand through, and turn the key.'

'Well, well, Mr Tanner, thank you for telling me. Why didn't *I* think of that?'

Sergeant Knollys successfully suppressed a smile. Tanner seemed quite unperturbed, waiting politely for the next question.

'So you keep those three keys on your own chain?'

'Just one key, sir. That key fits all three locks.'

'And what happened to the other two keys? There must have been three keys onginally.'

For the first time, the butler showed faint signs of confusion.

'Well, I don't know what might have happened to the other keys, sir. During my time here, as Lord Jocelyn will bear me out, there's only been the one key to these three windows.'

'That's perfectly true, Inspector. Both Tanner and his predecessor have fixed that key to their key rings. Do you think it's of any great significance? Aren't you going to examine the safe?'

'Bear with me, sir, if you please. I'll examine the safe in two minutes. I'll give it my undivided attention. But not just yet. Tanner, did you lock this particular window with your key last night, at eleven o'clock? And did you shoot the bolts, top and bottom?'

'I did, sir.'

'Very well. Now, as you can see, this door has been unlocked with a key, from the inside. There are no keyholes on the outer side of the three French windows. So the window's unlocked, but there's no key in the keyhole. What does that suggest to you?'

'Why, sir, that someone must have unlocked it later in the night, after I'd retired. But who could have done that? The key remained secure on my key ring.'

The man's face suddenly flushed with barely controlled anger.

'You're not suggesting that I left it open deliberately, are you? You're not suggesting—'

'That will do, Tanner,' said Lord Jocelyn, sharply. 'No one is suggesting anything. Mr Box is simply trying to establish what happened here last night. That is so, is it not, Inspector?'

'It is, sir. There's no call to take offence, Mr Tanner. It's very clear to me that someone crept in here last night, or very early in the morning, and using a spare key, opened this French window, and drew back the bolts. So, Mr Tanner, I'd like you to go now, and assemble all the indoor staff in one place, so that we can have a look at them. Sergeant Knollys will go with you. I'll take a look at the safe, now.'

All the time he had been speaking, Box had been watching Lord Jocelyn Peto's face, and had seen the curious amalgam of shock and vexation animating it. He was a handsome man, evidently accustomed to being admired, and he had never learnt the art of concealing his emotions. Yes, there was shock in that expression, which was understandable. But *vexation*?

'Sir,' he asked. 'did either you or Lady Marion Peto hear any sound of this break-in during the night? I expect Inspector Price has asked you the same question.'

'He has, Inspector. No, neither my wife nor myself heard anything untoward. Incidentally, Lady Marion was due to entertain her ladies of the Dorcas Society this morning, and I thought it advisable to let her do so, despite what has happened. Lady Marion would not be able to tell you anything useful.'

Somewhere, behind those dismissive words, Box caught a suggestion of belittlement. Perhaps this personable and noble banker had weighed his wife in the social balance and found her wanting? Such things did happen in circles where a public façade was judged to be a necessary ingredient of professional and marital success.

Box turned his attention to the safe. Two of its four shelves held a number of bound account books. Another contained locked deposit boxes, none of which had been disturbed. The fourth shelf, that nearest the floor, was empty.

Box took a hand lens from his pocket, and examined the two locks. Neither showed any telltale scratches or gouges, which would have told him of an attempt to insert force-locks into the keyholes. He inserted the top joint of his right little finger into the keyhole of the top lock, and looked at the smear of grease and metal filings that it had gathered. Lord Jocelyn's voice broke the silence.

'A professional burglar, you said, Mr Box. Obviously a very skilled one, as he was able to open the safe without leaving a mark on it. They listen to the tumblers moving into place, don't they?'

'Yes, sir. And when he's listened to the tumblers,' said Box, solemnly, straightening up from examining the lower lock, 'he executes a little tattoo with his fist on the panel, kicks the door with the heel of his right boot, seizes the brass handle, and – hey, presto! – Mr Milner's safe yields to his superior skills—'

'Good heavens, Inspector! Is that how it's done?'

'No, sir, it isn't. I hope you'll forgive my little joke. This robbery is what we call an inside job. That safe was opened with a key – it's all keys in this case. You've got a Judas in your midst, and, with a bit of luck, either myself or Sergeant Knollys will pick him out from among your servants. You see the black smear on my finger?

It's a mixture of hard wax and lead filings. The key that was used to open this safe was a recent copy of your own key.'

'A copy? But how can that be? I keep the key of that safe constantly about my person.' Box saw his hand stray to his waist-coat pocket.

'What about when you go to bed, sir?'

'I put it in my bedside drawer.'

'So it isn't constantly about your person, is it, sir? Most things aren't, when you come to think about it. At some time when you and your safe key have been separated, perhaps when you were asleep, or taking a bath, or preparing to change into or out of evening clothes, your resident Judas crept in, took a wax impression of your key, and later made a mould, into which he, or an accomplice, would pour molten lead. It's crude, Lord Jocelyn, and a lead key's only good for one job, but it's very effective. That's what's happened here.'

Lord Jocelyn Peto's face showed all too clearly his admiration of Box's professional expertise. He was a good-humoured, outward-going man, and Box's account of his deductions had made him want to clap his hands. But he couldn't do that, of course. That poor, inoffensive clergyman had been murdered on his doorstep, so to speak: the burglar had also been a murderer. And in any case, he was *vexed*. What on earth was he to tell this clever, eager young man?

'And now, sir,' said Box, 'perhaps you'd tell me what it was that our burglar was hired to steal? This job was plotted and planned, Lord Jocelyn. The burglar came to rob you of a specific item. Would you care to tell me what it was?'

'It was – it was a collection of old books, done up in a green baize bag. But I can't think that the burglar could have known of its existence. Surely he came here on the off chance that there was money in the safe? I'm known to be a very rich man.'

'Yes, I know you are, sir,' Box replied, treating the banker to a wolfish smile, 'and on this coming Friday I shall be one of the

police officers supervising the movement of your bullion reserve
from the Strand to Temple Pier.'

'What an odd coincidence, Inspector!'

'Yes, sir, it is. We live in a world of curious coincidences. So our
burglar turned murderer stole some old books, did he?'

'Yes. Old books, you know, from centuries ago.'

'Like the Complutensian Polyglot Bible, Lord Jocelyn?'

Arnold Box had the satisfaction of seeing the noble banker shy
away from him like a frightened colt.

'This is a very embarrassing situation, Inspector Box,' said Lord
Jocelyn Peto, frowning, and biting his lip. 'Very embarrassing. You
seem to know a great deal more about the Polyglot Bible than I
imagined any layman could know. You even know about
Sudermann. I want to tell you all, but if I do, I may compromise a
third party by linking him to this wretched robbery. Can't we just
let the matter drop?'

'No, sir.'

'Well, well, it's a silly, wretched business. I'd better tell you all
about it.'

Box, by drawing on his memory of the meeting with Mr M.R.
James, had duly dazzled the noble banker with his apparent expertise in the matter of ancient books and their wanderings.

Lord Jocelyn had preceded Box to a small writing room adjacent to the gallery, where they would be able to talk more
privately.

'You seem to know all about the rivalry between myself and Sir
Hamo Strange. It's a rivalry that extends not only to our dealings
as bankers, but to our success as collectors of ancient books and
manuscripts. I have been trying for many years to acquire the
unique Ferdinand and Isabella Bible, and Strange, too, was obses-
sively eager to obtain it.'

'And he secured the professional services of Herr Aaron
Sudermann in order to achieve his ambition.'

'He did, Mr Box. I can't imagine how you came to know all this! Sudermann's reputation as a procurer of antiquities is unequalled. But I used a very canny Scotsman called Macdonald. He conducts his business from a little crooked shop in Ediniburgh. It took him years to track the Bible down to Count Fuentes' castle in Andalusia, but when he had done so, he sped there like the wind on the third of July, and pipped Sudermann to the post.'

'I suppose there was an element of luck involved, Lord Jocelyn?'

'Yes, I suppose there was. And then, it seems that Fuentes had prepared a false copy of the unique Bible, concocted from a genuine edition which had been "doctored", if I may use that expression, and sold it to Sudermann before absconding to escape his debtors. Strange comes back to London with his prize, attempts to humiliate me by flaunting it in front of a couple of experts, only to have those experts pronounce it a forgery! I must say, Inspector Box, that it was an amusing business—'

Box angrily interrupted the banker's account of his triumph over Sir Hamo Strange.

'No, sir!' he exclaimed. 'It was not amusing at all, if I may say so. It was a sordid, wretched business all along! I am presented here, sir, with the prospect of two renowned bankers, one said to be broker to the crowned heads of Europe, the other – yourself – a nobleman, and a household word for probity in London, squabbling like jealous schoolboys over an overpriced second-hand book! And that petty behaviour, sir, has led indirectly to the violent death of a respected clergyman—'

'Inspector—'

'No, sir, hear me out! You thought it was amusing when Sir Hamo Strange was publicly humiliated. Did you let him see that you were amused? Did you gloat, sir?'

'Well, yes, I suppose I did. I pretended to commiserate with his loss, but he knew that I was secretly laughing at his discomfiture. The money was nothing to either of us. It was the loss of face that rankled with Strange.'

Box's anger was beginning to evaporate. Lord Jocelyn's behaviour had been typical of his class, and it had been idle to take him to task. Besides, the noble banker had shown no resentment at being scolded like a schoolboy. Perhaps Box's words had gone home.

'Loss of face? Yes, sir, I suppose that's true. And he would have guessed from your manner that you yourself had procured the Polyglot Bible. I'll save you the embarrassment of hinting that Sir Hamo Strange was behind this burglary by saying it for you. He wanted that Bible, and he was prepared to get someone to break in to your safe to get it. But, of course, Lord Jocelyn, you knew that, didn't you?'

'Yes, I did. And so, I made sure that Hamo would be disappointed a second time. When he opens that particular green baize bag – it's not the original, by the way – he'll find six bound copies of *The Cornhill Magazine*.'

'And where have you hidden the Complutensian Polyglot Bible, Lord Jocelyn?'

'It's where I intended it to be all along: in the vault of my banking-house in the Strand. Even Sir Hamo Strange can't cheat his way into that!'

Twelve people had been assembled in the servants' hall, a long stone-flagged room in the basement of Duppas Park House. Inspector Box and Sergeant Knollys stood near the door, and studied them. Tanner stood slightly apart, as though stressing his superior position as director of the household. A stern, starched housekeeper guarded her little flock of servant girls – the house parlour-maid, looking haughty and superior, three general housemaids, and a tearful little between-maid. Behind these stood the cook, her assistant, and the scullery-maid, a timid little creature who looked no more than twelve years old. Bringing up the rear, and ranged stiffly against the back wall, were the two footmen, resplendent in their knee breeches and blue and silver liveries.

'I am Detective Inspector Box, of Scotland Yard,' said Box. 'I've had you brought here so that I can ask you a single question: Did any of you hear or see anything that may be relevant to this robbery of your master's possessions during the night?'

Nobody answered, but one of the three housemaids started violently, and only just managed to stifle a sob. Box pretended not to notice.

'Nobody saw or heard anything? Are you all quite sure of that? A robbery has taken place, and a murder was committed in the grounds. A murder! If you've anything to tell me, you must tell me now. No? Very well. I think that's all, Mr Tanner.'

As the staff began to disperse, Box whispered to Knollys, 'The second of those two footmen – the lanky one, with fair hair – is Snobby Quayle, one of the Milton Fisher gang. He's been in service, and can pose as a footman, a skilled waiter, or a valet. He leaves doors unlocked, and windows half open – things like that. So when we get back to London we'll go after the Milton Fisher gang. It's interesting. . . .'

'Do you want me to arrest him, sir?'

'Yes. Then hand him over to Mr Price to keep locked up in Hatchard Street police station until we need him. He won't talk, though. The Fisher boys never do. Meanwhile, I'm going to have a word with that sobbing housemaid. She knows something.'

8

Sir Hamo Strange Dines Out

Box looked at the young woman who stood, pale and silent, waiting for him to speak. Alice Parkes was in her mid-twenties, a pretty girl with frightened blue eyes and a nervous mouth. She looked smart in the uniform of a housemaid, and Box guessed that she was the kind of young woman who performed her duties willingly and well.

'Now, Alice Parkes,' said Box, 'it's obvious to me that you saw or heard something last night – no, it's no good denying it, my girl, so you'd better tell me all about it! We're private here, in this little pantry, but if I have to haul you down to Hatchard Street, then everyone will know. So what was it?'

'Oh, sir,' cried the young woman tearfully, 'don't tell the mistress! If you do, she'll dismiss me straight away. I meant no harm. And neither did Bert—'

'Bert? Look, Alice, just sit down there in that chair, and tell me all about it. If you've done nothing wrong, then nothing's going to happen to you.'

'You see, sir,' said Alice, 'last year, when I was twenty-four, I had a baby, a little girl, it was. Well, Bert, my young man, swore he'd stand by me, and he did, and next year, when we've saved a bit more, we'll get married. Lord Jocelyn knows all about it, and agreed that I could stay. That's typical of his lordship, he's a wonderful, kindly man. But if Lady Marion ever found out – well, she's very strict, and she'd dismiss me immediately.'

'And where's the baby now?' For the moment, Box was more interested in Alice's story than in the burglary. He was beginning to regret his angry outburst to the noble banker. His regard for his wife may have evaporated, but in his treatment of Alice Parkes he had shown himself to be a far worthier man than Box had thought him.

'Baby is with my mother and father out at Selhurst. Bert's in service, too. He's a groom with Mr Sanders Clarke at Woodside. Mr Sanders Clarke is very strict, too, and won't let Bert visit, so once a month he walks in to Croydon from Woodside, and we meet in the trees by Jubilee Road to exchange news.'

'Ah! At last!' cried Box. 'A glimmer of light on the horizon! Your Bert was due to meet you last night, wasn't he? So, after the house was shut up, and everybody safely in bed, you slipped out into Jubilee Road, and waited in the trees for Bert to appear. Am I right?'

'Yes, sir. It was just after half past two. I slipped out of the front area door and across the lawn to the trees in Jubilee Road. The moon was ever so bright, and I could see the whole side of the house lit up. As I looked, a hulking great man appeared from the direction of Park Road. He was carrying a sack, which he threw down near the fire escape while he fiddled with some kind of lantern. Then he began to climb the iron steps. . . . I was terrified, sir, and when he turned on the first-floor platform and looked across at the trees where I was hidden, I nearly fainted.'

'He looked across, did he? I don't suppose you saw what he looked like, did you? Young women, when they're frightened, usually cover their faces with their hands.'

'Well, *I* didn't, Mr Box,' said the girl, pettishly. 'That man was after my master's goods, and I intended to get a good look at him. He was a huge fellow, with a big beefy face all pitted with smallpox scars. He stood there, hunched forward on the platform, looking more like an ape than anything human. Then he began to climb. I didn't wait to see if Bert would turn up. Instead, I made my way back to the house and crept up to my bed. I thought I'd dream about that man all night, but in fact I went to sleep straight away.'

'When you left the house, Alice, did you lock the door behind you?'

'Oh, yes, sir. I have a latch key to that area door. I'd never have left my master's house open in the middle of the night.'

Alice suddenly began to cry.

'I wasn't going to say anything, sir,' she sobbed, 'but when we heard that poor Mr Vickers had been murdered by that man, I didn't know what to do. You won't tell the mistress, will you? I'll lose my place—'

'I won't tell anyone, Alice, apart from my police colleagues, so don't worry about it. I hope all goes well for you, and Bert, and the baby. Meanwhile, if you recall anything else that you think I ought to know about, write a note to me. Inspector Price will give you my address.'

'This is a very sinister business, Sergeant Knollys,' said Box, drawing on his slim cigar. They had left Croydon on a train that would take them straight through to Victoria. Their compartment was empty, so that they could talk freely.

'Sinister, sir?'

'Yes, Sergeant. At first, it looked as though we were investigating a silly prank perpetrated by one spoilt millionaire upon another. But then, we find that one of the spoilt millionaires, Sir Hamo Strange, had access to a specialist villain like Snobby Quayle, one of the Milton Fisher gang of high-class robbers. How is it that a renowned banker has access to villains of that calibre?'

'It suggests something very unpleasant, sir. There's a whiff of corruption in the air.'

'There is, Sergeant. And then, we come to murder. Alice Parkes had the courage to look at Mr Vickers' murderer, and gave me a description of him. It was Francis Xavier Mahoney, a man with a trail of corpses behind him. He doesn't usually have any grudge against his victims, Sergeant. They're just people who got in his way while he was engaged on a job. He usually batters them to death in minutes, and then gets on with whatever he's doing. We know all about him, but we've never been able to bring him to book. Dead men tell no tales.'

'What's a man like that doing in the pay of Sir Hamo Strange? Incidentally, sir, if ever I catch this beauty, I'll not let go until I've brought him in. Mr Vickers was a good man, and a first-rate rugby player.'

'We've got to look into the matter of Sir Hamo Strange, Sergeant,' Box replied. 'Anyone who can call on the services of the Milton Fisher gang and Basher Mahoney needs to be investigated. But in three days' time millions of pounds' worth of gold are to be moved out to the East India Export Dock. Until that's done, Sir Hamo and his criminal associates will have to wait.'

Police Constable Lewis Lane sat at a corner table in the back bar of a public house near Long Acre, and thought about the business of his dead daughter, Catherine Mary. He had both heard and seen her, and tomorrow – Friday, 28 July – he would witness her final revelation before she was taken away to the Garden of Innocence.

PC Lane stirred uneasily. Was it all true? How *could* it be? There had been Mrs Pennymint and her platitudes, the reptilian Mr Portman, and then – and then the elegant and accomplished lady, Madam Sylvestris, who could bring back the spirits of the dead. Inspector Box was clearly an unbeliever, too ready to scoff at what he didn't understand. He'd been that way himself, once.

And yet. . . . This public house, the Sarah Siddons, was firmly anchored in reality. It was brash, very noisy, and very glittering, but it held its own quality of realism and common sense. Over in the far corner, an articulate old fellow was holding forth to an audience of a half-a-dozen theatrical customers, folk who worked at Covent Garden or Drury Lane. He had a fine, old-fashioned theatrical voice, and his long story was punctuated by laughter from his listeners. A broken-down old actor, by the look of it, but he, and his audience, belonged to the real world. Was he right about Madam Sylvestris? Or was the whole business a fraud, as Mr Box believed?

And had he been right in accepting an offer from a sergeant he'd never clapped eyes on before? Sergeant Webb, he'd called himself. The letters on his collar showed that he was from 'N' Division, at Islington. He'd heard on the grapevine, this Sergeant Webb had said, that he urgently wanted to attend a seance on Friday, the twenty-eighth of the month. Webb was a spiritualist himself, and sympathized with Lane's dilemma. He'd be able to send a substitute, a Constable Edwards, also of 'N', to take his place on guard at Sir Hamo Strange's private pier below Carmelite Pavement.

PC Lane looked at the old actor, who was still regaling his friends with amusing stories. He was a man nearing sixty, with an elfish, good-humoured face. In his imagination, Lane suddenly began to hear the strains of Bach's 'Jesu, Joy of Man's Desiring', which had been played on the phonograph at the seance in Belsize Park.

The blood rushed to Lane's head, and for a moment he thought he was going to faint. That expressive, fleshy mouth . . . the last time he had heard the old actor speak, he had told him that he was Roger Wilcox, his wife's uncle on her mother's side.

It was a fraud! It had all been lies. And little Catherine Mary's memory had been violated by that woman, by Portman, and by that superannuated old villain holding forth in the corner, and being repaid with tots of gin.

'Are you all right, mate?' enquired a man who was threading his way towards the bar. 'You look as pale as a ghost.'

'Just a little turn, friend. The fresh air will put that right. I don't suppose you know who that old chap is, the one telling funny stories in the corner?'

'That? That's Sebastian Tolmache, the old character actor. He's more or less retired now. I'd drink up and leave, if I were you, mate. You don't look well at all.'

Villainy. . . . He'd been got out of the way by someone. Well, fate had put paid to their little trick. He'd go after all to Carmelite Pavement tomorrow, and have a look at this Constable Edwards, who was supposed to take his place. And when the bullion assignment was over, he'd go after the so-called Sergeant Webb, and arrange for Pennymint, Portman and Sylvestris to be taken up on a charge of conspiracy.

Meanwhile, little Catherine Mary was where the vicar had said she was: safe in Heaven, with the angels. PC Lane finished his Guinness, and hurried out into Long Acre.

Louise Whittaker, thinking about her friend Inspector Box of Scotland Yard, stepped out of the Ladies' Dining Room in High Holborn, and almost collided with a distinguished bearded gentleman who had just alighted from a cab.

'Why, Miss Whittaker! You remember me, I trust? How nice to see you again!'

'Professor Verner! I'm so sorry to have barged into you like that. My mind was preoccupied with a friend of mine who's connected with the investigation of this terrible murder and robbery out at Croydon. How are you, Professor?'

'Very well. And hearing you mention that robbery at Croydon – at the home of Lord Jocelyn Peto – makes me recall that you told me, when we last met, that you banked with him. With Peto & Company in the Strand, I mean.'

'Yes, I do. For my twenty-first birthday my parents opened an account for me there. I was tremendously proud of that, you know! Even today, the private banks have a certain cachet—'

Professor Verner glanced conspiratorially at Louise, and lowered his voice.

'That may well be, but if I were you, my dear young lady, I'd take my money away from Peto's as soon as possible. There's a rumour going round that Peto's vaults are virtually empty. Take your money out, and put it somewhere safe, like in the Westminster Bank. A word to the wise, you know.'

When the professor had bidden her good day, Louise Whittaker walked thoughtfully up towards Holborn Circus. She'd wondered herself about Peto's. A stationer's clerk who had called at her house in Finchley had told her of a conversation he'd overheard in one of the City public houses. One of Peto's clerks had stoutly defended the bank, but in such a wild way as to arouse immediate suspicion.

If only she could entice dear, shy Arnold Box out to Finchley that very day, so that he could tell her all about the robbery at Peto's house in Croydon! There was something odd about the whole Peto business, and she'd take shrewd old Professor Verner's advice. Better safe than sorry.

'You continue to spoil me, Lord Jocelyn. I'm constantly flattered by your little attentions.'

Madam Sylvestris opened the large, flat box of marrons glacés that Lord Jocelyn Peto had placed on the occasional table beside her *chaise-longue*. She admired the rows of sugared chestnuts in their little silver foil cups, but forbore to eat one. She adored marrons glacés, but they were a confection best eaten in private.

'This is a beautiful room, Almena,' said Lord Jocelyn. 'It complements your exotic beauty. I suppose I can't persuade you to drop the "Lord", and just call me Jocelyn?'

Madam Sylvestris treated her friend to a languid, amused smile. What a dear, florid fool he was! And how weary she'd become of his increasingly insistent demands. The trouble with Lord Jocelyn was that he was an incurable romantic. To him, these visits furnished him with harmless excitement in what had become a life of drab domesticity. He thought that his wife, Lady Marion, lived

in guileless ignorance of his doings. It was like him to underesti-
mate, as well as undervalue, a woman who could prove to be a
deadly and ruthless enemy. . . .

'No, Lord Jocelyn. To do that would be to yield to a very bour-
geois kind of vulgar familiarity. Ours is a fine and noble friendship.
Come, now, Lord Jocelyn, tell me about this poor clergyman who
was murdered in the grounds of your house. What a shock that
must have been for you!'

'It was. Poor fellow, he was very highly valued in Croydon. He
was killed by a burglar who'd managed to break into Duppas Park
House and rifle the safe. It's not a pleasant thing, Almena, to have
the police trampling all over the place. It looks bad. And it's bad
for business. Did you like your new carriage?'

'It's beautiful. You're so generous, and yet I've done nothing to
merit such kindness. Oh, sometimes I wish that we could flee to
Paris! Wouldn't that be too marvellous? You and I, arm in arm,
strolling along the boulevards, with no disapproving English eyes
to look at us askance. . . . But there. I'm being foolish. You must go
now, Lord Jocelyn, and take yourself back to Croydon. One day,
perhaps. . . .'

Madam Sylvestris looked wistfully at Lord Jocelyn Peto, and
sighed. It was beautifully done.

'Paris. . . . Well, perhaps something could be arranged. I am
sometimes there on business for a week or more. Paris! Yes, I'll
think about that. Meanwhile, goodbye, my dear.'

'Not goodbye, surely? Merely *au revoir*. Go! Away with you!'

Lord Jocelyn murmured some compliments over her hand, and
departed. A few moments later, Madam Sylvestris's maid entered
the room.

'I don't know what to think, Céline,' said Madam Sylvestris.
'I'm tired of him, and his romantic fantasies. He thinks we're both
in a Jane Austen novel, for ever trading platitudes and elevating
small talk to a fine art. What do you think I should do?'

'This Lord Jocelyn, *madame*, is a foolish dreamer riding for a fall. You live well in this house, but the house is *his*. Bah! Does he think that the good Lady Marion will do nothing to avenge her honour? Even now, her spy, the man with the tinted glasses, stands at the road's end, making notes. And the spirits . . . well, you're playing with fire in that direction. There are too many people involved for your safety—'

'You are right!' Madam Sylvestris rose from her *chaise-longue*. 'It's been very good for the last six months, but this business of luring away poor PC Lane was a dangerous risk. The police will become suspicious. So, I think the time's arrived for me to retire from mediumship, and take up spirit healing. There's money in that, Céline, and no tell-tale apparatus to cause one embarrass-ment.'

'You could return to Newcastle, *madame*. Old Mr Ironsides would love to set you up in comfort once more.' The maid laughed. 'Those conversations you had with his deceased father! Every morning I would read his father's letters in the study, where he kept them bound up with tape in a secret drawer, and every evening you would tell him what I had recounted to you! There would still be rich pickings, *madame*, in Newcastle.'

'Well, we will see. Or perhaps I should transfer my attentions to Jocelyn's rival, Sir Hamo Strange? I've heard a few rumours about Peto's Bank, and I've no intention of going down with that partic-ular sinking ship.'

'Strange? Bah! He is a dried-up stick, that one! Do not waste your charms in that direction. Heal, if you will: create a healing sanctuary somewhere in the countryside, and summon your clients there. Or go to Newcastle. Whatever you do, *madame*, get away from Belsize Park. There's danger in the air.'

'You were always a blundering fool, Mahoney,' said Mr Curteis, 'and now you've saddled us all with a murder! He was beside himself with rage when I told him. I thought he was going to have a fit. And then, when he opened the green baize bag, and found a few bound volumes of magazines in it – well, I feared for his life! He staggered, and clutched at his heart. And then, do you know what he did? He started to laugh. He laughed and laughed, with the worthless books strewn across the desk in front of him. I was relieved to see that he wasn't going to die, but I thought that perhaps he'd gone mad.'

'What did he say then?'

'He said that Peto had won that particular round, but he was damned if he was going to let him win the match. I asked him what he meant, but he just smiled, and shook his head.'

The two men were sitting in a sparsely furnished room above a French polisher's shop in Islington. It was there that Curteis had hurried the fugitive thug only hours before the police had raided his mean dwelling in Stepney.

Francis Xavier Mahoney seemed to have lost interest in what Curteis was telling him. His brutal face held an expression of sneaking self-pity as he contemplated the events of the last few days.

'Honest to God, Mr Curteis,' he said, with the hint of a whine in his voice, 'I never meant to croak that old parson out at Croydon. Everything had gone well. Snobby Quayle had left the French window open, and the key you gave me, done up in a little parcel, opened the safe a treat. He's a good boy, that Snobby. He'd make a fine peter man if he put his mind to it.

'I was coming down the fire escape when I saw this figure lurking in the garden. He came right up to the steps, and I threw the loot down, so that it caught him across the shoulders. I got down to the ground, and there he was, struggling to pick up a walking stick to tackle me with. Well, I took it off him, see, and walloped him across the head with it. How did I know that it'd kill him? The trouble is, I don't know my own strength. These people just get in my way, and have to be stopped.'

'I wish *you*'d stop, Mahoney,' said Curteis, with a mocking smile. 'I don't know why you're telling *me* all this. Anyone would think I was your father confessor, or the magistrate. "It wasn't my fault, Your Honour, I don't know my own strength". That defence won't save you from the gallows, you stupid big stiff. And just wait till you get to Heaven!'

With an oath, Mahoney flung himself on his tormentor, and threw him to the floor. He knelt down over Curteis, and clutched his throat with one of his big, sinewy hands.

'Maybe it's time I did for *you*, as well,' he snarled. 'I'm going to choke the life out of you—'

The next moment he found himself flying though the air. He landed with a clatter of fire irons in the empty fireplace. Curteis, in time-honoured manner, hauled him to his feet.

'No doubt the exercise will do us both good,' he said. 'Now, we were able to rescue your police uniform from Stepney before the Law descended. Make sure you're there at Carmelite Pavement on the twenty-eighth. Portman and his friends arranged to keep PC Lane busy in Belsize Park while the job's done.'

'Old Strange – do you think he'll dump me, after this business in Croydon?'

'He may, and who'd blame him? But if it's any consolation to you, you murderous thug, I'll never "dump" you, as you so elegantly put it. So lie low here, and make sure you're sober and diligent on the twenty-eighth. Just do as you're told this time and all will be well.'

At the house of a great merchant prince in Brook Street, Mayfair, a small but exclusive dinner party was nearing its end. Dessert had been cleared, and the deft waiters had brushed away the imaginary crumbs from the table with folded white napkins. Soon, the ladies would retire, leaving the men to their port, but conversation lingered for a while.

Sir Hamo Strange sat back in his chair, and regarded his host, hostess and fellow guests with an almost proprietary air of satisfaction. Sir Moses and Lady Herscheimer, whose home this was, were old acquaintances, and it was they who had arranged this dinner at Sir Hamo's request. Herscheimer was London's most celebrated commodity broker, and a noted arranger of desired meetings.

Sir Hamo had been placed to Herscheimer's right. To Sir Hamo's right sat the Russian Ambassador, Prince Orloff, looking, as always, very stiff and proud in his evening dress, and sporting the star and ribbon of the Order of St Stanislaus. His wife, the elegant and cultured Princess Orlova, sat opposite him across the table, and to Lady Herscheimer's right. Between her and Prince Orloff sat Count Kropotkin, the Head of Mission. They had all, Sir Hamo mused, been carefully set in their respective places like the pieces on a chess board.

Prince Orloff had proved a cheerful guest, despite his natural hauteur, and had joined in the conversation at dinner with gusto. Whenever he failed to catch a remark, he would turn to Kropotkin, who would rapidly translate it into Russian for the Prince's benefit.

At last, everyone rose as the ladies prepared to retire to the drawing-room. As the port decanters were placed on the table, Sir Moses Herscheimer asked to be excused, as he had one or two important letters to write. Everyone colluded in this fiction, and the great merchant prince followed the ladies and the waiters out of the dining-room.

'The Emperor,' said Prince Orloff, without preamble, and glancing benignly at Sir Hamo Strange, 'occasionally does me the honour of confiding in me. Yesterday, he sent me a cable at the embassy, instructing me to give you his personal greeting and fe-licitation.'

'I am deeply honoured, Your Excellency.'

Was that the right answer to give? He was unused to the many-tiered and nuanced language of diplomats. Yes; Prince Orloff looked even more cheerful, and Count Kropotkin was smiling quietly to himself.

'In addition,' Prince Orloff continued, 'the Emperor mentioned to me a singular service that you had rendered him, so much appreciated, indeed, that he has decided to confer on you a knighthood in the Order of the Holy Seraphim, First Class.'

In the approved Russian manner, the Prince and the Head of Mission clapped their hands for a few moments as a sign of congratulation. Sir Hamo's head spun. He deeply valued his own title of Knight Bachelor, which the Queen had bestowed on him for his part in averting the collapse of Baring's Bank in 1890. But a Russian title, conferred upon him by the Tsar and Autocrat of All the Russias – well, there was something headily exotic about that!

'Prince Orloff could bestow the honour upon you here in London, Sir Hamo,' said Count Kropotkin in his quiet tones. 'That would be entirely in accordance with protocol, as you are not, of course, a Russian subject.'

'However,' said Orloff, 'the Emperor is anxious to award the honour in person. So, later in the year, you will receive an invitation to come to St Petersburg, as a guest of the Grand Duke George Constantine. It is he who would present you formally to the Emperor when he conducts you by railway to the Peterhof Palace.'

The port circulated, cigars were lit, and the conversation turned to politics and money. Later, they joined the ladies, and talked of the more exciting events of the London season. At half past eleven the carriages arrived, and Sir Hamo Strange began his journey across town to Medici House.

All was going well. After years of total devotion to the creation and distribution of money, he was beginning to show himself in Society. He had long ago outclassed Jocelyn Peto as a financier; soon, he would outclass him as a nobleman. The Order of the Holy Seraphim. . . . Exotic. Wonderful. Evidently the Tsar had appreciated the great loan that would let him play with his new Trans-Siberian Railway! Yes, all was going well.

What about the wretched impasse at Croydon? Could that be in any way traced back to him? Perhaps. He would hope and pray that everything went well on the twenty-eighth, when the great movement of bullion took place. A great deal depended on the success of that operation. Till then, he would occupy himself with his daily business. The Holy Seraphim. . . . The Grand Duke George Constantine. . . . Tomorrow could take care of itself!

9

On Carmelite Pavement

When Box left his lodgings in Cardinal Court, a quiet enclave of old houses behind the *Daily Telegraph* offices in Fleet Street, the gas lamps were still glowing, but a rosy flush had already appeared in the eastern sky as the morning of 28 July dawned. He imagined the early sunlight spreading its rays across Borough and Southwark, before making its strong assault on the early morning gloom and mists of the City.

As he made his way down Bouverie Street, turning up his collar against the early morning chill, he thought of the six forays that he'd made during the week, three on foot and three by omnibus, tracing Superintendent Mackharness's carefully planned routes for the movement of the four million pounds' worth of bullion down to the waiting steam launches. Apart from a dug-up gas main at the opening to New Change Lane, there had been no impediments to any of the planned movements. The whole exercise, given a reasonable measure of luck, should pass off without a hitch.

Box turned abruptly left into Tudor Street, where he paused for a minute or two at an arched iron gate, giving immediate access to a small brick-built lodge. A steep flight of granite steps led down from the back of the little lodge to a deserted paved yard in front of what at first sight looked like a warehouse. A notice fixed to the iron gate read:

CARMELITE PAVEMENT BULLION VAULTS
NO ADMITTANCE TO THE PUBLIC

It was here that Sir Hamo Strange kept his unimaginable stores of gold and silver. It was just half past six. In half an hour's time, that empty yard at the foot of the steps would be a hive of activity as one million pounds in sovereigns was conveyed through a tunnel under the Embankment and so on to Sir Hamo's private pier, where the first of the six special steam launches would be waiting. It would be numbered C1 on its white funnel.

He'd detailed Sergeant Knollys to keep an eye on the morning's work at Carmelite Pavement. According to information passed to them from Inspector French at Whitehall Place, poor young PC Lane, who was well known to Sir Hamo Strange and his staff, would be on duty. It might be prudent to have the massively strong Jack Knollys down there to give him some kind of reassurance. Young Lane, grieving for his baby girl, and seduced by spiritualists, would not be at his best that morning.

Although it was very early, Blackfriars Bridge was carrying a brisk stream of horse-drawn traffic, mainly canvas-covered vans and lorries coming across with goods from the Surrey side, though one or two early omnibuses were running. At that time of morning, as Box noted with wry amusement, the companies tended to put on their old white-painted 'bone-shakers', perhaps on the assumption that as it was so early, the yawning passengers wouldn't notice the discomfort.

Everything was going to be all right. Box smiled to himself as he recalled something that Mackharness had told him at the end of the previous day's shift. 'I think it would be prudent, Box,' he'd said, 'to provide each police detail with a Very pistol and cartridges, so that, if anything goes amiss, the other details can be immediately alerted.' Where on earth could Old Growler have got such a far-fetched idea as that? Perhaps he'd also hired the band of the Irish Guards to play a little victory march when the operation was concluded!

Still, where these bankers were concerned, there were some very odd things going on. How had Sir Hamo Strange managed to secure the services of Snobby Quayle, and the Milton Fisher gang? There was nothing of the amateur about those shady folk, and you had to know where to find them before you could do business with them. Snobby was still locked up in Croydon, stubbornly refusing to say anything. When this bullion business was done, Box would go after slimy Milton Fisher.

The very idea of Sir Hamo Strange contemplating burglary was grotesque in itself, but then, he'd somehow become involved with Basher Mahoney, first-class burglar, and unconvicted killer. As far as Box knew, Mahoney didn't work for the Milton Fisher gang. It was time to cast a discreet eye over the private activities of Sir Hamo Strange.

As Box neared the end of Blackfriars Bridge, the sun finally won its victory over the early morning gloom. He stopped for a moment and turned to look back at the dome and towers of St Paul's Cathedral, towering over all other buildings in its vicinity, and bathed in a splendour of golden light. What a marvellous city London was!

By the time Box came off the bridge, the lamplighters had begun their task of extinguishing the gas lamps along the magnificent sweep of the Embankment, though the morning chill still held. He took out his watch and flicked open the lid. A quarter past seven. Plenty of time for him to take a leisurely walk along to Morgan's Lane Pier, where Mackharness had told him to position himself at a quarter to eight, in order to watch the six bullion launches sail safely under Tower Bridge.

He made his way along Bankside, and stopped to refresh himself at a working-men's coffee stall that was still open for business. He cradled the thick mug between his hands, and watched a couple of City gents buying newspapers from a crippled vendor who had stationed himself beside the man who was dispensing coffee.

'Still nothing much in the papers about this robbery at Peto's,' said one man to the other. 'I expect the police know more than they're prepared to say.'

'Funny about Peto,' said his companion. 'There's a rumour running round our place that Peto is in Queer Street.'

'You don't say! Peto the man, or Peto the banker? I've not heard anything.'

'It doesn't make much difference which Peto. There's some say that he's been riding for a fall for the whole of this past year.'

The two men hurried off towards the bridge, and Box made his way thoughtfully to Morgan's Lane Pier.

Sergeant Jack Knollys came into Tudor Street at 7.35. He was surprised how quiet it was, but then saw that most of the buildings lining the narrow thoroughfare were shops and warehouses, most of them still shuttered.

He'd promised to take Vanessa to the Palace Theatre of Varieties in Cambridge Circus that evening, and had bought two 2/- tickets in advance. He'd learnt late last night that he would be on duty all Friday, including the evening until nine, and had sent his fiancée a note, cancelling their treat. That had not been the first time.

Would Vanessa tire of his constant submission to the demands of duty? He couldn't bear the thought of losing her. Before her previous fiancé had been killed he had started to neglect her, and she had begun to realize that poor Arthur Fenlake was not the right fellow for her.

Suddenly, Knollys felt a warming conviction that all was well between him and Vanessa Drake. At the same time, he was convinced that someone unseen had tried to reassure him: it was almost as though a voice had spoken in his ear. But the street was quite deserted. He shivered, but not from cold, and dismissed his personal preoccupations from his mind.

Knollys walked across to the arched iron gate, which was set in stout railings rising from low brick walls. He looked down through the railings to the yard below.

There was a police constable standing at the foot of the steep flight of steps leading down from the miniature lodge behind the iron gate. He was a heavy, ungainly fellow, his arms dangling at his sides, his huge fists clenched. His uniform seemed too small for him, and he was writhing in what looked like impatient discomfort.

The constable looked up towards the road, and Knollys saw a brutish, pock-marked face, sweating beneath the regulation helmet. Something about the man suggested that he had just experienced an enervating shock. As the constable began to run up the steps towards him, alarm bells began to ring in Knollys' head.

The man disappeared into the lodge, and a moment later a stout door behind the iron gate was thrown open. Knollys saw the silver letter Ns on the collar of the constable's tunic, and wondered what he was doing so far out from Islington, where he must have been stationed. Still keeping his eyes on the pockmarked face, Knollys showed the constable his warrant card.

'PC Edwards, Sergeant,' the man said. 'You'd better come inside the lodge. All's well down at the pier— But look, who's that, lurking in the doorway over there? Surely that's the glint of a pistol?'

Later, Knollys was to wonder ruefully how he had allowed himself to fall for such an old trick. For a brief moment he turned his back on the pockmarked constable, and was instantly felled by a terrific blow to the back of his head. As he began to lose consciousness, he was dimly aware of a pair of strong hands dragging him by the ankles, and face down, into the lodge.

Morgan's Lane Pier was a stubby stone construction jutting out into the river from the grass-grown yard of Morgan & Company's burnt-out warehouse. A hundred yards to Box's right, Tower

Bridge rose in all its pristine glory of iron, steel and masonry, 120 feet up to the summer sky. They said it would be opened next June.

Box's vantage-point lay among a medley of trawlers and strings of barges, looking as though they'd been tossed carelessly towards the bank by the strong river currents. Black, soot-caked smoke stacks rose from the open decks, visible through the forest of slender masts. A smell of tar and coke fumes mingled with the strong salty tang of river water and rotting flotsam moving around the vessels. Men seemed to be at work everywhere, but no one paid the slightest attention to the solitary man in smart overcoat and curly-brimmed hat, standing with binoculars at the ready on Morgan's Lane Pier.

At 8.30 the first of the steam launches came into view. Box could see it through his binoculars, moving low in the water, its gleaming white funnel with the red band standing out clearly against the drab warehouses on the opposite bank. The inscription C2 painted on the funnel told him that this fast and powerful boat held the consignment of gold from N.M. Rothschild & Sons. It would have left Swan Lane Pier, beside London Bridge, some ten minutes since.

The launch proceeded under Tower Bridge, and was lost to sight. Some ten minutes later, an identical steam launch hove into sight, escorted by a flock of screaming gulls. From a list of timings that Mackharness had given him, Box knew that this was Sir Abraham Goldsmith's offering, from Queenhythe Steps. Yes, there was the inscription C3 on the funnel. All was going well.

The next two launches, C4 and C5, arrived in procession, the vessel from White Lion Quay having caught up with that from Grant's Quay. The precious consignments of Brown's of Lothbury and Thomas Weinstock & Sons proceeded safely and securely under Tower Bridge.

At 9.15, Box began to feel uneasy. Where was C6, the launch from Peto's Bank? It had been due to appear at 9.10. Had something happened? Nonsense! It was all this Croydon business, and the rumour-mongers gossiping at the newspaper stand that was making him nervous.

There! The sixth launch suddenly came into sight, chugging merrily towards the bridge. Lord Jocelyn Peto's consignment had arrived safely. Box slipped his binoculars into one of his overcoat pockets, and felt in the other for a packet of cheroots that he'd bought earlier that morning at a tobacconist's in Fleet Street. Somewhere nearby, a clock struck half past nine.

From the knot of trawlers and barges below Morgan's Lane Pier a long, black rowing boat appeared. It moved heavily, propelled by three oarsmen wearing the heavy black serge uniforms and low-crowned peak caps of the River Police. A fourth man, dressed identically to his companions, sat on a narrow seat in the stern, guiding the police galley by means of rudder strings. The man in the stern caught sight of Box, and shouted an order to his crew. They immediately rested their oars, and looked up at Box where he stood in splendid isolation on the stone pier.

'What's the matter, Arnold?' shouted the man in the stern. 'Has Mackharness banished you? What did you say to him?'

'You cheeky man, Inspector Cross,' Box called back. 'I'll have you know I'm here on very important business—'

'I know you are, Arnold. I've heard all about it. Counting launches, isn't it?'

Inspector Cross of the River Police seemed to have been rolling in mud. His uniform was wet and stained, and his narrow, saturnine face was smeared with black oil. These men, Box mused, spent their whole working life on the river, rowing in an open boat. They were rough and irreverent, constantly suffering from bronchitis, and liable to die an early death. The luxury of a steam launch with an awning was not for the likes of them. One of the constables tied up the boat to a mooring ring. Inspector and men produced pipes and spirit flasks, and enjoyed a morning break, leaving Box to his own devices.

It was 9.45, and Sir Hamo Strange's launch, C1, had not yet arrived from Carmelite Pavement. It should have passed under Tower Bridge at 9.30. Box threw his half-smoked cheroot into the river, and glanced nervously towards the opposite bank. There wasn't much to see, apart from the shining roof of Billingsgate Market, and the splendid façade of the Customs House. Strain your eyes as much as you liked, you couldn't see Blackfriars Bridge from this far up the river.

At 9.50, Box called down to Inspector Cross, who was sitting once more on his little seat in the stern of the galley.

'Bob, would you be prepared to row me across the river to Blackfriars? There's something wrong. There were six launches, and five of them have passed safely under the new bridge. But the sixth— There's something wrong. I'd be easier in my mind if I was on the river, and going in the direction of Blackfriars. Perhaps the launch had to set off late from Carmelite Stairs.'

Inspector Cross looked thoughtfully at Box for a moment, and then made up his mind.

'There's an iron ladder just below where you're standing, Arnold,' he said. 'Climb down that, and step into the galley. *Step*, mind! Don't jump, or you'll have us all in the drink. You'll have to crouch down here with me, in the stern. Right, you lot, pipes out, and back to your oars. Keep on this side until we're under Blackfriars Bridge, then strike out across the river to Carmelite Stairs.'

It was as they emerged from under Southwark Bridge, hugging the embankment wall along Bankside, that they heard a sudden loud report. It was followed by the explosion of a scarlet Very light, which hovered eerily, as though suspended in the air, high above Blackfriars Bridge.

The first person Box saw when he clambered up an iron ladder and on to the stone flags of Carmelite Pier was Sergeant Knollys, a bloodstained bandage round his head, talking to an old acquain-

tance of theirs, the patient and quietly spoken Inspector Saville of
Thames Division. A dozen police officers were stationed in the
yard, apparently taking written statements from a number of men
in overalls. Presumably, they had been summoned to the scene by
Mr Mackharness's Very light. The unthinkable had happened.
Inspector Cross waved a nonchalant farewell to Box, and then his
galley struck out once more for the Surrey side.

Carmelite Pier, Box saw, was entirely enclosed by the blank
walls of the surrounding buildings. The only ways off the pier,
then, were the river, and a low tunnel facing it, which he knew led
under the Embankment to the Bullion Vaults on Carmelite
Pavement. It was through this tunnel that the bullion consignment
would have been wheeled – to where?

This, thought Box grimly, is no time for formal niceties.

'So the bullion's been stolen, has it, Mr Saville?' he asked.

'It has, Mr Box, and your Sergeant Knollys here was battered
about in the process. He'll tell you all about it in due course. For
the present, I want you to come with me to ask a few questions of
the man in charge here. He's waiting up above in his office.'

The three men hurried through the tunnel to the main building
of the bullion vaults, where a further phalanx of policemen
thronged in the big yard, talking to some of the workmen. An
audience of gaping civilians lined the railings along Tudor Street
above them. They entered a vast empty hall, where they glimpsed
stacks of wooden pallets and an orderly line of heavy iron trolleys.
The gated entrances to a number of wide lifts filled one entire wall.

Waiting for them in a glass-walled office near the entrance was
an anguished, middle-aged man dressed in a black suit, who was
clutching the rim of his bowler hat so tightly that his knuckles had
turned white.

'Mr Garner,' said Inspector Saville to the elderly man, 'this
plain-clothes officer is Detective Inspector Box of Scotland Yard.
The injured man, as you know, is Detective Sergeant Knollys. I
want Mr Box to hear your story from the beginning. Mr Box, this

is Mr Horace Garner, Chief Warden of the Carmelite Bullion Vaults.'

'I came down here to Carmelite Pavement, gentlemen,' said Horace Garner, when the four men had sat down at a table in the little office, 'at seven o'clock sharp. Everything was in order. The consignment had already been brought up from Number 3 vault on the hydraulic lift. Let me be quite precise about this consignment. It consisted of seventy-eight mahogany bullion chests, each eighteen and a half inches square, secured with flat iron bands, and fastened with padlocks. Each chest contained twelve thousand eight hundred and twenty pounds in gold sovereigns, all minted in the same year: 1858. What we call "old specie".'

'Why were there so many chests, Mr Garner?' asked Box. 'Surely larger containers would be preferable to all those little boxes.'

'Gold is a very dense metal, Inspector, as well as being very heavy. Those "little boxes", as you call them, each weigh two hundredweight, and need two strong men to lift them. It's very interesting, working out all these precise details for each major movement—'

The chief warden's eyes suddenly filled with tears, and his face was contorted with anguish. He was, Box judged, well over sixty, and his neatly trimmed hair was turning white.

'What will Sir Hamo Strange say, when he comes down here? We've already sent messengers up to Medici House. I've worked here since I was twenty years old. He'll dismiss me without a character—'

'Of course he won't,' said Inspector Saville. He sounded to Box like a kindly schoolmaster coaxing a frightened boy to tell the truth. 'Why should he? It's not your fault, Mr Garner, and the more you tell Mr Box and me now, the easier it'll be for us to find out what's happened to all that gold.'

'So there were seventy-eight mahogany bullion chests already waiting to be shifted?' asked Box.'

'Yes, that's right. They were laid out here in the main shed on eight pallets, all ready to be lifted on to the trolleys, and taken down to the pier.'

Horace Garner stopped, and the two policemen could sense that he was recollecting the events of the morning.

'There was a policeman – I stepped out from this office into the yard at half past seven, to see that all was well, and was reassured to see a police constable in uniform standing halfway up the flight of steps to the public road. I mention him, because. . . .'

Garner's voice died away, and he seemed once again to be plunged deep in thought. Arnold Box looked at the sorely tried chief warden and, with a sinking heart, he suddenly sensed the truth.

'This policeman whom you saw, Mr Garner: had he replaced another man who'd come earlier?'

Garner's face lit up with something approaching pleasure.

'Why, yes, Mr Box. How did you know that? When I came in at seven o'clock, I was greeted in the yard by Police Constable Lane, who is very well known to us. Seeing him there reassured me, I must confess. Well, by seven-thirty the complete assignment of gold was ready to be lifted on to the trolleys and taken through the tunnel on to the pier.

'I went out into the yard, and saw that PC Lane had been replaced by this other man, a big, lumbering fellow who saluted me, and then ran up the steps to the lodge. I saw that another man, a giant of a fellow, was opening the gate from Tudor Street. Presumably, the new police constable was going up to find out what he wanted.'

'The "giant of a fellow" was me,' said Sergeant Knollys. 'I felt there was something wrong about him at once. He was nervous — shivering, almost. In any case, I wondered what a constable from "N" was doing this far out. Well, he got me to turn away from him for a moment, giving him the chance to flatten me with a baulk of timber. When I came to, I found myself lying in a corner of that lodge on the road. That was when I staggered out on to the steps and fired the Very pistol.'

'Dear me, Sergeant,' said Box, shaking his head, 'you shouldn't have fallen for his tricks. Always trust your sixth sense.'

The chief warden seemed to be recovering from the shock of the daring robbery.

'At ten minutes to eight, gentlemen,' he continued, 'the seventy-eight bullion chests were put on to the trolleys by my twenty gangers, and wheeled down through the tunnel and on to the pier. The steam launch was waiting – a white-hulled boat with specially strengthened bulkheads – and the loading of the bullion proved to be a smooth and efficient operation, lasting no more than half an hour.'

'Did you notice the funnel?' asked Box. 'Was there a number painted on it?'

'There was, Inspector. The funnel was white, with a red band, and the inscription "C1" was painted on it.'

'Then it's the genuine launch, right enough,' said Saville, 'which makes me wonder what happened to its legitimate crew. We'd better find out. What did the strange policeman do, Mr Garner?'

'He climbed into the launch, and stayed on board. The launch already had steam up, and at eight-thirty it moved away from the pier, and I watched it chugging out across the river. How on earth was I to know that anything was amiss?'

'A little question, Mr Garner,' said Box. 'When the launch was moored at the pier, was it pointing upstream or downstream? By which I mean, was it pointing towards the Tower Bridge end of the river, or towards Waterloo Bridge?'

'Well, of course, it was pointing towards the Tower Bridge end. What a peculiar question! But when it left the pier, I must admit, it struck across the river towards Stamford Wharf, on the Surrey side. I assumed it was some special manoeuvre.'

All three police officers rose from the table, as though by

common consent. There was nothing further to be learnt from Mr Garner. Once outside in the yard, Inspector Saville glanced anxiously towards the tunnel leading to the pier.

'If we're to catch these villains, Mr Box, it's up to Thames Division to move into action. We'll get after them straight away, before the trail goes cold. Garner thinks they crossed the river towards Stamford Wharf. There's a lot of derelict property and disused basins between there and Hungerford Bridge. Our own launch will be in the river by now. Never fear, Mr Box, we'll get them before the day's out.'

Saville almost ran down the yard, and was lost to sight in the tunnel. Box turned to his injured sergeant.

'Are you all right, Sergeant?' he asked. 'That bandage is clotted with blood.'

'I'm fine, sir. It'll take more than a crack on the head by a hulking brute like that fellow to put me out of action.'

'You know who that so-called constable was, don't you?'

'I can guess, sir, though you must remember I'd never seen him in the flesh before. It was Mahoney, the man who murdered the Reverend Mr Vickers out at Croydon. It looks as though our ugly friend is a maid of all work – robber and killer combined.'

'Francis Xavier Mahoney's a high-class burglar – beautiful work he does – but he's always been a dab hand at murder. Maybe we'll get him, this time. I think his number's up.'

'What are we going to do now, sir?'

'I'm going out to the West India Import Dock, to find out what happened there. I'd like to know whether those other five launches that passed under Tower Bridge actually arrived at their destination safely!'

'And what do you want me to do, sir?'

'You? I want you to go back to King James's Rents. You'd better take a cab. And when you get there, go and find Dr Cropper in Whitehall Place, and get him to fix your head properly. You're no use to me, bleeding all over the place.'

'But, sir—'

'Do as you're told, Jack. Go and see Dr Cropper. You and I will discuss all this business later. I'm off now to the West India Docks.'

10

In Corunna Lands

From where he stood on the roof of one of the eleven huge warehouses rising up on the north side of the West India Import Dock, Box could see the Swedish merchant steamer *Gustavus Vasa* lying at anchor in Limehouse Reach. Her masts and spars gleamed in the mid-morning sun, and a plume of black smoke hung over her dark-red funnel. It was just after eleven o'clock.

Out beyond Tower Bridge there was a strong breeze, which was a welcome change from the smoke-filled carriage of the little train that had brought Box along the dock railway to the gritty and grimy platform of West India Dock Station. Behind the breeze Box could discern the unmistakable salty tang of the sea.

'So all went well at this end of things, Captain Mason?' he asked of the dock supervisor standing beside him on the roof. A gnarled, bearded man in faded Merchant Navy uniform, his eyes were quick and intelligent. He was smoking a short clay pipe.

'All went as smoothly as butter, Inspector Box. The five launches sailed into my dock – little things they looked, too, beside these great merchant vessels – and their cargoes were offloaded on to the steam tender.'

'So all went well?' Box repeated. He sounded as though he remained to be convinced.

'Yes, that's what I've told you, isn't it? The tender conveyed the whole consignment of gold out to the *Gustavus Vasa* yonder. The entire operation took forty minutes. There were riflemen at hand to see fair play, as you might say.' The elderly captain shook his head sadly. 'But it's bad news, Inspector,' he continued, 'about Sir Hamo Strange's gold. Somebody must have got wind of what was going on, though it was hardly a state secret! Still, shifting gold isn't really our affair. All we did was lend them one of our docks.'

He turned away from the river, and regarded the complex of dock buildings with pride.

'Do you see these warehouses, Inspector? They're holding a hundred thousand tons of goods – sugar, coffee, flour, cocoa, all kind of spices. That's what our business is all about.'

While Captain Mason was speaking, Box had been surveying the busy quays of the great dock. A figure in a flapping Ulster cape and a high-crowned beaver hat had just emerged from the sooty little station, clutching a ticket in one of his gloved hands. The man glanced up at the roof of the warehouse, and Box saw to his surprise that it was Superintendent Mackharness.

'Box,' he shouted, in his unexpectedly powerful voice, 'down here, if you please. I shan't keep you more than a minute.' Box bade farewell to Captain Mason, and hurried down the vertiginous spiral staircase of the warehouse. Mackharness's 'minutes' had been known to last an hour.

Mr Mackharness said nothing until he had led Box to a rough alehouse, evidently the exclusive domain of the dock force. It had no name, but the man inside, a hard-bitten Irishman, said his name was Pat, and that the premises were known as Pat Mooney's.

'Box,' said Superintendent Mackharness, 'I'm minded to buy you a glass of something. What will you have?'

'Why, thank you, sir,' Box replied. 'A glass of India Pale Ale would be very welcome.'

'One India Pale Ale, Mr Pat Mooney,' said Mackharness, 'and a pint of Irish stout. Is that your little office there, behind the bar? We'll take it in there, if you don't mind. We're Scotland Yard officers, here on Government business.'

The landlord, subdued by Mackharness's designedly overbearing manner, did as he was told, and left the two men alone in his office, which was little more than a cupboard with a grimy window looking out on to the dock railway.

'Now, Box,' said Box's master, 'Sergeant Knollys told me that you were coming out here, so I decided to come out after you. There's nobody to overhear us here, and I've something I want to tell you. Just over half an hour ago I was called upon at the Rents by my friend Lord Maurice Vale Rose – I think you know that his lordship and I are acquainted?'

'Yes, sir. A great honour on both sides, if I may say so.'

'Well, the honour's all on *my* side, Box, though I expect you meant your remark kindly. But what was I saying? Yes, Lord Maurice Vale Rose is one of the Permanent Under-Secretaries at the Treasury. He told me that the Government, on hearing of the robbery at Carmelite Pavement, has immediately made available the sum of one million pounds in gold bars to complete the Swedish Loan.'

'The Government? Well, sir, that's very interesting. It makes you think. . . .'

'Yes, doesn't it? I thought you'd be intrigued. This consignment of gold bars will be brought down the river on a Royal Naval light cruiser, and will arrive here in the West India docks at three o'clock this afternoon. The bullion will be loaded on to the tender under armed guard, and taken out to the *Gustavus Vasa*, which will immediately raise anchor and set out for Göteborg. What do you think of that?'

Mackharness had nearly finished his pint of Irish stout, but he paused for a moment and looked steadily at Box over the rim of his tankard.

'I'm thinking that it's very quick work, sir – far too quick for my liking. It's as though someone in the Treasury had been expecting this robbery to happen.... Somebody appears to be oiling someone else's wheels. It makes me nervous.'

'It makes *me* nervous too, Box. It suggests that someone outside the Treasury knew that the loan would be guaranteed. Incidentally, Lord Maurice Vale Rose told me that the Bank of England had insured the whole consignment of four million pounds against loss by theft or accident. Maybe somebody knew *that*, as well. Think about it, will you, Box?'

'I will, sir. What do you want me to do now?'

'You'd better stay out on the river all day, in case that missing launch is found holed up somewhere. This robbery is a shocking affair, Box, and I myself am not going to emerge scot-free from the affair. I planned the whole thing, so that, if the need arises in higher quarters, I can be made a convenient scapegoat.'

'But it's not your fault, sir—'

'Not, it's not, but one must learn to take the rough with the smooth. So do as I say, and stay on the river, will you? That heavy launch can't have got very far. I think that's all, Box. I'll leave you, now. The Commissioner's asking for me, and I must get back to Whitehall Place before noon.'

'Paper, paper! Big bullion robbery! Millions lost! Read all about it!'

The City rang with the news, and the vendors did excellent business as the early afternoon papers were all but snatched from their hands. Men in dark frock coats and silk hats congregated on the pavements, discussing the robbery. Poor old Strange! He stands to lose a million. It's a vast sum, even for someone like him. . . . Oh, don't worry about Strange. Somebody told me that the Bank had insured the whole consignment with the Prudential Assurance Company. Strange will be all right.

'Paper, paper! Desperate villain posed as policeman! Latest! Mahoney sought!'

The gold robbery at Carmelite Pavement monopolized the

conversation in The Recorder public house near Barbican. Mr Arthur Portman had contrived to ignore the banter of his fellow clerks for the last half-hour, but the arrival of yet more sensational accounts of the robbery made him judge the time right to reply to the question that one of the company had just asked him.

'A statement? From me? What kind of statement do you want, my friend? The theft of old Strange's gold has nothing to do with us at Peto's.'

'Did Peto's consignment make it safely to the West India Docks?'

'It did, all six hundred thousand pounds of it. It'll be safe on board that Swedish ship by now.'

The verbal give and take between Portman and the others was good-humoured, and the background murmur of conversation in the crowded public bar had continued. But then someone else asked a question, and both its truculent tone and indiscreet content brought the bar chatter to an abrupt stop.

'Is it true that Peto's vaults are empty? The word's going round that Peto's half-million contribution left the cupboard bare.'

Mr Arthur Portman sprang from his seat, upsetting the remains of his sherry on the bar top in his agitation.

'Nonsense! What a mischievous lie! There's . . . well, there's sufficient money down there to stock the tills for a month. In any case, any shortage of specie would be only temporary, as you know quite well – Government loans are always repaid on time. There's no call for panic, I tell you—'

'But *you're* getting out, aren't you? That's what you told old Joey Beadle in here, the other day. Sounds as though Peto's is a sinking ship—'

'It's not true, I tell you! For God's sake, shut your mouth – it's rumours of that kind that can bring a solvent house crashing down to ruin.'

It was the rough-mannered and weather-stained Inspector Cross of the River Police and his men who discovered the steam launch C1. Nosing their heavy galley in and out of a maze of stagnant waterways penetrating the vast derelict commercial site of Corunna Lands below Waterloo Bridge, they had found the launch scuttled in a disused repair basin, its white funnel tilted drunkenly above the black and greasy water. Cross had alerted Inspector Saville of the Thames Division, and then he and his men had rowed away to their base at Lower Station, Blackwall Hulks.

Arnold Box arrived at Parr's Basin as dusk was falling. Corunna Lands, abandoned by its proprietors in the late '80s and awaiting development, was a dismal sight. Derelict buildings sagged on the grass-grown quays; sheds and workshops had collapsed in ruin; many structures had been burnt down by gleeful young incendiaries.

During the late afternoon, the great steam pontoons of the London Salvage Company had eased their way through the dereliction, and the firm's skilled operators had commenced their preparations to lift the sunken launch from the basin. Sixteen nine-inch-thick wire hawsers had already been passed under the hull by divers, and attached to cable drums, which had been positioned by crane on either side of the basin. Box, standing on a platform some six feet above the quays, listened as the company's chief engineer explained what was going to happen.

'We've positioned those two great steam engines on either side of the basin, Mr Box. Each engine, with its attendant cable winder, is heavier than the launch. They're massive affairs, those engines, and they can only be moved and put into position by the big steam cranes you can see over there.'

The engineer motioned towards the cranes, towering up over the ruined landscape from an adjacent waterway.

'When the drums are turned, Inspector, the hawsers under the hull are tightened and raised, and the vessel is brought up to the surface. Of course, it'll tilt over to one side as soon as it leaves the water. The hawsers attached to the right-hand cable drum are then raised at an angle – the drum and its housing are lifted bodily on a moving platform – and the vessel slides down towards the opposite quay. We'll use grappling irons to drag it bodily on to the wide paving.'

Flaring torches had been lit all round the basin, and the flickering light glanced off the black, impenetrable water. The men went about their tasks with the detachment born of long practice. The steam engines roared and thundered on either side of the basin, as they were brought to their highest pitch of power. Looking at this scene, Box was strongly reminded of the oil flares lighting up the backyard of 14 Back Peter Street, Soho, when he and PC Lane had unearthed the evil graveyard beneath the outside privy.

There came a hiss of steam, and a thunderous clanging roar from the vast hawser drums. Nothing seemed to happen for more than five minutes, and then a shriek of protesting steel rose from the disturbed water. The sound set Box's teeth on edge. From the depths below they heard a dull boom as the submerged cables hit the keel of the stricken launch. The busy engines roared away, the light from their fires spreading across the paving of the quays.

Slowly but steadily the steam launch C1 rose out of the water. The superstructure was only a little damaged, though the light awning that had covered the deck had been sloughed off and lost below the water. The hawsers shrieked as they were tightened, and as the whole structure cleared the surface, streams of water began to flow down from the launch, cascading like so many waterfalls into the disturbed basin.

When thirty minutes had passed, the engines were shut off for a moment, while a man in oil skins clambered out on the perilous cradle. He seemed to Box to be patting the dented side of the launch with a leather-gloved hand. Apparently satisfied, the man slithered cautiously back to the quay, and shouted something to his mates. The steam engines roared back into life.

With a renewed hissing of steam and a heavy rumbling of

machinery, the cable drum on the quay to Box's right began to rise on its moving platform. It was a slow process, occupying all of half an hour, during which time the last light of day receded, and the flaring torches seemed to burn more brightly. At last, with an echoing scraping reverberation, the launch began to slide towards the left-hand quay. Skilled hands reached out with long grappling hooks to drag it off the hawsers and on to the wide flagged walkway on the rim of the basin.

Box's attention turned to the shadowy figures standing near him on the platform above Parr's Basin. The company's chief engineer, an elderly be-whiskered man in a bulky overcoat and a black bowler hat, had excused himself and climbed carefully down to the quay. From the darkness emerged the familiar figure of Inspector Saville of the Thames Division. Like Box, he had been working all day without a break, but his tired face broke into a smile. Box recognized in his uniformed companions some of the police officers whom he had seen earlier in the day at Carmelite Wharf

'Now that she's out of the water,' said Saville, when he had greeted Box, 'you can see that she was bigger in every way than you'd have thought. There was certainly plenty of room to store seventy-eight bullion chests. But I don't suppose we'll find anything in her, Mr Box. The thieves must have sailed her into here and out of sight, removed the gold, and then scuttled the launch to hide her. Very clever of them. They'll have conveyed the gold out of this wilderness and up on to Waterloo Road, as like as not. That's how I read the situation. From there, they could disappear into Southwark and lie low for a while.'

'You say they'd have "conveyed" the gold somewhere, Mr Saville. What exactly do you mean by that? How do you "convey" one million pounds of gold in seventy-eight chests, each weighing two hundredweight? They'd need a positive army of men to drag their booty out of all this ruin and decay.'

'Well, maybe they had such an army! They'd need twenty gangers of their own, not an impossible thing for a first-class criminal to organize. That's for us to find out, Mr Box. Either way, they'll have left traces of their activity. So, at first light, I'll take my officers up on to Waterloo Road, and we'll move on from there. What do you intend to do?'

'I'm going to take a look in that launch. Perhaps they took fright, scuttled the boat and fled, leaving its cargo behind. In any case, I'm going to take a look.'

Accompanied by two seasoned men, Arnold Box clambered over the stricken launch's side. He had been given a hooded lantern, and its light glittered off little pools of water marooned in the well of the boat. He edged his way along the glistening deck, and past the silent engine house. He could glimpse the white funnel with its red band and numeral rising crazily at an angle above him.

As he reached the stem of the launch he stumbled over something bulky lying in the scuppers. He directed the light of his lantern downward, and met the open, incurious eyes of the dead Police Constable Lane.

By seven o'clock the steam machinery had fallen silent, and the body of PC Lane had been carried from the wreck. Fresh torches had been lit, and it was by the light of these that a hastily summoned civilian doctor, a young man attached to one of the hospitals, examined the remains.

Arnold Box remained aloof, sitting on a broken wall. So much, he thought, for the thrill of the chase. Strange and his millions were as nothing in comparison to the life of that young man. . . . He stirred as the doctor straightened up, and looked in his direction. Lane's body had been placed on the flags of the quay, as there were no roofed buildings in sight.

'There's not much that I can tell you, Inspector,' said the young doctor. 'But for what it's worth, I can assert that this man was not drowned, as you might have thought. He would have been dead before he was placed into that launch.'

'How did he die, Doctor?'

'His neck was broken, probably as the result of a massive blow to the throat. The trachea seems to be crushed. . . . I can't see anything properly. I'd be able to tell you more if I could examine the body in a decent mortuary.'

Box glanced down at his dead colleague. Someone had closed his eyes, and his boyish round face looked peaceful, but his head lay at a grotesque angle, and even in the flickering light of the torches Box could see the massive bruising at the throat. It was a fortnight to the day since he and Lane had attended the seance in Spitalfields.

'Poor fellow!' said the doctor. 'He looks so young. I've never been called out to a case like this before. How old was he, Inspector?'

'He was twenty-three, Doctor— I didn't catch your name.'

'Miller. Donald Miller. I'm only twenty-five myself. I'm a house surgeon at Charing Cross Hospital.'

Box looked at the young man, with his clean-shaven face and eager eyes. He was only a couple of years older than poor Lane. He was suddenly aware of his surroundings, of the dark expanse of Corunna Lands, where little fires glowed among the vast area of ruins. He could see the bright line of the river, and the brilliantly lighted north side of the Thames glowing beyond the bridges.

'His name was PC Lane, Dr Miller, and, as I said, he was twenty-three years old. A few weeks ago he and his wife lost their little girl, aged two and a half. Now Mrs Lane's lost her young husband as well. She's got three other children, two boys and a girl, to look after. She lives near Bevis Marks, just by the Baltic Exchange.'

'Terrible. . . . I suppose you have your own doctors, don't you? After tonight's exprience, I'd love to be of some use to the police.'

'Well, Doctor, there are always vacancies for police surgeons, and I think you'd be more than welcome. In any case, I can ensure that you're retained for the post-mortem on poor Lane, if that's what you want. When you have the time, call on me at 4 King James's Rents, Whitehall Place, and I'll tell you something about a police surgeon's work.'

'Thank you very much, Inspector. What about this body? Shall I—?'

'Some police officers will be arriving soon, Doctor, with a shell in a police hearse. They'll convey the remains to the Metropolitan Police Mortuary in Horseferry Road. Perhaps you'd call there tomorrow morning, and make yourself known to them. I'm certain that you'll be invited to assist. Mention my name: Detective Inspector Box. Thanks for all you've done here, Dr Miller. Don't forget my address: 4 King James's Rents.'

As the doctor picked his way carefully through the rubble and up to the main road, Sergeant Knollys appeared on the opposite side of the basin. Box watched him while he stood motionless, taking in the bizarre scene – the silent machines, the still taut mesh of cables, and the salvaged launch lying drunkenly on its side. Slowly Knollys walked round the rim of the basin, until he stood beside the corpse which lay, still uncovered, on the flags.

'It's PC Lane, Sergeant,' said Box. 'His neck was broken, and his body hidden in the launch. Then the launch was scuttled. The gold wasn't in it.'

'We should be out looking for Mahoney,' said Knollys, looking down at the corpse. There was a smouldering anger in his voice that Box was quick to notice. Was Knollys about to start a personal vendetta? Any such notion needed to be nipped in the bud.

'It was pointless to go looking for Mahoney at this juncture,' said Box impatiently. 'He's gone to earth – him, and his accomplices, and the one million pounds in gold. Or so it would seem. We'll hunt him down and bring him in when the time's right.'

A rumbling sound on the road above announced the arrival of the police hearse. Box plucked Knollys by the sleeve.

'Come on, Sergeant,' he said, 'let's make ourselves scarce. Inspector Saville will do the necessary for poor Lane. You and I have further work to do here in Corunna Lands.'

'What *can* we do, sir? It's as black as pitch.'

'Is it? What about all those pinpoints of light among the acres of ruin? They're fires, Sergeant, which means that there are people living here in this wilderness – tramps, for instance, and destitute men who collect firewood and scrap to eke out a living. I don't like the smell of this bullion business, Jack. There's something odd about it. So let you and me go and seek out those islands of light.'

As Box and Knollys emerged from the Stygian blackness beyond Parr's Basin and into the circle of orange light cast by the flames of a bonfire, an old man in tattered clothes rose to greet them. He smiled, and the smile revealed a mouthful of crooked and broken teeth. The old man motioned to some piles of broken timber and bales of rotting newspaper surrounding him.

'Sit down and warm yourselves, gentlemen,' he said. 'You're police, I expect? Yes, I thought so.' His voice was roughened by a combination of drink and exposure to the elements, but there was a ghost of a chuckle behind his words. Box knew from experience what kind of man this was. He would once have held a respected position in society, but drink had reduced him to the status of vagrant. Box searched his pocket for some coins, making sure that the man could hear them clinking as he did so. The old man's rheumy eyes brightened.

'So how can I help you, Officers? Is it about the men from the launch? Bold as brass, they were – too bold, because they didn't realize there were folk like me living rough in the Lands.'

Box drew a couple of half-crowns from his pocket, and handed them to the man. He saw that he was wearing woollen mittens, the palms of which were full of holes.

'Tell me what you saw, gaffer,' said Box, as he and Knollys settled themselves as best they could on two hillocks of tied-up newspapers, part of the old man's stock in trade.

'It was daylight, gentlemen, when that boat was sunk in the old basin. From where I'm sitting now, you can see a steep path running up through the ruins towards Waterloo Road. I can't say exactly when it was, but it was still afternoon. Ten men toiled up that path from the basin, dragging heavy square chests behind them, two men to a chest. In a moment or two another gang of ten men, muffled up in pea jackets and scarves, scrambled down from the main road, and helped the men from the launch. None of them had any idea that I was watching them.'

'How many chests were there?' asked Box.

It's hard to say. Twenty, perhaps, maybe twenty-five—'

'There weren't seventy-eight chests, by any chance?'

The old man laughed, and waved an admonitory finger at Box.

'Seventy-eight? 'Course there wasn't! I can still count, you know. They'd still be there now if it had been seventy-eight. They were heavy, those chests, but two men apiece was enough to drag them up the slope and on to the road. Twenty or twenty-five. The men all worked as quietly as they could, with no talking to interrupt what they were doing. The whole business lasted about twenty minutes.'

'Weren't you afraid that they'd see you?'

'No, I wasn't afraid. I was quite hidden from their sight. And in any case, I thought perhaps that they were on police business of some sort, because they were led by a giant of a man in policeman's uniform. But they weren't police, were they?'

'No, gaffer, they weren't. They were robbers, and the one who looked like a policeman is a murderer several times over.'

Box took one of his official cards from his pocket, and scribbled some words on it by the light of the old man's fire.

'What's your name, gaffer?'

'Thomas Edwards, aged seventy. Fallen clerk.'

'Well, Thomas Edwards, if you present this card to Mr Field at the Southwark Board of Guardians, he'll arrange for you to get some outdoor relief. Come on, Sergeant. It's nearly ten o'clock, and we were due off at nine. It's time for you and me to sign out and go home for the night.'

11

All That Glisters. . . .

When Box came into 4 King James's Rents at eight o'clock the next morning, he found that everyone was talking about the murder of PC Lane. He pushed open the swing doors of his office, and stood by the fire, looking into the big, fly-blown mirror above the mantelpiece. He saw that there were dark shadows under his eyes, and his usually perky face looked drawn. He felt worn out and tired.

Two fresh notes had been pasted on the mirror among the clutter of ancient visiting cards and dead messages that both Knollys and he had agreed to clean up some time. One note, scrawled in green ink, read: 'There's no Cedarville Road in Harpenden.' Why had he wanted to know that? The second note, written in capital letters, told him that Paul Lombardo was watching a house in Melbourne Avenue, Belsize Park. Lombardo? Well, well – that was very interesting. If he got a moment, he'd track Lombardo down to one of his haunts, and have a little chat with him.

There was a stir in the tunnel-like passage joining the office to the drill hall, and in a moment a burly uniformed police sergeant, an impressive figure with a flowing spade beard, came into the room. He was carrying an enamel mug of steaming hot tea, which he placed on the table. He regarded Box with a look compounded of respectful affection and concern.

'Sergeant Kenwright!' said Box, sinking into his accustomed chair at the big table. 'So you're back from Brighton. I was away from the Rents all day yesterday, so I didn't see you when you returned. How are things here, this morning?'

'Well, sir, there's a lot of bad feeling about, as you can imagine. Poor young Lane had been going through a bad patch, and everyone across the cobbles was sorry for him. Now his wife's left to bring up three young children alone. He died in the course of duty—'

'Yes, he did, Sergeant, so there'll be a pension of sorts to help out. And there'll be enough collected for a decent funeral and a private grave, like we did for PC Daniels last year. Do you remember him?'

'I do indeed, sir. Choked on his false teeth while helping another constable to arrest a thief. I went to his funeral. It was a simple affair, but there was a proper glass hearse with two black horses between the shafts, and six uniformed constables as bearers. Yes, there's a lot of ill-feeling about this morning.'

Box had finished his tea, and Kenwright had just retrieved his mug when Sergeant Knollys came through the tunnel from the drill hall. At the same time, Box heard the shrill scraping sound of the big double gates to the rear yard being pulled open.

'Sir,' said Knollys without preamble, 'Inspector Saville's here. He's come straight from Corunna Lands in a police van. He's found the rifled bullion chests, and he's brought some of them along with him. I met the van as I was coming down Aberdeen Lane, and arranged for the big gates to be opened for him.'

At that moment Inspector Saville of Thames Division came through the tunnel. He looked as mild and cheerful as ever, despite his long night's labours. Sergeant Kenwright saluted, and the inspector rather absentmindedly returned his salute.

'Sit down, Mr Saville,' said Box. 'So you've found the bullion chests? Don't go, Sergeant Kenwright. You'd better hear what Inspector Saville's got to tell us.'

Saville sat down at the table, and took out a notebook from one of the pockets of his uniform frock coat. Knollys and Kenwright remained standing near the fireplace, while the inspector told his story.

'At first light, Mr Box,' Saville began, 'my constables and I climbed up out of all that ruin and on to Waterloo Road. Not a hundred yards along, just near the opening to Roupell Street, one of my men discovered a long, open gully, part of a blocked waterway beside the footings of a demolished workshop. There were twenty-five bullion chests lying smashed in the gully. The hasps on most of them had been forced with jemmies, though one or two had evidently been attacked with axes. Of course, they were all empty. As I suspected when we were still down at Parr's Basin, there must have been plain vans waiting for the villains, to which they transferred the bullion.'

'Did anyone see any vans? Did you ask around?'

'Oh, yes, we asked a good number of people living in the area. No one saw any vans, but that's the only way in which they could have conveyed that great amount of gold away. You don't need me to tell you that most people don't notice anything.'

'According to my arithmetic,' said Box, 'there are fifty-three chests unaccounted for. What happened to them?'

'I think the gang started to open the chests when they reached that gully — the whole location must have been chosen beforehand. But as the minutes passed, they began to take fright, and loaded the remaining fifty-three chests directly on to their vans.'

'Why did they want to empty the chests in the gully in the first place? Why not load the whole lot on to the vans at once?'

'I reckon they'd have thought the combined weight of the gold and the heavy mahogany chests would be too much for the horses. In the event, though, they had to take that risk. And evidently it paid off.'

A little silence fell on the room when Saville had stopped speaking. They could all hear the asthmatic hissing of the old gas mantle suspended from the soot-stained ceiling, and the crackling of the coal in the grate. An angel's passing over, thought Box, wryly.

'An angel's passing over, Mr Box,' said Saville. 'Maybe he's gone, now. I've brought the wreckage of all those chests along for you to see. I'm not quite sure why, but there's something about the whole business that seems odd, and I think it needs detectives to examine some of the evidence.'

Inspector Saville turned to look at the impassive, bearded figure of Sergeant Kenwright, whose eyes, he noted, had gleamed when he'd mentioned the bullion chests.

'I've heard all about you, Kenwright,' he said, 'and the skilled work that you did in that business of Sir William Porteous's coach, and then in assembling the fragments of the Hansa Protocol. I thought you'd like to take a close look at those chests.'

Sergeant Kenwright blushed with pleasure. Fancy being remembered by busy senior officers like Mr Saville! Kenwright had spent most of his working life as a beat constable, but a year ago he had nearly died of rheumatic fever, and had been transferred to King James's Rents to aid his recovery. He had taken to the dilapidated place immediately, and had been able to exercise his skills in such a way that he had been promoted to sergeant. He hoped desperately that he would not be sent back to the divisions. It was lovely at the Rents.

Inspector Saville rose, and carefully replaced his uniform cap, glancing in the mirror to do so. It was time to go in pursuit of the villains along Waterloo Road. He took his leave of Box, and followed the eager Sergeant Kenwright through the tunnel.

'I don't believe a word of it, Jack,' said Box. 'This is a gang who carry out a daring robbery, seizing a launch – what's happened to its original crew, and why has nobody reported them missing? What was I saying? They seize a launch, and take it across the river

145

in full daylight, and then stop on a derelict site to break open the chests. They could have been seen at any time. Robbers on this scale don't behave like little grab-and-snatchers, stopping to shake money out of a purse before throwing it away. What was the point of stopping in that gully?'

'You say you don't believe a word of it, sir,' said Knollys. 'Nor do I. That old man we met in Corunna Lands counted twenty-five chests being hauled up on to the road. Mr Saville's brought twenty-five chests here for Sergeant Kenwright to examine. Where are the other fifty-three?'

Both men were silent for a moment, listening to the noise of activity in the drill hall as the broken chests were brought in across the yard from Aberdeen Lane. They could hear Sergeant Kenwright unfolding the trestle tables, and dragging chairs about.

'There's only one place they *can* be, Jack, but it just doesn't make sense.'

'No, sir, it doesn't – unless—'

'Let's leave it for the moment, Sergeant. Evidently we think alike, but we'd better wait until friend Kenwright has examined those chests before we develop a theory. Meanwhile, it's time for us to pay a visit to Mr Milton Fisher, one of whose gang, that so-called footman Snobby Quayle, is still languishing in Inspector Price's gaol at Croydon. Fisher owns a billiard saloon at the Tottenham Court Road end of Oxford Street. He'll be there now.'

Box got up from the table, and began to struggle into his smart overcoat.

'And on Monday, Sergeant, we'll go and make a few enquiries in Batt's Lane, near Bevis Marks.'

'You want to talk to PC Lane's widow? That's very kind of you, sir—'

'It's nothing to do with kindness, Jack. PC Lane was supposed to have been got out of the way when the bullion robbery occurred, and I've a shrewd idea how it was going to be done. Why he turned up at Carmelite Pavement anyway is another matter, which can keep for the moment. You see, I've not forgotten Mrs Pennymint and her merry band of fortune-tellers. They're tied up somehow with this robbery, and I want to find out how they worked that business of poor little Catherine Mary.'

Fisher's billiard saloon was a tawdry affair, its walls, once green, faded to a drab grey. Three heavy billiard tables occupied the smoky room above a stationer's shop in Oxford Street, and at one of them Mr Milton Fisher was playing a solitary game of billiards. Box looked round the bare-boarded room with distaste.

'I don't know how you can bear to stay cooped up in this filthy den all day, Fisher,' he said. 'Why don't you go out on a job occasionally, with one of your high-class villains? A breath of air would do you the world of good.'

Milton Fisher, a stout and perspiring man whose acne-scarred face was badly in need of a shave, wore a loud check suit that was too tight for him, so that his fat wrists protruded from the sleeves. He continued his lonely game, pausing only to glance balefully at Box, and to notice the presence of Knollys, who stood, arms folded, with his back to the door.

'What do you want, Box? What gives you the right to swagger in here, making accusations?' The cue clicked, the billiard balls rolled, and Fisher continued to avoid any direct eye contact with his visitors. Knollys looked at him with growing animosity. Fat parasites of Fisher's kind held no appeal for him.

'I suppose you know,' Box continued, 'that your man Snobby Quayle was involved in the robbery at Lord Jocelyn Peto's house at Croydon? It was too bad for him, Fisher, that I was called out on the case.'

'Yes, I heard that you'd nabbed him. Is that why you've come here today? To tell me that poor Snobby's in choky? Well, I knew that already. Snobby won't mind. It's the luck of the draw. Good morning.'

'I want to know how you became involved in that Croydon

robbery, Fisher. Who employed you? What's your connection with Francis Xavier Mahoney? I've no time to be bandying words with you. I'm investigating this bullion robbery at Carmelite Pavement, which involves the murder of a policeman, PC Lane.'

Milton Fisher moved round the table, his eyes fixed on the green baize. He stooped down and squinted along his cue. There was just a trace of a smile on his face.

'Lane? Well, I'm sorry to hear that. I've no doubt he was a fine, upstanding—'

Sergeant Knollys suddenly hurled himself at Fisher and pinned him against the wall with a massive forearm across his throat. The colour drained from the gang-leader's face. His cue clattered on the floor.

'Listen, scum.'

Knollys' voice came low and terrifying, with the sibilance of a deadly snake fascinating its victim before the venomous strike.

'Your friend Quayle was present in a house where murder was done, the murderer being Basher Mahoney. Just hours ago, Mahoney murdered our colleague PC Lane, who's worth more than all you scum put together. So we're talking murder, see? We're talking about you and your pals taking the eight o'clock drop one fine morning. You, and Quayle, and Mahoney. So unless you want a billiard ball rammed down your throat, you'd better tell us a few things that we want to know. And you can keep a civil tongue in your head while you do it.'

'Get him off me, Box, do you hear?' croaked Fisher. 'Snobby Quayle was working on his own. That robbery had nothing to do with me and my boys. I don't know who found out about Snobby's talents, but it wasn't through me.'

'Did you employ Mahoney to help in the Croydon robbery? Was it your boys who shifted the bullion up from Corunna Lands and on to Waterloo Road?'

'I don't know what you're talking about, Mr Box. I never employed no one. It's God's truth, I never had anything to do with

Croydon. If Snobby was there, then he was working for someone else. And I've never employed Mahoney. You must know that yourself. I'm a thief, not a murderer. And this bullion – I don't know what you're talking about. Now, call this killer off me, will you?'

'That'll do, Sergeant Knollys,' said Box. 'You could have told me all this when I came in, Mr Fisher, then there wouldn't have been all this unpleasantness. I believe what you say. You're too much of a sneaking coward to risk murder. Next time I call, try to be a little more co-operative. Come on, Sergeant.'

Jack Knollys withdrew his arm from Fisher's throat, and the man gasped and sagged with relief The sergeant picked up the stout billiard cue from the floor, and snapped it in two across his knee.

'Yours, I think, Mr Fisher?' he said. He threw the pieces down on the table, and followed Inspector Box out of the stale room.

Lady Marion Peto, sitting on a sofa in a small private apartment in the Coburg Hotel, Carlos Place, near Grosvenor Square, put up her lorgnette, and looked with scarcely concealed distaste at the man standing with his back to the window. Mr Paul Lombardo was certainly a man of distinguished appearance; and in the Coburg he had chosen a first-class hotel for their meeting. But the waxed beard and moustaches, and the rose-tinted spectacles, appeared to be rather outré.

'Now, madam,' said Mr Lombardo in a quiet, confiding tone, 'it would be better if I were to give you a plain, unvarnished account of my investigation, rather than wrap up the business in a stream of soothing platitudes.'

'That would be by far the better way,' Lady Marion agreed.

Lombardo had noted the look of grim determination in his client's face, and realized that, for all her lack of dress sense and social nicety, Lady Marion Peto was an aristocrat of the old school. It would be pointless and impertinent to trifle with her.

'Your husband, Lord Jocelyn Peto, pays frequent visits to a woman living in Melbourne Avenue, Belsize Park. He calls there usually between eleven and twelve in the morning, Tuesdays and Thursdays, and frequently, but irregularly, in the early evening. He has on two occasions remained in the house for a complete day, by which I mean from early morning to late afternoon. My agents and informants can prove that Lord Jocelyn is engaged in immoral physical commerce with this woman.'

'You mean they are lovers?'

'Madam, with due respect, that is a novelist's word in this context. We are not talking about a young man's romantic attachment. Lord Jocelyn and this woman are engaged in immoral commerce.'

He paused delicately, and heard his client's rapid hiss of indrawn breath. His insistence on the sordid nature of the affair had gone home. Lombardo saw Lady Marion's face grow pale, but he knew that a woman of her breeding would show no sign of emotion.

'What is this woman's name?'

'She calls herself Madam Almena Sylvestris, though she was born Ada Mullins, daughter of a Birmingham corn chandler. When she was eighteen she married a Mr John Silvers, tobacconist, of Eltham. Silvers died of liver complications in 1887.'

'How old is she now, this Madam Sylvestris? And why did she adopt such a ridiculous, tawdry name?'

Lady Marion, he saw, was trying very hard to keep her venomous contempt from revealing itself in her words, but the struggle was unavailing.

'Madam Sylvestris is thirty-three. By any standards she's a beautiful woman, and very charming with it. She adopted that name when she became a spiritualist medium.'

Lady Marion Peto started violently, and the reticule that she had been clutching slid to the floor.

'A *medium*? How appalling . . . Lord Jocelyn must have lost his senses to consort with such degenerate people. Has he lost all sense of caste? Very well, Mr Lombardo. I'm most grateful to you for this information. How you found it all out is beyond me.'

Mr Paul Lombardo smiled deprecatingly.

'Well, madam, it's my business to find out things. There is more, if you'd care to hear it.'

'Tell me. Tell me all!'

'The house in which Madam Sylvestris lives – 8 Melbourne Avenue, Belsize Park – is wholly owned by Lord Jocelyn. Its deeds are lodged with Ephraim & Sons, the land agents in Poultry. Lord Jocelyn recently ordered a new carriage for Madam Sylvestris, at a cost of three hundred and fifty pounds. That's all I have to report, Lady Marion. I beg the favour of awaiting your further orders.'

Lady Marion Peto recognized the request for payment. She retrieved her reticule from the floor, opened it, and removed a purse.

'What do I owe you, Mr Lombardo?' she asked. She had recovered her sang-froid, and looked at the private enquiry agent with what she imagined was haughty indifference. Lombardo suppressed a smile.

'Twelve guineas, madam.'

Lady Marion opened her purse and counted out twelve sovereigns, a half-sovereign and a silver florin, which she handed to Lombardo, who bowed his thanks.

'In matters of this nature, Lady Marion,' he said, 'it is better not to ask for a receipt, though I will write you one readily if you so desire.'

'A receipt is not necessary. I may wish to employ you further, and I know where you are to be found.'

Lady Marion stood up, and moved towards the door.

'Should you be contemplating divorce—'

He was stopped by an exclamation of disgust from his titled client.

'You forget yourself, Mr Lombardo! People of our sort do not resort to the divorce courts. There are other, more acceptable, ways of righting these grave wrongs.'

In a moment she had gone, leaving Paul Lombardo with a profound sense of unease. There had been something in Lady Marion Peto's demeanour during their interview that had frightened him, leaving a sense of danger in the air. He wondered, with an ill-defined feeling of foreboding, what Lady Marion would do next.

Sergeant Kenwright had reassembled the fragments of ten of the smashed bullion chests, and had laid them carefully on ten trestle tables in the drill hall. It was a large, forlorn place, used mainly for meetings and storage. There was a row of windows high up on one wall, and closed double doors at the end. At night, and on dark winter days, the room was lit by candles, placed in a series of tin candle sconces fastened along the walls.

Kenwright had donned spectacles for his work, and was sitting on a folding chair in front of one of the ten chests. He had made the four sections of it hold together by tying them with rough parcel string. From time to time he uttered a little grunt of satisfaction as he peered at a splinter or indentation through a hand lens. Eventually he rose from the chair, and crossed the room to a lectern, where he had placed a few sheets of paper, an inkwell, and a pen. It was time, he thought, to write up a few notes for the guvnor.

After some minutes, he looked up, as Inspector Box and Sergeant Knollys came into the room through the tunnel from the front office. He took off his spectacles, folded them, and slipped them into a little tin case.

'Well, Sergeant,' said Box, 'have you found anything of interest? You've practically rebuilt some of those chests, I see. Well done! You're a careful man, with delicate hands and a sharp eye for the irregular, So what have you found?'

'Sir,' said the big bearded sergeant, 'if you look at these boxes, or chests, you'll see a regular pattern of marks and dents on the interiors which are very interesting. I'll say a few words about those in a minute. The hasps and staples were forced with jemmies, leaving the heavy padlocks intact, which is what you'd expect. I've placed four of those locks on that table over there. Perhaps you'd care to look at them, sir?'

Box picked up each of the four padlocks in turn, and examined them. They were still fastened to the hasps and staples, which had been contorted when the jemmies had forced them from the wood.

'They just look like regulation padlocks to me, Sergeant Kenwright.'

'They are, sir. But three of them were actually open. They'd never been locked at all.'

Box's eyes gleamed with a sudden speculation. He tried the locks, and found that the sergeant's assertion was true. Whoever had secured those three chests, with their priceless contents, hadn't bothered to turn the key in their padlocks. He glanced at Sergeant Knollys, and met an answering look of understanding. Very soon both men would put into words what they thought, but dared not articulate.

'Well done, Sergeant Kenwright! And what's so peculiar about those marks and dents on the inside of the chests?'

'Well, sir, some of them are like heavy pencil lines, all horizontal, and occurring in the same place inside all ten chests. The dents, too, are all of the same depth, and all blackened, as though rubbed inside with a soft lead pencil.'

Box peered into one or two of the reassembled chests, noting the marks, all of which Kenwright had ringed in white chalk.

'Lead? Are you suggesting—? You know, Sergeant, the gold coins stored in chests of this type are laid between layers of lead foil.'

'Yes, sir, but foil is only a thirty-second of an inch thick at its edges. Foil would leave no marks at all. Look, sir.'

Kenwright stooped down to the floor, and picked up a weighty lump of metal, which had once formed part of a lead gutter. He had battered it roughly into the shape of a brick. Without saying a word, he thrust the lump of metal firmly into one corner of the first chest, and then removed it. Box and Knollys saw the dark indentations made in the wood, and realized that they were more or less identical with the marks that Kenwright had ringed in chalk.

'And what do you deduce from that, Sergeant Kenwright?' asked Box.

'I deduce, sir, that these boxes were filled with lead ingots, and that they'd been crammed rather roughly into the chests to make them fit. Lead, sir, not gold: that's what we're looking at here.'

12

The Good Neighbour

Batt's Lane, a terrace of workmen's brick cottages facing a builder's yard, lay dozing in the strong sun of the last day in July, 1893. Box tapped on the door of PC Lane's little house, noting the black crape tacked around the door knocker. There was no reply, and he was just about to knock again when a ponderous, genial old man appeared from the house next door.

'They're not there,' he cried. 'Are you from the benefit club?' The old man's voice rang loud but uncertain, as though he were slightly deaf. 'You'd better come in here, and talk to the wife and me.'

The cottage at the end of the terrace nearer to Bevis Marks had been expanded at the rear with a long yard, at the end of which was a milking-shed. A sign along its front read, 'Simon Lovett, Dairyman'. Box and Knollys followed the old man into a shady stone-flagged kitchen. A plump, contented-looking woman was sitting behind a short counter. She looked at the two detectives with absorbed interest.

'Mr Lovett?' said Box. 'I'm Inspector Box of Scotland Yard, and this officer is Sergeant Knollys—'

'There, Martha, didn't I tell you? The gentleman from Whitehall Place who came to see poor Mary on Saturday told me that you'd probably be coming, sir. He wasn't an inspector, he was a big man, covered in buttons and flaps and frogs, with silver braid on his hat.'

'He was a superintendent. Superintendent Fitzgerald of "A" Division.'

'Yes, that's right. Very nice, he was. As I said, he'd come to see poor Mary next door. Poor girl, she'd already lost the baby, and now her husband's dead. They came first thing Saturday morning to tell her the news. It was dreadful. The wife and I went in, of course, and poor Mary was crying, and the children were all howling. . . .'

This big, genial man exuded goodness from every pore. He was obviously a kindly and concerned neighbour, a man whom PC Lane would have trusted as a confidant. He was also, if his opening salvo was anything to go by, an inveterate talker.

'Now, Inspector,' Mr Lovett continued, 'is there anything special you want to hear about?'

'I'd just like to hear about the baby, Mr Lovett, and what happened to her. You see, I was working with PC Lane on a very distressing case, and he told me that he and his wife had just lost a baby—'

'Dreadful! It broke her heart, and he was never the same afterwards. Catherine Mary was a lovely little thing She'd toddle in here from next door, through the back yard, clutching her doll – Polly, she called it – and then she'd say, "Cathy come". She called herself Cathy . . . she didn't have many words. "Dada", she'd say, and "Mammy". Didn't she, Martha?'

This man, thought Box, is a good neighbour, kind-hearted and generous. But he has a tongue that runs away with him, which makes him one of the most dangerous kind of neighbours in the world. . . .

'And where's Mrs Lane now?' asked Box.

'Her brother came on Saturday night – came on the railway to Paddington – and took Mary and the children away with him,' said

Mr Lovett. 'She was calmer by then, and agreed to go down with him to the country for a while – until the funeral, you know. Her brother's a farmer, from a place called Marsh Gibbon, in Oxfordshire.'

'And what's his name, Mr Lovett? This brother?'

'Miller. Joe Miller. I think he's her only living relative.'

Simon Lovett launched out on to a sea of reminiscence. He spoke at length about Mary Lane's late grandmother, Theodora, and about Mary's scapegrace uncle, Roger Wilcox, who had died in the Malay Straits in 1865.

'You're a mine of information, Mr Lovett, if I may say so,' said Box. 'A positive cornucopia of knowledge. Could you tell me exactly what happened to the baby? I don't want to ask her mother.'

'She took ill in Wellclose Lane, just near the railway bridge, while she was playing with some older children who knew her. Diphtheria, it was. Doctor Morland was summoned, but there wasn't much he could do. They took her to the hospital, of course, but it was hopeless. I remember that the ward sister wept when poor little Catherine Mary died. She was buried out at Putney Vale, in her favourite little pink dress.'

Mr Simon Lovett suddenly ran out of words, and a large tear rolled down his cheek. For the first time since Box had entered the house, Mrs Lovett found her voice.

'Mary had started to go to these seances – wicked, I call them. Poor Mr Lane told me that he was going to attend some of them, in case he could discover anything like fraud going on. He forbade Mary to go. And then, on the day before Mr Lane was due to go to one of these sittings out at Belsize Park, a little girl called Nora Maitland was knocked down and killed by a runaway cart. Dreadful, it was.'

Box glanced at Knollys, who had been quietly listening to the conversation. It was a signal for the sergeant to ask a question that Box and he had prepared before ever they had set foot in Batt's Lane.

'I expect you've told this story of poor little Catherine Mary to other folk, Mr Lovett? People who called on you to ask how the Lanes and their children were coping with their loss?'

'Well, Sergeant, that's true enough. We're friendly people, Martha and I, and it was only natural for the neighbours to ask us how poor Mr Lane and his wife were coping.'

'There was that well-spoken gentleman who called, Simon,' said Mrs Lovett. 'Don't you remember? It was only a day or two after the baby died. He asked us a lot of questions, sitting in that chair where you are now, Sergeant. He said he was from a police charity, but that it would be wise not to say anything to Mary in case nothing came of the matter. I remember him particularly, because as he left the dairy, I saw him stop and peer through the Lanes' front window. Then he pushed an envelope through their letter-box. And what do you think was inside it? Five sovereigns, wrapped up in tissue paper. So whoever he was, he was genuine enough.'

'What was he like, this gentleman?' asked Box. 'To look at, I mean.'

'Well, he was a narrow-faced kind of a man, aged about forty, with black whiskers meeting beneath his chin. He was wearing a well-tailored morning coat, and his silk hat was shiny-new. But for all his smart appearance, Inspector Box, I think there was more of the clerk than the gentleman to him. He told us his name, but I can't remember it now.'

Box rose to his feet, and Knollys followed suit.

'Thanks very much, both of you,' said Box. 'You've been of great help to the police, and when I write up the record of this case, your names shall stand as evidence of your part in its solution.'

Uttering little cries of pleasure, husband and wife accompanied Box and Knollys into the street. The last thing they saw, as they turned the corner, was Mr and Mrs Lovett waving cheerily to them from the front door of their cottage.

The morning's work, not all of it connected with the bullion robbery and Lane's murder, took Box and Knollys from Bevis Marks to the City, and then to Oxford Street, where they interviewed a man suspected of concealing a dead body. As a neighbouring clock struck twelve, they settled themselves in an empty bar in the rear of the Horse and Groom public house, and refreshed themselves with a pint of Bass's ale, and a generously-conceived bacon sandwich.

'It was Portman,' said Box. 'Mr Arthur Portman, chairman and secretary of the Temple of Light, and chief counter clerk of Peto's Bank in the Strand. He was careful not to call directly on the Lanes, because they were to be his dupes, though he did look through the Lanes' front window, and no doubt saw the portrait of that scapegrace uncle on the mantelpiece. So he visited our friends Mr and Mrs Lovett, and found in Mr Lovett the answer to his prayers.'

'What do you mean by that, sir?'

'I mean that Lovett is one of nature's gossips,' said Box, 'and everything he told us, he told Portman. When the time's ripe, we'll pay friend Portman a surprise visit at his place of work in the Strand.'

'You don't know that it was him for certain, sir.'

'Not as a gospel fact, no, but there are times, Sergeant, when you've got to accept something as fact for the sake of a workable theory. Everything that Lovett told Portman – the baby's name, the baby's name for herself, how she addressed her ma and pa, etcetera and so forth, was then repeated to those two harpies, Pennymint and Sylvestris. That's how the seance was worked. That's how poor young Lane was duped.'

'What do you propose to do about the spiritualists, sir? You can have them up for purporting to tell fortunes, or charge them under the vagrancy acts.'

'I've worked out a kind of timetable in my mind for dealing with these intertwined villainies. Pennymint first, then Portman – interview them, and put the wind up them, if you'll excuse the expression. I'll need warrants, though, to search Madam Sylvestris's house, and Sir Hamo Strange's bullion vault. So tomorrow, Sergeant, you and I will go down to Brookwood and tackle Mrs Pennymint. From what I saw of her, she'll panic and confess all when she hears that her dupe PC Lane has been murdered.'

'Sir, it's Tuesday tomorrow, and those trains to Brookwood—'

'Yes, I know all about the Brookwood trains, Sergeant, but the Pennymints live just a stone's throw from Brookwood Station, so there's no point in taking a direct Woking train. So it's to Brookwood tomorrow, Jack, to beard Mrs Pennymint in her den.'

Knollys smiled to himself, and changed the subject.

'Why did Portman post an envelope with five pounds in it through the Lanes' door?'

'I think that was conscience money, Sergeant, which says something for Portman and his associates, I suppose. It's a point worth bearing in mind as a mitigating circumstance once we round up this gang of sinners.'

Box bit into his bacon sandwich, and swallowed a mouthful of ale. The Horse and Groom was a dark place, on the shady side of Oxford Street. The little room where they sat smelt of stale tobacco and beer. Box pushed open a frosted glass window, and a miasma of putrescent air came in from the middens in the backyard. He pulled the window shut, and sat down again.

'What about the spirit baby?' asked Knollys. 'Lane told you that he'd actually seen a baby at the Belsize Park seance. Did he make that bit up?'

'No, it would have been a real baby, a toddler, introduced into the room through a false door or panel. The so-called medium does the voice, and they make sure the toddler's too young to speak. The sitter's in such a turmoil that he believes anything he sees. They have music, and perfumes, and – it makes me sick, Sergeant, and they're going to pay for their chicanery.'

'Wouldn't it be a risk, sir, using a real live child?'

'Oh, yes. Some of them don't take that risk. There was a Mrs Niedpath taken up last year, who sent a little monkey into the darkened seance room, and said it was a little boy come to comfort his mother. She got three months in the House of Correction.'

Despite the dismal surroundings, the sandwiches were excellent, and the beer very welcome on such a hot day. For the next few minutes both men gave all their attention to the business of refreshment. When they had finished, they sat back contentedly on the oak settles. Box lit one of his thin cheroots, and blew smoke towards the blackened ceiling.

'Why?' asked Knollys, and the word came so unexpectedly in the silence that Box jumped in alarm.

'Why? What do you mean, "why"?'

'Why did they go to all those lengths to deceive poor Lane and his wife?'

'It was done to lure PC Lane away from Carmelite Pavement on the morning of the twenty-eighth. He was given a very powerful inducement to arrange a substitute, that substitute being the murderous Mahoney. You can see, now, can't you, the connection between those spiritualists and the bullion robbery? They're not just linked, Sergeant: they're entwined.'

'But PC Lane turned up for duty after all.'

'Yes, he did. Perhaps the call of duty was greater than his desire to see his little daughter's spirit. . . . No, that won't do. He must have found out something about Madam Sylvestris that made him see the whole seance business as a wicked fraud. That would make him recall his responsibilities. He'd have known that I'd have helped him later to haul in that gang of spiritual bloodsuckers.'

'And so Mahoney killed him, sir. I believe now that he'd only just done the deed when I turned up at Carmelite Pavement. He looked agitated and ill at ease, but he left me no time to ask him any inconvenient questions.'

Sergeant Knollys rubbed his head ruefully, and recalled Mahoney's sudden attack upon him. What a fool he'd been, to turn his back on the man! He'd unfinished business to do with Mahoney.

'And so PC Lane died, Sergeant, simply because he failed to keep out of the way. I expect Mahoney waited until the yard was empty for a moment, and then carried Lane's body down to the pier. He'd have concealed it there until the steam launch arrived. Something like that.'

'Who were the men in the launch? And where are the original crew?'

'Well done, Sergeant! You're asking all the right questions today. So sit still, and listen, while I propound a theory. The original crew of the launch have not been reported missing by the owners, because – because there never *was* an original crew. It must be that. . . . The men in the launch had been hired especially for the task—'

'From the Milton Fisher gang?'

'No, Sergeant. I believed Fisher when he said he'd nothing to do with this business. That crew – the crew who sailed the launch into Corunna Lands and scuttled her – was hired to do the job by someone in the consortium who hired the launches in the first place. When we've finished here, we'll go out to Rotherhithe and interview the people who hire out the launches – what were they called? – Moltman. Moltman & Sons, They'll tell us why one launch – Number C1 – was to be provided without a crew.'

'Sir—'

'Yes, I know, Sergeant. I'm skating on thin ice, as the saying goes. Fools rush in where angels fear to tread. But this is all between these four walls, Jack. That sinister crew who came in their launch to Carmelite Pier could only have been provided by—'

'Hold on, sir! With all due respect, haven't you considered the possibility that a professional gang as yet entirely unknown to us engineered this robbery? After all, no other launch was affected. Maybe this unknown gang planned all along to seize this huge assignment of bullion.'

'You're not thinking straight, Jack,' Box interrupted. '*There was no original crew.* You won't find ten sailor men with their toes turned up, floating down towards the sea. These villains were the intended crew all along, and they were hired by the man who started this whole operation – the man whose bullion chests contained not gold, but *lead*.'

'Sir Hamo Strange.'

'Yes, Sir Hamo Strange! There, that's in the open, so we can pause there, Sergeant, and pass on. Twenty-five chests were recovered, artistically smashed, and with some of the locks still open on their hasps. Fifty-three chests went missing. But we know where they must be, don't we, Sergeant? Go on, don't be shy: tell me!'

'They're at the bottom of Parr's Basin, sir, in Corunna Lands. They sailed the launch into that wilderness, and threw the whole lot, apart from the twenty-three they kept back to create the illusion of a robbery, into the deep water of the basin.'

'And why did they do that?'

'Because to them, those chests of lead were quite worthless.'

'And why did they pretend to force open twenty-five of the chests in the gully?'

'Because, sir, they'd already opened them on the launch, and thrown their contents into the river. Those empty boxes were there to create the illusion that a robbery had taken place.'

Box offered his cigar case to Knollys, who accepted a thin cheroot. Box lit both cigars with a wax vesta, which he dropped into the dregs of his beer. He sat back luxuriantly on the settle, and regarded his sergeant with twinkling eyes.

'You're doing very well, Sergeant Knollys,' he said. 'Now, let's see whether you can complete the theory. You said that the villains wanted to create the illusion that a robbery had taken place. So are you saying that *no* robbery took place? That *no* gold was stolen from Sir Hamo Strange's vaults? In that case, who's gained from all this rigmarole? As far as I can see, no one's gained anything at all.'

Knollys drew thoughtfully on his cigar. It was some time since the guvnor had subjected him to one of his splendid barrages of questions. They were designed to clarify matters in a case that was particularly obscure, but they were also part of a conscious effort to refine his sergeant's skills in the art of detection.

'Who's gained? Well, sir, I'd say Sir Hamo Strange has gained, because the whole consignment of the Swedish Loan was insured by the British Government. For reasons of his own, Sir Hamo Strange had kept his million pounds in gold intact, and defrauded the Government of one million pounds.'

'Well done, Jack! So our great financier has cheated the British Government of one million pounds by a very clever and very dangerous piece of villainy. Others are involved, including Mahoney, and possibly our prim and proper Mr Arthur Portman, spiritualist and bank clerk. Excellent, Sergeant! But you still haven't seen what it's really about, have you?'

'What do you mean, sir? What else is there to see?'

'What was in the chests?'

'Lead.'

'Well, then. What if Sir Hamo Strange's vast holding of gold below Carmelite Pavement is *all* lead? Perhaps the colossus of finance is down to his last few pounds, Sergeant, and defrauding the Government of a million pounds may be the first step in rebuilding a battered fortune. If that's true, then it's gaol for our Sir Hamo.'

'We'll never know what's really in those vaults, sir. What you say can only remain supposition.'

'Oh, no, Sergeant Knollys. Remember, we're still investigating this so-called robbery, so it would be entirely in order for us – and Sergeant Kenwright – to carry out a thorough inspection of all the chests held in Sir Hamo's vaults. I'm going to tackle

Superintendent Mackharness about it. He's had his own suspicions from the start, and I think you'll find that in this matter of the fake bullion robbery, he'll be entirely on our side.'

Box stood up, and brushed some imaginary breadcrumbs from his fashionable overcoat.

'Come on, Sergeant,' he said, 'it's getting late. Time that you and I set out for Rotherhithe.'

The boat-yard of Moltman & Sons lay alongside one of the many large basins of the Surrey Commercial Docks, near the opening of the Grand Surrey Canal. In a brick-walled office reached by means of a flight of steep wooden steps, Box and Knollys found the yard foreman, a heavy, hunchbacked man who introduced himself as John Hodge. His sun-bronzed face looked as though it had been sculpted from mahogany, but his bright blue eyes were alert and humorous. Box had never before seen a man who stowed the stub-end of his current cigar behind his ear.

'Inspector Box, hey? And Sergeant Knollys?' said Hodge. 'Well, this is an honour! I suppose you've come about our scuttled launch? Disgraceful. Mr Moltman's very angry about it, as well he should be. Still, it can be salvaged, and we'll make it as good as new in a couple of weeks. The insurance will cover the cost.'

Mr Hodge glanced out of the office window at the busy yard. Three new launches were taking shape on the stocks, and beyond them, lying at anchor, lay a dozen trim craft, part of Moltman's celebrated boat-hire business. Finally, he gave his full attention to Box.

'So what can I do for you, Inspector?'

'Mr Hodge, I want to know why Moltman's didn't provide the crew for launch C1, the vessel assigned to collect Sir Hamo Strange's bullion from Carmelite Pavement, and deliver it to the West India Docks. All the other launches in the operation had crews provided by you.'

For answer, John Hodge began to rummage through a pile of

165

dog-eared letters lying in a wooden tray on his desk. His fingers, Box saw, were heavily stained with tobacco, the nails bitten and cracked. Perhaps being foreman of a large boat-yard affected the nerves? With a little yelp of triumph Hodge found the document that he was looking for, and handed it to Box.

'Here we are, Inspector. Here's your answer. On Wednesday, the twenty-sixth, two days before the gold was moved, that letter was delivered by hand. It came from Mr Horace Garner, Chief Warden of the Carmelite Pavement Bullion Vaults. You can read what it says yourself.'

The letter, written by hand on the printed notepaper of the Vaults, begged to inform Messrs Moltman & Sons that Sir Hamo Strange would provide his own crew for the launch C1, that they had contracted to supply. The letter was signed by Horace Garner, who begged them to believe that he was their humble servant.

'And did this crew turn up here on the Friday morning?' asked Box.

'They did. There were ten of them, decent-looking men in navy-blue jerseys, pants, and caps. Very respectable, they were, and obviously used to launches and their funny little ways. I never thought anything of it. Why should I? So off they went, out of the basin and into the river.'

'Did they say anything to you?'

'Not a word. They just nodded and smiled, you know. They were French.'

'French?'

'Yes. At least, I think they were. They jabbered a bit among themselves, and it sounded like French to me. Is there anything else?'

Mr Hodge was clearly aching to get out among the boats. Box had heard enough.

'May I keep this letter, Mr Hodge?' he asked. 'I'll give you a receipt, and return it in the post when I've done with it.'

'Certainly, certainly. Now, if you'll excuse me, Inspector. . . .'

Without waiting for his receipt. John Hodge strode out of the office, and clattered down the wooden stairs. Box scribbled a few words on a piece of paper, and left it on the foreman's desk. Then he and Knollys followed him.

Later that afternoon, a special courier delivered a note to Box at King James's Rents. The envelope also contained the letter that Mr Hodge had loaned to Box earlier in the day.

Medici House.
Blomfield Place,
London, EC
31 July 1893

Dear Inspector Box,
The letter that you sent us, purporting to come from Mr Horace Garner, is an impudent fiction. I can confirm that neither Sir Hamo Strange, nor Mr Garner, knew anything of the matter. We assumed that the crew who arrived with the launch C1 was a crew furnished by Messrs Moltman & Son. The signature, 'H. Garner', is a bold and wicked forgery.
Your obedient servant,
William Curteis
Private Secretary to Sir Hamo Strange

13

Wrestling with the Spirits

The 9.30 train for Brookwood moved ponderously out of the private station at Waterloo, its polished black carriages gleaming in the morning sunshine. A crowd of people standing mournfully on the long platform watched it begin its dignified progress out of London along the tracks of the London & South Western Railway.

Arnold Box sat back in his upholstered seat, and observed his five fellow passengers. Jack Knollys sat beside him, reading the *Morning Post*. To Knollys' right an elderly man, clad in funereal black, was nursing a black bowler hat on his knee. In the seats opposite sat two ladies in deep mourning, and a little boy in a sailor suit. The ladies were weeping, occasionally lifting their black veils to dab their eyes with small black-bordered lace handkerchiefs.

'It seems to me, Sergeant Knollys—' Box began.

'Shh!' hissed the elderly man. He regarded Box from reproachful faded grey eyes, The two ladies burst afresh into tears, and the elder of the two pointedly snapped open the clasps of a black prayer book, and pretended to read. Knollys smiled. Box, who had not thought to buy a paper, sat in frozen embarrassment, staring ahead of him. Dense black smoke drifted past the window of the carriage.

'Mama,' asked the little boy in the sailor suit, 'why are those two men sitting in our carriage?'

'I don't know, dear,' muttered the elder of the two ladies. Box saw her dart him a venomous look through her veil. 'Maybe they got on the wrong train.'

'In the midst of life we are in death,' declared the elderly man, and the two ladies began to weep again. Box rose from his seat, and with a mumbled apology slid open the carriage door and stepped out into the corridor.

He remained there, observing the changing scenery as the train passed through the London suburbs and then out into the Surrey countryside until it slid to a gentle stop at Brookwood Station, a long platform set pleasantly among a grove of trees. Box gratefully opened the carriage door, and stepped down on to the platform.

As though obeying a hidden command, all the other carriage doors opened, and the black-clad passengers alighted. They stood motionless, looking fixedly towards what appeared to be two long guard's vans at the rear of the train. Sergeant Knollys quietly joined Box on the platform.

A number of men in frock coats and top hats came into sight, moving slowly towards the train. At the same time, the van doors were slid open.

'Sir,' whispered Knollys.

'What?'

'Hats off.'

Again, as though orchestrated by a hidden director, four dark elm coffins were solemnly borne from the vans, and lifted at a slight angle up on to the platform. The men in frock coats were joined by a number of clergymen. Box's fellow passengers threw him a look of reproach, and the little boy in the sailor suit managed to stick his tingue out at him without being detected by his mama. The elderly man with the faded grey eyes joined them, and they attached themselves to the first of four separate cortèges that had travelled down from London on one of the special funeral

169

trains provided by the London Necropolis and National Mausoleum Company.

As they emerged from the station on to the public road, Inspector Box sighed with relief. Knollys had been right to warn him about taking one of the Necropolis trains. They were, in effect, hearses with mourners' carriages attached, pulled by a steam locomotive, and not really suitable for ordinary passengers. Still, it had got them there!

Brookwood Cemetery, originally planted out in 1854, was a vast sylvan burial ground for London's dead, occupying 2000 acres. Box had been there once, as a boy. Over the years it had developed into a strangely beautiful, almost rural, estate, and many of the crowded London parishes had their own sections there.

A short walk along a winding path brought the two detectives to Charnelhouse Lane. Number 24 proved to be a pleasant villa of modest proportions, with a green-painted veranda running along its front. It stood in a very well tended garden, bright with summer flowers. This, as Knollys had ascertained, was the home of Mr Alfred Pennymint, market gardener, and his wife, Minnie. Box pushed open the garden gate, and the two detectives walked up the path to the front door.

A man was sitting at a rustic table in the garden. He had no coat, and his shirt sleeves were rolled up to the elbow. He wore a battered straw hat to protect his sparse silver hair from the strong sun. A large jug, and a collection of earthenware cups, stood on the table. This, Box surmised, would be Mr Alfred Pennymint.

'You've come in by the wrong gate!' cried the man. His voice was cheerful, and his eyes humorous. 'The entrance to the market garden is another hundred yards along the road, just beyond the turn.'

'We're police officers, Mr Pennymint,' said Box. 'We're here to have a few words with your wife. I'm Detective Inspector Box of Scotland Yard, and this is Detective Sergeant Knollys.'

'You'd better come in then, gentlemen, and slake your thirst. It must have been a dusty journey from London today. Pour your-selves out some cider. That's right. So you want to see Minnie? I expect it's about that poor young man Lane?'

'It is, Mr Pennymint. You see, he'd visited one of your wife's seances shortly before he was murdered. As a matter of fact, I was there with him. I think there may be a connection between the Temple of Light and the people responsible for PC Lane's murder.'

Mr Pennymint shook his head, and sighed. Box saw that his words had not really registered. The hint that his wife may have been involved in a murder plot had been quite lost on him.

'It's not something I hold with, myself, Mr Box,' said Pennymint. 'This spiritualism business, I mean. But it keeps the wife happy, and she loves her meetings up there in London. They seem a decent lot of folk, as far as I can make out. Very respectable. And that Mr Portman of hers is a real gentleman. But it's all a bit – well, funny, isn't it?'

'This cider's very welcome, Mr Pennymint,' said Box. 'Thanks very much. So you don't really believe that your wife has special powers?'

'Oh, I wouldn't say that, Mr Box. She picks things up, you know. She'll suddenly know that something's happened before anyone's brought news of it. Things like that. It's uncanny, really. Very clever, I suppose. But Minnie's not one for study and perse-verance, so she's never really trained herself. It's all haphazard, if you know what I mean— Ah! Here's Minnie now. I'll leave you, gentlemen, to have your chat with her, and get back to work.'

Mrs Pennymint had appeared on the porch. She looked as homely and natural as when Box had first seen her over a fortnight earlier. She was wearing a sprig muslin dress, which was far too young for her, and a vivid scarlet kerchief draped loosely round her neck. Her husband introduced her to the two detectives, shook hands with them, and made his way through the garden to a gate that led out on to the main road. His wife joined them at the table.

It's about poor young PC Lane, isn't it?' said Mrs Pennymint.

Her eyes were troubled, and she spoke in a low voice. 'He should never have gone to visit Almena. Madam Sylvestris, you know. He was in such a state over the loss of his little girl that he'd have believed anything he was told.'

'Do you mean that Madam Sylvestris deceived him, ma'am?'

'Dear me, no!' Mrs Pennymint sounded shocked. 'I mean that Mr Lane was not ready to approach so near to the other world. It was too early, and I was surprised that Madam Sylvestris didn't realize that. Yes, I was very surprised at that. . . .'

Mrs Pennymint frowned, and Box could sense her perplexity and confusion. Watching her, he had a sudden conviction that she was wholly innocent of any attempt at deception. Deluded she may have been, but deceitful? No, not that.

'Do you hold all your seances at the Temple of Light in Spitalfields?'

'Yes, that's right. Twice a week I go there. Oh, I'll arrange a little private sitting for neighbours here in Woking, but mainly they're at the Temple of Light.'

Her eyes suddenly closed, and they saw her eyelids tremble for a second before she opened them again.

'I shouldn't worry about that girl if I were you, Mr Knollys,' she said. 'She'll be quite safe on her own. She knows you're not another – another – what is it? Fenton? Fenlake.'

Mrs Pennymint seemed hardly conscious that she had spoken at all. She sat politely, waiting for one or other of her visitors to speak. Jack Knollys had gone pale, so that the ugly scar across his face stood out white and fearsome. Box felt a leap of superstitious fear in his stomach.

Jack Knollys' fiancée, Vanessa Drake, had been neglected by the young man to whom she had previously been engaged, a Foreign Office courier called Lieutenant Arthur Fenlake. It was that neglect to which the spiritualist medium was referring. How could she have known such an intimate detail of a young woman's life? Or of Knollys' nagging worry that Vanessa would think that he, too, was neglecting her in favour of his official duties? Box placed a reassuring hand on Knollys' sleeve, and the sergeant took another swig of cider. From that moment, he never took his eyes off Mrs Pennymint.

'Now, ma'am,' Box continued, 'I want you to tell me whether or not you have any financial interest in the Temple of Light? Have you ever paid for any repairs, or matters of that kind?'

He had thought that the medium would have taken offence, but she merely laughed.

'Repairs? Stuff and nonsense! To be quite honest with you, Mr Box, I know very little about the place. As far as I know, the premises belong to a trust, with Mr Arthur Portman as principal trustee. I've never been interested in that kind of thing. My concern is to bring a bit of comfort to the bereaved. That's my work.'

'And do you travel up by train for your seances? It must be a heavy day if you have to come all the way back again on the railway.'

'My goodness, what a nosy man you are! I travel up by the early morning train from Woking on seance days, and I'm met at the station by Mr Portman, who takes me to his lovely little house in Henrietta Terrace, off the Strand. And there I stay, enjoying the company of his wife Mildred, until it's time to go to Spitalfields. Mr Portman takes me there in a cab.'

'And when the seance is over?'

'When the seance is over, Mr Box, Mr Portman takes me back to his home, and I stay there the night. Next morning, I catch a train back here to Brookwood. I hope you're satisfied with all that, young man?'

Again, Mrs Pennymint's eyes closed, and her eyelids fluttered and trembled before they opened again. She added: 'Your father's very happy today, Mr Box, because the doctors say that he'll be measured for an artificial leg, soon. . . . Yes, and the next morning, I take a train back home to Brookwood.'

Once again, the medium sat patiently, waiting for one or other of her visitors to speak.

What was going on? Was this woman making it all up? But how could she be? How—'

'What can you tell us about Madam Sylvestris, Mrs Pennymint?' asked Knollys. He had seen that Box was, for the moment, beyond speech.

'Well, of course, she's very famous, Mr Knollys. She's what they call a physical medium. I can only do thoughts and mental communications of all kinds, and there are occasions when I can see spirit beings. But Almena – Madam Sylvestris – she can conjure up discarnate entities, fully developed spirits that can talk. It's quite wonderful, what she can do. You . . . you can—'

Mrs Pennymint suddenly clutched Box's arm. At the same time, her eyes closed again, and her head sagged forward. She began to speak, and her voice was harsher and deeper than her normal tones. Around the three of them the August sun touched the trees with gold, and the birds sang lustily.

'The man who killed PC Lane has a pockmarked face. He's a big, brutal man. M. I see the letter M. And an X. *He was dressed like one of us, Inspector. For a moment I was deceived – the uniform. And then he came at me.* . . . This man who killed PC Lane is hiding. He's being sheltered by an accomplice. But he'll not survive this month. He's marked with the dark cone, the black flame. Darkness.'

Mrs Pennymint opened her eyes, and shook herself like a terrier, at the same time removing her hand from Box's arm. She smiled apologetically.

'There, now,' she said, 'I'm dropping off to sleep! It's this warm weather. They say it's going to change by mid-month. But then, they're always saying things like that. How do they know what the weather will be like before it's happened? You can't foretell the future.'

Some minutes later, Box and Knollys set out to walk to Woking station. Both men felt shaken to the core by their experience at Mr Pennymint's home.

'Sir,' said Knollys, 'while Mrs Pennymint was telling us about Mahoney – which in itself was a bit of a shaker – PC Lane himself started to speak in his own voice—'

'Yes, I know, I heard him, and I don't believe it, even though it was true. I'd rather *not* believe things like that. But I don't know what to make of it, Sergeant, and that's a fact.' Box shook his head in bewilderment before continuing.

'I suppose she could have gathered together a whole dossier of little facts, just like Portman must have done to feed that harpy Sylvestris with the details of poor little Catherine Mary and her death. Maybe she's right about Vanessa, and about Pa's leg. But what about my so-called Uncle Cuthbert? She slipped up there, right enough.'

Jack Knollys made no reply, and the two men walked in silence for a while along the leafy lane that would take them out of Brookwood.

'That woman's innocent of any collusion in this business of Lane and the bullion robbery,' said Box at length. 'She knows nothing. But the same can't be said of Sylvestris. Mr Mackharness has secured three warrants, one for the Temple of Light and the other two for Belsize Park – search and arrest. Tomorrow, Sergeant, we'll kill two birds with one stone.'

Outside the Temple of Light in the nameless alley off Leyland Street in Spitalfields, a throng of devotees, some hysterical, others belligerent, had gathered to witness the desecration of their sanctuary by unbelieving officers of the Metropolitan Police. 'Blasphemy!' 'The Antichrist is here!' 'Where is Freedom now?' These, and other cries assailed the air. A police van, its rear door open, stood outside the building, a patient horse between the shafts. Hidden by the van was the notice board announcing to the passers-by that 'There Is No Death'.

Inside, the building was alive with policemen. Two of them had taken down the plush curtains behind the platform, revealing a number of wires descending from the ceiling, and attached to pulleys. Some of them had heavy lead weights attached, and Inspector Box had just concluded an experiment in which, by letting one of the weights drop to the floor, he had reproduced the loud report that had accompanied Mrs Pennymint's trance. He remembered, too, that she had not flinched at the sound. Either she had expected it, or her trance was genuine. After his visit to Brookwood, Box was inclined to the latter explanation.

Sergeant Kenwright, whose burly, bearded presence had over-awed the crowd in the alley, slowly appeared on the platform, rising up inch by inch from some kind of pit below. It would have been a comic sight, if Box had not recalled the spirit of Tom Prentice, appearing before his overawed brother, Alexander.

'How's it done, Sergeant?'

'It's a rising platform, sir, raised and lowered by a cranked wheel down in the cellar. You see these thin tubes, attached to the under-side of the platform? They're fastened to a tiny little furnace with bellows, to pump coloured smoke up into the church. There's a host of tricks and traps down there.'

Box had spotted the man calling himself Alexander Prentice in the crowd. He was now sitting forlornly in the police van outside. Like all the others connected with this den of superstitious deceit, he would be charged under the Vagrancy Act of 1824.

The search continued. Sergeant Knollys had found a little cramped office in the cellarage, and looked up from reading a book as Box entered.

'Do you see this book, sir?' said Knollys. ' "The Psychic's Warehouse Catalogue. High quality mechanical appliances to assist the medium. Only the finest materials used." ' He flicked over the glossy pages, showing Box some of the items for sale from a private address in the Edgware Road. A clockwork rapping hand, for table tapping, 4s. Telescopic reaching-rods, from 2/6d. The

Complete Spirit Rapping Table, 'for use in private apartments', 21/- Slate writing; Sealed letter reading; Self-playing guitars. Luminous materialistic ghost. Phosphorescent paint Coloured spark wheels. Percussive light boxes. All at reasonable prices.

'What a rotten place this is, sir!' Knollys cried, throwing the book down on the table of the little office.

'Yes, Jack, it is. Rotten to the core. I don't suppose you remember the book on this shady business that came out in '91? It was called, *The Revelations of a Spirit Medium*, and was a true confession by one of these so-called psychics It had to be anonymous, of course, but I happen to know that it was genuine. That book tells you all about the things for sale in that catalogue. By the time we've finished here, I expect we'll find quite a few objects of that nature hidden in cupboards.'

They made their way back upstairs, where the searchers had discovered more false panels, sliding floorboards, and other devices calculated to deceive. Sergeant Kenwright was busy paying out a thin wire through his gloved hands and, as he did so, a fine white 'ghost' rather like a kite with a round head attached, floated down from a trap in the ceiling.

'What will happen to these bloodsuckers, sir? We'll round up the whole gang of them very soon, I should think. They'll be so frightened after our raid that they'll betray each other out of sheer funk, though Portman might be a tough nut to crack.'

'Yes, Portman. We'll save him to the last, Sergeant. By visiting him at his precious bank, we may be able to shake his confidence a little. As for all this deceit and chicanery, we can only see it punished under the terms of the 1824 Vagrancy Act.'

'And what kind of punishment is that, sir?'

'Hard labour in the House of Correction for a period not exceeding three months. Most of them get a month. We've seen enough here, Sergeant. All this rubbish will be collected, and produced in evidence before the magistrates. If I had my way – which I haven't – I'd burn the whole place down.'

Outside, the devotees renewed their clamours on seeing Box and Knollys emerge. Several elderly women were kneeling on the pavement, holding up beseeching arms to Heaven. The men, silent now for the most part, regarded the police officers with surly defiance.

'They'll change their tune, sir,' said Knollys, 'when we produce all that proof of fraud and deceit. This will be the end for Madam Sylvestris.'

Box shook his head. Poor Jack! He'd seen many terrible things in his career, but evidently he'd never come across spiritualism before.

'Change their tune? Oh, no, Jack, they won't, you know! Madam Sylvestris will become a martyr. These devotees will pour fresh money into her coffers, and condemn the police as brutal unbelievers, conspiring with the Government and the Church of England to suppress the 'truth'. Exposing rogues of this type, Sergeant, is a very unrewarding occupation. Still, we're not in this job for rewards. We'd better get out to Belsize Park, now, and complete the morning's good work.'

The police van halted at the beginning of Melbourne Avenue, Belsize Park, and Box, accompanied by Sergeant Knollys and the Scotland Yard Matron, stepped down into the road. Box pointed to an elegant closed carriage, with a glossy black horse between the shafts, drawn up in front of one of the opulent villas on the right side of the leafy road. An elderly coachman was busy loading a quantity of luggage on to the roof.

'It looks as though we're just in time,' he said. 'Word must have reached Madam Sylvestris of our visit to Mrs Pennymint. That's number eight, and those trunks on the pavement suggest that our spiritual lady friend is doing a flit.'

The matron, a capable-looking woman in her forties, dressed discreetly in civilian clothing, treated her companions to a grim smile. Also known as the 'female searcher', or more prosaically as 'the search woman', she had a long experience of consorting with the more unspeakable specimens of her own sex.

'You may have trouble with this lady, Mr Box,' she said. 'They usually like to make a fuss, these fake mediums, in the hope that their plight will get into the papers. There'll be no need to search her, though. We're not taking her *in flagrante*, producing spirit babies from her leg-of-mutton sleeves.'

'I hope there's no trouble, Kate,' Box replied. 'But after what happened to PC Lane, I'm in no mood for compromise. She'll walk down the road with us to the van, and behave herself, or she'll be carried there! Come on, let's get it over and done with.'

They walked up the garden path, and Knollys rapped sharply on the door. A face peered briefly at them through a stained-glass panel in the door, which was opened cautiously. A housemaid, her face darkened by a suspicious frown, peered out at them.

'Who are you? Madam can see no one today. She is about to embark upon a journey—'

'We are police officers,' said Box curtly. At the same time he pushed the door open. He, Knollys and the matron entered the house.

Madam Sylvestris stood halfway up the stairs. She was dressed in the height of fashion, and from her shoulders hung a beautifully cut travelling cloak. A wide-brimmed hat adorned with trimmed ostrich feathers proclaimed itself as being one of the latest Bond Street creations. Handsome and haughty, she looked every inch a lady.

'Who are you?' asked Madam Sylvestris in icy tones. 'Upon what pretence do you force yourself into a lady's house? I am at this very moment leaving for a visit to the North. Céline, fetch my mauve silk parasol.'

Box slowly mounted the stairs, fixing the lady all the time with his steady gaze. He placed his hand lightly on her arm.

'You are Ada Silvers, née Mullins,' he said, 'alias Almena Sylvestris. I am arresting you under the terms of the Vagrancy Act,

1824, in that you did, at London, in several and divers locations, pretend or profess to tell fortunes, and did use subtle crafts and other means or devices, by palmistry or otherwise, to deceive and impose on any or several of Her Majesty's subjects; and that you did falsely purport to raise up the spirits of the dead; for all which things you are to be deemed a common rogue and vagabond, and taken up accordingly.'

He had scarcely finished speaking when the maid, Céline, flung herself up the staircase, collapsed at Madam Sylvestris's feet, and turned to face Box and his companions like a terrified animal at bay.

'Assassins!' she shrieked. 'Murderers! Why do you wish to butcher a saint? Who will help us? Cowards!'

'Hush, faithful one,' said Madam Sylvestris calmly, and with infinite dignity. 'This gross man and his companions are imprisoned in their envelopes of clay. Such people cannot discern the spiritual in mankind. But we know that the Powers will come to our aid – look! There, in the hall' – her voice dropped to a hoarse whisper – 'standing beside that cruel woman: it is the Archangel Michael!'

'Strewth!' muttered Box. Kate had been right. They were going to make a show of him. He could see a few curious neighbours already hovering in the porch. He couldn't cope with all this fancy talk.

'Holy Michael, Archangel,' Céline shrieked, now clutching her mistress's knees, 'defend us in the day of battle! Be thou our defence against the wickedness and snares of the Devil!' Abandoning English, she launched into a volley of French. To Box's infinite relief, Kate the Matron suddenly took charge of the situation.

'Hold your noise, young woman,' she said, at the same time prising Céline's arms away from Madam Sylvestris's knees. 'One more peep out of you, and we'll take you in, too, to keep your mistress company. And no more talk of angels from either of you, do you hear? We'll have no blasphemy here.'

Céline, suddenly subdued, walked meekly down the stairs, and stood beside Sergeant Knollys.

'And you, madam,' said the matron, 'must obey the warrant and come with us. You can walk with dignity, and unmanacled, to the police van on the corner, or you can be handcuffed, and carried there by police officers. Which is it to be?'

Madam Sylvestris walked calmly downstairs into the hall. She treated Box and Knollys to a cold bow. Both men marvelled at her impudent audacity.

'Céline,' she said, 'you had better secure the house, and make the journey up to Newcastle yourself. I will join you there as soon as my business with these people is over and done with. Go now, dear girl. Say no more. The Powers are with us both.'

After Madam Sylvestris had been safely lodged in the local police station, Box and Knollys, armed with their search warrant, returned to the house in Belsize Park. The French maid, and the elderly coachman, had departed in their mistress's carriage, but a kind of woman caretaker readmitted them to the house, and raised no objection to their conducting a search. Evidently, she had not been in her mistress's confidence.

In the first-floor seance room they found the curtained alcove. A thorough examination of the floor beneath the medium's chair revealed yet another contraption for pumping coloured smoke into the room. Behind the chair, concealed in the panelling, there was a secret door, leading into a small windowed room.

'They'd pump up the ghostly smoke, Sergeant,' said Box, 'and then through the swirling mists the spirits would appear – accomplices, making their entrance through that secret door.'

'And not only accomplices,' said Knollys, glancing quizzically at Box.

'No, Sergeant, not only accomplices. Because on one occasion at least it was a little baby girl who was pushed through that panel

– a little toddler, who could scarcely yet speak. And so poor Lane saw his Catherine Mary, and was promised that, the next time he came, he could hold her. He sent me a note, telling me that. Unless I'm very much mistaken, our haughty Madam Sylvestris will do three months' hard labour for this.'

The hidden room contained an array of reaching-rods, hand bells, and other paraphernalia of fakery. One cardboard box was full of strips of muslin, some of it unpleasantly damp.

'Ectoplasm,' said Box. 'It exudes from the medium's mouth, and is supposed to give form and substance to the spirit visitors. They swallow it first, and regurgitate it to order. Disgusting. Come on, Jack. Let's get back to town and make our way to the Strand. It's time to deal with Mr Arthur Portman, the man behind the mediums.'

14

The Bank Crash

They saw the frantic, screaming crowd besieging Peto's Bank as they rounded the corner from Wellington Street. Box estimated their strength at over 200 desperate souls, all driven by the single desire to get their deposits back in gold. The traffic in the Strand had ground to a halt. Passengers on the open top decks of omnibuses were standing up to get a better view of the frightening scene.

'Blimey! It's a run on the bank, Sergeant,' said Box. 'There have been rumours about Peto's for weeks. Look, here's a crowd of our lads pouring out of Southampton Street. Let's join them, and see what we can do.'

'What about Portman, sir?'

'He's probably in need of being rescued at the moment, Sergeant Knollys. His connection with the Temple of Light can keep for the moment. Look at that!'

The tall double doors of the main entrance to the bank were heaving to and fro as the incensed crowd tried to pull them open, and terrified members of staff inside the bank attempted to keep them closed. A dozen police officers, their minds intent on their duty to restore public order, had begun to restrain parts of the crowd, and to corral them in the gardens adjoining the stricken bank. One burly sergeant recognized Box, and saluted him.

'Sergeant Davies,' said Box, 'I want to get inside that place. Can you help?'

'Come round to the back of the premises, sir. We're already in full control there. There's a rear entrance to the bank – a staff entrance, it is – you can gain access to the banking hall through that.' Sergeant Davies, an elderly, weather-bronzed man, shook his head sadly. 'It's a shame to see respectable folk behaving like savages, sir. A good number of them are gentlemen. There was a sudden rumour this morning that the bank was failing, and within half an hour the place was besieged.'

'What's it like inside?'

'All hell's let loose, sir. Inspector Paulet doesn't want us to draw truncheons, in case it leads to bloodshed, so we've left them to it. What we *should* do—'

'Yes, Sergeant, go on.'

'Well, Mr Box, I think we should do a baton charge and drive them all back into the Strand. Emotions are high, as they say, and it's like a tinderbox in there. Anything could happen. Assault, battery – maybe arson, in which case they'll all perish together.'

They had been hurrying along the narrow alley beside the gardens while Sergeant Davies was talking, and in moments they had reached the rear of Peto's Bank. What looked like a whole company of police were drawn up in a formidable line from the rear entrance to the detached coach house belonging to the bank.

'In here, sir,' said Sergeant Davies, unlocking a door. 'I'll leave this door unlocked and guarded while you're in there. If you need— What's that?'

A tremendous noise of shattering glass came to them, followed by a kind of hysterical cheer.

'The crowd's breaking the front windows, Sergeant,' said Box. 'They're turning into a mob by the sound of it, and if they're not stopped, they'll start looting, and it won't just be Peto's who'll suffer. Tell Mr Paulet, will you? Tell him to charge and disperse, before it's too late. Come on, Sergeant Knollys, it's time for you and me to venture inside.'

Even as the door was closed behind them they could both hear the terrifying baying and shouting coming from the banking hall at the front of the stricken building. As they walked along the corridor facing them, the noise became louder, and when they pushed open a door half concealed behind a pillar, the full force of the bedlam made them stagger with shock.

The main hall of Peto's Bank was a lofty and magnificent chamber, flanked by massive pillars of variegated marble. The long mahogany counter faced the main doors, and above it stood a long ornate balcony, its front balustrade incorporating a magnificent gilded clock. The vaulted ceiling was painted to resemble that of the Sistine Chapel.

Box and Knollys recorded all this grandeur almost uncon- sciously, because it was not dead marble but living and enraged humanity that riveted their attention. What must have started as an anxious crowd of clients had developed into a mass of strug- gling, fearful men, most of them clutching pass-books, and surging forward towards the counter.

There were a dozen pale-faced clerks manning the long counter, and Box could see their mouths moving as they indulged in hope- less conversations and entreaties with a string of men who were shouting and banging their clenched fists on the counter. Among the clerks Box saw the elegant figure of Arthur Portman, the Chief Counter Clerk, his face as ashen as those of his colleagues. Soon, Box, thought, some frantic depositor is going to leap over that counter. . . .

The general bedlam suddenly soared into a howl of execration as Lord Jocelyn Peto appeared on the balcony. He was flanked by a number of directors, but Box had eyes only for the man whom he had interviewed at Duppas Park House just over a week earlier. Lord Jocelyn's face was entirely drained of colour, so that he looked like an image of wax. He was trembling violently, and one of the directors had taken hold of his arm in order to support him. His lips moved, at first without sound, and then he attempted to speak.

The noise in the banking hall rose to a crescendo. Objects standing on the counter were seized and hurled up at the balcony. Box saw a steel inkwell rise in an arc and then fall, scattering ink on to the frantic crowd. Why didn't Paulet do something? Lord Jocelyn staggered back, and was hustled away out of sight. Poor man! thought Box. His face had expressed a knowledge of his total ruin.

It was then that Arnold Box, casting an eye over the crowd from the safety of the pillar where he stood, saw Louise Whittaker. Half fainting, she was still clutching her pass book, and was being supported by an elderly man whose attentions were divided between his concern for a young woman in distress and the prospect of his own impending beggary.

Jack Knollys had also seen Louise, and without waiting for Box to speak, suddenly began to carve his way through the crowd. It was impossible for anyone to impede the giant sergeant's progress, and Box had the sense to swallow his pride and follow in his wake.

When Louise saw Arnold Box, she burst into tears. It was obvious to both men that she was terrified, and that their priority was to get her out of that raging, mindless bedlam. She tried to speak, but Box put a finger to his lips, while Knollys, circling her with his massive arms, all but dragged her back through the throng to the safety of the pillar. They slipped through the door to the rear passage, and immediately the hideous noise receded.

'Jack,' said Box, scarcely looking at his weeping lady friend, 'will you get her out of here? Take her in a cab to Miss Drake's rooms in Westminster. I must go back in there. Inspector Paulet's let this business go on too long.'

It was then that Box spared Louise a glance. He put a hesitant hand on her arm.

'You'll be all right, won't you? Jack will take care of you.'

Louise Whittaker managed a smile through her tears.

'Yes, Mr Box,' she replied, 'I'll be all right.'

Jack Knollys hurried her away, a brawny arm round her shoulders. Box returned to the fray. As he re-entered the stricken banking hall the tall front doors suddenly crashed open, and a dozen constables, truncheons drawn, poured into the bank. They were led by a very smart, middle-aged inspector with bristling, indignant moustaches, who glanced briefly at Box, and then put a whistle to his lips. The piercing blast had the effect of immediately silencing the crowd, and Box wondered why he hadn't thought of such a simple and obvious expedient.

As the police took up their positions along the walls, Box saw the embryo mob quite suddenly revert to a collection of individuals, fearful for their immediate future, and privately appalled at what they had been doing. Inspector Paulet disappeared from sight for a while, and then re-emerged on the balcony where the unfortunate Lord Jocelyn had tried and failed to address his frantic depositors.

'Gentlemen,' said Paulet, in a firm, calm voice, 'Peto's Bank is closed for business today. I suggest that you all go home now, and wait for an official announcement from the chairman and directors. No charges of any kind will be made against you, and you are free to go about your business. Please disperse now.'

The raging mob had turned into a docile and bewildered flock of sheep. In less than five minutes the banking hall was empty. One of the constables closed and barred the heavy doors.

'Mr Paulet,' said Box, raising his hat, 'is it in order for me to congratulate you?'

Inspector Paulet smiled wryly, and glanced round the deserted room. Pass books, trodden hats, sticks and umbrellas littered the inlaid marble floor.

'Congratulate me if you must, Mr Box,' he said. 'I've no objection! I left them in here to stew in their own juice while I cleared the outside. They were trapped in here, you see, by the mob pressing against the doors. Had they panicked in here when they thought they couldn't get out, there would have been deaths. Asphyxiation, you know. And what were you doing here, anyway? Surely you didn't bank with Peto's?'

'No, Mr Paulet, the Post Office Savings Bank's good enough for me. I came here to speak to Mr Portman, the Chief Counter Clerk – where are they, by the way? The clerks, I mean. The counter's deserted.'

'They've been sent home. Superintendent Rice is out at the back While the poor clients were making themselves scarce, he told all the bank staff to go. We'll secure the premises until we hear from the directors.'

'I wonder what became of Lord Jocelyn Peto? He appeared on the balcony for a few moments, and tried to speak, but he was howled down. He disappeared, then.'

'He came out through the back entrance, Mr Box, together with two of his directors. He looked devastated. Ruined. I don't think he heard half of what was said to him. He's been taken back to Croydon. Well, I can't stand round gossiping. I must make all safe here, and then go about my business. Good day, Mr Box.'

'It was terrible, Vanessa. Men I had seen in the bank before – gentlemen – were howling like beasts in a zoo. Then Arnold appeared, and you, dear Mr Knollys, and dragged me out of the nightmare— Oh, dear!'

Louise Whittaker broke down in tears, and hid her face in her hands. She lay on the sofa in the little living-room of her friend Vanessa Drake in her lodgings near Dean's Yard, Westminster. It was a tall, gaunt building, once the convent of an Anglican sisterhood, that had been converted into sets of rooms for single women. Jack Knollys thought: she's very beautiful, and very clever, and I don't wonder that the guvnor fell for her. But she can't stand up to physical stress. Not like Cornflower. . . .

He looked at Vanessa Drake, who was talking quietly to her

friend. Vanessa's blonde hair was pulled back in businesslike
fashion behind her ears. Her intensely blue eyes shone with the
eagerness of youth – she was still only twenty – but also with an
excitement born of her reckless physical courage. He had loved
her from their first encounter. What Cornflower had seen in *him*
was still beyond his comprehension!

'Lie there quietly, Louise,' Vanessa was saying. 'I'll make us both
a cup of tea, and yours shall have a dollop of medicinal brandy in it!'

Vanessa and Knollys left the room, and walked down the
corridor that led to the small communal kitchen. Jack Knollys
paused at a window overlooking one of the ornate parapets of the
neighbouring Westminster Abbey.

'Vanessa,' he said, 'twice in as many weeks I've disappointed you
by cancelling visits to the theatre. I'm worried in case you think
that I'm deliberately neglecting you – putting my duty to the police
before my duty to you, like poor Arthur Fenlake.'

Vanessa Drake smiled up into her fiancé's eyes.

It's not the same thing at all, Jack,' she said. 'With Arthur, I was
an outsider. He was forced to stay silent about his Foreign Office
work, and so there was a more or less permanent gulf between us.
But it's different with you, and with Mr Box. We've all worked
together for the secret services, and we've all had the most incred-
ible adventures together. So when you send word that you can't
come out with me to the Alhambra, or wherever it is, I know
there's a good reason. Just as you'd understand if Colonel Kershaw
were to come here one morning and tell me to take a train to
Scotland, or a boat to Norway. You're not to worry about it, do
you hear, you great silly boy! Now, leave me alone to make some
tea for poor Louise.'

On his way back to King James's Rents Jack Knollys thought of
Mrs Pennymint's sudden intuition that he was worried about
Vanessa, and her assurance that he was worrying needlessly. She'd
been right. Whatever the truths or otherwise of spiritualism, that
lady had been able to read minds.

The City began to panic that very evening, 2 August, 1893. Two famous discount houses, both dependent on Peto's Bank, suspended business, and by eight o'clock it was learnt that Samuel French, the merchant banker, had ceased trading. It was predicted that there would be further failures, and that the frail structure of financial credit was in imminent danger of collapse.

The late editions of the newspapers contained a statement from the Bank of England, declaring that Peto's Bank was still solvent, and that if depositors would only stay their hand, the stricken house would soon recover. The statement was of no avail. The evening crowds in the Strand stopped to look at the black and white posters pasted over the door and windows of Peto's Bank, looking like newspaper placards. CLOSED. CLOSED. CLOSED. There was a finality about the notices that convinced more than any declaration to the contrary from the Bank of England.

In Superintendent Mackharness's mildewed office on the first floor of 4 King James's Rents, Box listened to his superior officer, who sat behind his big desk. The special warrant to search Sir Hamo Strange's vaults at Carmelite Pavement lay on his blotter. It was a close, dull evening, with a thin rain falling.

'I want you to tread very carefully over this matter, Box,' said Mackharness. 'I may say that I had great difficulty in securing this warrant, which, as you see, has been signed by the Deputy Commissioner. You have told me your suspicions about Strange, and I am inclined to believe you. But I want you to exercise discretion. Make it appear that you are pursuing the so-called robbers, and insist on being allowed to open those chests. I think that's all. Go down to Carmelite Pavement first thing tomorrow.'

Inspector Box seemed disinclined to dismiss himself. There was something he wanted to know, and the superintendent could supply the answer.

'Sir,' asked Box, 'what are we to think about this failure of

Peto's Bank? Why was there that sudden run? Lord Jocelyn Peto and his affairs have been bound up with this bullion business from the start—'

'Yes, yes, Box, that's very true, and I can understand your bewilderment at one of these princes of commerce suddenly failing.' Mackharness folded his large hands together on his desk, and composed himself to deliver an explanation.

'You see, Box, credit survives only on trust. A bank takes your money on deposit, gives you a spot of interest, and expects you to trust them to return your money on demand. Now, no bank, no matter how eminent, can survive the sudden decision of all its depositors at once to ask for their money back. There simply isn't enough gold in the vault to stock the tills if that were to happen. Do you follow me? Well, Peto's credit has been assailed in certain quarters recently. Lord Maurice Vale Rose told me that rumours of Peto's insolvency have been circulating in the City for a couple of weeks now.'

'And were those rumours true, sir?'

'As a matter of fact, Box, they weren't. That's the tragedy of it. Lord Jocelyn, presumably for reasons of personal pride, agreed to empty his vaults in order to pay his share of the Swedish Loan. He knew that, on application to other private banks in the City, they would transfer part of their own gold to him until such times as the Swedish Loan was repaid. Lord Maurice Vale Rose assures me that it is standard practice.'

'But in this case, news of the empty vault coincided with these rumours of insolvency. . . . I begin to understand, sir. And once the depositors demand their money back all at once, the bank must fail.'

'Exactly. It's a precarious thing, this business of credit – taking a man's word on trust that he can repay on demand the money you've lent him. So there it is. Peto's were never "bankrupt", as people put it. But now they've closed. Sad, but there it is. So get down there to Carmelite Pavement tomorrow, will you? Take

Sergeant Knollys and Sergeant Kenwright with you. And be careful.'

Box opened chest after chest, throwing back the heavy mahogany lids, and in every instance, the harsh electric lights in the ceiling of the Carmelite Pavement bullion vaults revealed not shining ingots of gold, but sullen, lifeless slugs of lead.

Mr Garner, the chief warden, had received the three police officers with an almost studied calm, in marked contrast to his frantic demeanour on the day of the bullion robbery. He had merely glanced at their search warrant, and then surrendered to them a massive ring of keys.

'You will not want me beside you, Officers,' he had said, 'while you conduct your search. You'll see from the tags attached to those keys that each of them will open the bullion chests in a particular vault, and in a specified row. It is a simple and efficient system for the safe storage of over twelve million pounds' worth of gold.'

He had conducted them to one of the three wide hydraulic lifts, where a pull on a lever had opened the gates with a hiss of released air that had sounded like a sigh of pain. When they reached the brilliantly lit main vault, they saw that the bullion chests were arrayed in long lines on heavy wooden pallets, and that the lines seemed to stretch to infinity in the tunnel-like whitewashed chamber.

'There are two further vaults beyond this one,' Garner had told them. 'They are interconnected by short tunnels, and each of them has a lift to the ground floor. When you've finished your work, you may take any one of those lifts back to the surface.'

And now, after nearly an hour, they had opened over a hundred specimen chests, and found each one filled neatly with slugs of lead. The tread of their boots had echoed from the barrel-vaulted ceilings.

'We could stay down here all day,' Box whispered, 'and I think we'd find that the contents of all these chests is lead. It confirms my own suspicion that the great Sir Hamo Strange is a fraud and an impostor.'

'Do you think that man Garner knows about it, sir?' asked Knollys.

'He might do, but I doubt it. All he has to do is move these chests around when he's told to do so. Don't forget that Strange seems to have his own gang – the people who carried out the so-called "robbery", and left their convenient clues for us to find in Corunna Lands.'

'So what do we do now, sir?' asked Sergeant Kenwright.

'This man Strange, Sergeant, had defrauded the Government and the Prudential Assurance Company of one million pounds sterling, his "compensation" for a robbery that never took place. Others must have been involved, in which case it's conspiracy to defraud. Our next step is to apply for a warrant. I think the application will have to be made by Sir Robert Bradford. Only the Commissioner could persuade a magistrate to sign a warrant for the arrest of Sir Hamo Strange.'

Box suddenly shivered. Although it was high summer, it was cold in the vaults, and rather eerie. The place was used to silence, and that silence effortlessly swallowed up their voices. The electric light, a novelty to them all, shone unblinkingly and with an intangible air of menace.

With a clanking and hissing that made all three men start in alarm, the heavy doors of the lift seemed to close of their own accord. It was then that Box realized that there were no staircases into or out of the vault. They stood for a moment in apprehension, and had begun to hurry towards the lift when all the electric lights went out, leaving them in total darkness.

None of them spoke a word, but they could hear each other's breath coming in frightened gasps. Had someone decreed that the Carmelite Pavement bullion vaults was to be their tomb?

A moment later the lights flickered on again, flooding the vaults with light. Then the doors of the lift rumbled open, as though inviting them to leave. It was an invitation that they hurriedly accepted.

'I'm so sorry, gentlemen,' said Mr Garner, 'that you were left in the dark. One of the wardens conducted the daily test of the lift mechanism and the switching for the electric lights without realizing that there was anybody down there. I quite forgot to alert him to that fact. Did you find what you were looking for? Really, this bullion robbery seems to be an impenetrable mystery.'

'Thank you, Mr Garner,' said Box, smiling. 'We certainly did find what we were looking for, but of course I'm not at liberty to tell you what it was.'

'Quite so. Well, I'll bid you good day, Mr Box.'

The three officers climbed the steep steps from the yard, walked through the open brick lodge, and passed under the arched iron gate into Tudor Street. Box glanced back, and saw Mr Garner climbing up an outside staircase to a glazed office overlooking the yard.

'So they have taken themselves off?' asked Sir Hamo Strange.

'Yes, sir,' Mr Garner replied. 'They seemed quite satisfied.'

Sir Hamo permitted himself a wintry smile, which was followed by a hearty laugh.

'I'm sure they were, Garner! Well, my little subterfuge seemed to have frightened them out of the vaults a little before their time. Just as well, I suppose. Had they opened every single chest, I should have been mightily embarrassed.'

'They seemed to think that I knew nothing about your customary use of lead when the need arose, sir, and, of course, said nothing.'

'Quite right, Garner. But you knew nothing of the impending charade of the bullion robbery, did you? I thought you were going to die of fright when I came down here that Friday! I should have warned you what was going to happen, but thought you'd be more convincing when the police arrived if you thought that a genuine robbery had occurred.'

He looked at the array of huge ebony and brass electric light switches on the wall, and at the valves and levers operating the lifts and their heavy doors. Yes, it had been amusing to plunge the celebrated Inspector Box and his clodhopping giants of companions into pitch darkness.

'Garner,' he said, drawing on his gloves, 'I've urgent business to transact in Whitehall, as you'll readily appreciate. You've been with me many years, now, and I've found you the soul of loyalty and discretion – both sovereign assets in my line of business. It's time, I think, that you received a considerable rise in salary.'

'Oh, sir—'

'There, there, Garner, say no more. I must go straight away to Whitehall.'

As Box, Knollys and Sergeant Kenwright entered the vestibule of 4 King James's Rents, they were accosted by an elderly police sergeant in uniform, who stepped out of the narrow front office near the door. Like Kenwright he was a heavily bearded man, but he was older, walked with a limp, and regarded Box over a pair of wire spectacles perched on the end of his nose.

'There's a gentleman to see you, Mr Box. I've got him there, in the office. He said he'd wait.'

'Best show him in, Pat,' said Box. 'We're just back from Carmelite Pavement, and there's a lot for us to do in consequence, but I expect we can spare a few minutes.'

Box went into his office, and sat down in his favourite chair near the fireplace. Knollys was already writing up an account of their visit to Sir Hamo Strange's vaults. Sergeant Kenwright had disappeared through the tunnel to the drill hall.

'Mr Arthur Portman, sir,' said the duty sergeant.

'What? Good Heavens! Mr Portman – what are *you* doing here? That'll be all, thank you, Sergeant Driscoll.'

195

Mr Portman looked pale and shaken. He glanced uneasily around the rather bare and utilitarian room, and Box saw him make a little wry face when he glanced up at the soot-stained ceiling. Whatever his troubles, he had evidently not lost his aesthetic sense.

'Inspector Box, may I sit down? Thank you. I remember you from your visit to the Temple of Light the other week. You came with poor young Mr Lane. Dear me, what times we live in! What is one to say? And then yesterday, Mr Box, you were present at the collapse of our bank—'

'A disaster for you, Mr Portman, I expect.'

Sergeant Knollys had been watching the Chief Counter Clerk of Peto's Bank as though he were a specimen mounted on a slide and placed under a microscope. His sudden question seemed to hold a hint of mockery that Box was quick to detect.

'A disaster? Yes, indeed. I am now quite without employment, and through no fault of my own. Poor Lord Jocelyn! One sympathizes, of course, but a married man like myself, with a handsome town property, has to look to his own interests.'

'And why exactly have you come to see *me*, Mr Portman? Do you want me to write you a reference?'

'Certainly not. What an extraordinary idea. Evidently you are not able to feel any sympathy for my plight. Well, I'm not here to talk about the fall of Peto's Bank; I'm here to tell you that I went down on the train to Brookwood last night, and talked to Mrs Pennymint about the, er – raid – that you conducted at the Temple early yesterday.'

'And what do you gather from your talk with Mrs Pennymint?'

'Like her, Inspector, I was shocked and horrified. She was told that quantities of apparatus and other deceitful paraphernalia were removed in a van. In particular, she told me about that whited sepulchre, Almena Sylvestris. Any breath of scandal, as you know, is fatal to the cause of spiritualism. She betrayed a very noble cause with her wicked tricks and deceptions.'

'You knew nothing about that, of course?' asked Box. 'Nothing about the secret panels in her house, the devices beneath the floor to produce spurious ghosts—'

'Nothing! I was a trustee of the Temple of Light, and a credulous dupe of that wicked woman. So was poor, feckless Mrs Pennymint. I knew nothing whatever about all this deceit. You must pursue that woman Sylvestris. Do not rest until you have apprehended her. I place all my records at your disposal.'

'That's very good of you, Mr Portman.'

'Not at all, Inspector. I am armed in innocence, and place myself entirely at your disposal. Here is my card. I will bid you good day.'

'So there it is, Sergeant,' said Box, when Portman had left the office. 'He's going to wriggle out of it. He's got in with his story first, and there's no concrete evidence that he was in any way involved in all that chicanery. He's wriggled out of it.'

'He's a liar, sir, and a rogue. He'll cross the wrong fellow's path one of these days, and find himself floating in the river with a knife in his back.'

'Maybe so, Jack. But for the moment, he's "armed in innocence", as he kindly informed us. We've lost him, I think. But never mind. We've bigger fish than him to fry.'

15

Profit and Loss

'Oh, Mr Box! Have you heard the news?'

Mrs Peach, Box's landlady, deposited a freshly fried kipper on his little round table in the sitting-room of his lodgings in Cardinal Court. As Box had not yet left the house for work, Mrs Peach must have known that he had not heard the news. But then, he mused, there was a delicious thrill in making people wait until you chose to tell them.

'What news, Mrs Peach?' he asked, knife and fork poised to tackle his breakfast.

'Lord Jocelyn Peto! He's committed suicide, Mr Box. Shot himself in the conservatory of his house in Croydon.'

'Who told you that, Mrs Peach? I saw the poor man only yesterday—'

'The milkman told me. He's up so early that he can buy the three o'clock edition of the *Daily Chronicle* from old Anderson's shop in Shoe Lane. I expect Lord Jocelyn couldn't face the shame of being ruined, poor man.'

Box made as though to rise from the table, but his landlady was not going to allow him to waste a perfectly good kipper, to say nothing of freshly made toast and tea.

'Now, don't go rushing out like that, Mr Box,' she said. 'You can't bring poor Lord Jocelyn back to life. Sit down and eat your breakfast. You've got to keep your strength up.'

When Mrs Peach had left the room, Box did as she'd commanded, and ate his breakfast which was always something tasty and nourishing, followed by quantities of tea – proper Londoners' tea that you could stand your spoon up in – and buttered toast. His landlady, who took only gentlemen boarders, was a firm believer in feeding the inner man.

So Lord Jocelyn Peto, a ruined man, with his credit as a banker shattered, had taken the gentleman's way out. . . . Box had thought him to be a flippant, trivial sort of man when he'd first met him, but in the end he'd succumbed to the banker's boyish directness and charm. Yesterday, he had looked both desperate and frantic. It was a sad and terrible end to a once honourable career.

Box buttered a piece of toast. Louise had emerged physically unscathed from her ordeal. Jack Knollys had accompanied her out to Finchley, where he had abandoned her to the tender ministrations of little Ethel, the maid. Had she been ruined by Peto's fall? How was he going to find out?

The little clock standing on his mantelpiece among a welter of ornaments and photographs told him that it was already half past seven. Time to walk into work. As he left the table, and picked up his overcoat, there came a businesslike rap on the door. A telegraph boy had called with a message.

'Mr Arnold Box?' asked the smart lad in uniform and pill box hat who stood on the landing. 'A message from Inspector Price, of Croydon. No answer expected— Oh, thanks very much, sir.'

Box had given the boy a threepenny bit. He tore open the flimsy telegraph form, and read Inspector Price's message.

Box, King James's Rents, SW. Come at once to Duppas Park House Croydon. Advice urgently needed – Price.

Within the minute, Arnold Box had hurried out of secluded

199

Cardinal Court and into the noise and bustle of Fleet Street, where he hailed a cab to London Bridge Station.

Box was admitted to Duppas Park House by the butler, Tanner. No longer calm and aloof, he looked shocked to the core. And well he might, thought Box. This was the second violent death to occur at Lord Jocelyn's elegant house. Box put a finger to his lips to prevent the butler from bursting into speech. A sound of uninhibited sobbing had come to his ears from somewhere along the rear passage.

'Who is that sobbing, Mr Tanner? Is it Lady Marion Peto?'

'No, sir,' Tanner whispered. 'It's Alice Parkes, the maid. She's taken it very badly. Shall I show you through to the conservatory, sir?' The man's voice began to tremble, and he added, 'Poor Sir Jocelyn! There was no one to come to his assistance in his hour of need.'

Box found Inspector Price standing among the potted palms, cool ferns and exotic plants of Lord Jocelyn's extensive conservatory at the rear of the mansion. Somewhere in the room a fountain was splashing gently into a basin.

Price greeted Box in his lilting Welsh voice, and without further preliminaries he pointed to a spot somewhere behind a bank of tall ferns growing in wooden tubs.

'He's still there,' he said, 'where the housemaid Alice Parkes found him, at a few minutes after midnight last night. She's very incoherent, but it seems that she had been out late, Thursday being her day off. She'd met some young man—'

'Bert,' said Box. 'He and Alice are getting married next year. No wonder the girl's upset. First, she witnesses the murder of the Reverend Mr Vickers, and now she discovers her master's dead body. I'd best take a look.' Box stepped beyond the ferns.

Lord Jocelyn Peto lay on his back on the terracotta tiled floor. There was a congealed wound in his right temple, and a pool of dried blood on the floor. A pistol lay a couple of feet away from his right hand. Yet another .38 Colt. Every villain seemed to have one, these days.

A wickerwork table stood beside the body, and a basket chair of the same material lay on its side. It was clear that Peto had been sitting in the chair when the shot was fired, and that he had then slithered out of it to the floor.

'Why did you send for me, Mr Price?' asked Box.

'Because his eyes are closed. I've not seen a suicide of this kind where the eyes have been closed. And somehow – well, I'd have thought Lord Jocelyn would have weathered this particular storm. He'd many friends in the City, and was much liked here in Croydon. Quite frankly, I never imagined that he would commit suicide.'

Box knelt down over the body, which was dressed in day clothes – the very clothes, Box realized, that the frantic man had worn when he had last seen him, standing despairingly on the balcony of his ruined bank. He tentatively breathed in, near to the dead man's partly open mouth. Price saw him frown. Then he inhaled a second time, more deeply and prolonged. He got to his feet and examined the wickerwork table. It held a silver tray with a coffee pot, a half-empty coffee cup, and a decanter of brandy. Box raised the glass to his nose, then put it down quietly on the table.

'It was murder, Mr Price,' he said. 'First, he was rendered senseless by chloral, introduced into the brandy decanter, and perhaps into the coffee, too. He fell into a sleep here, in the chair, and then somebody came in and shot him dead. It's very warm in here, and it's going to be necessary to remove the body very soon.'

'Murder? I thought so. I'll make arrangements for the remains to be removed to our police mortuary—'

'Would you mind if I took charge of it? There's a brand new police surgeon at Horseferry Road, Dr Donald Miller, a house surgeon at Charing Cross Hospital. It was he who performed the post-mortem on poor PC Lane, and confirmed that he'd died of a broken neck, as the result of a massive blow to the throat. I know who did that, incidentally, and when I'm ready, I'll bring him in. I'd like to cultivate this young Dr Miller, and doing a post-mortem on Lord Jocelyn would be an enormous boost for him.'

'Just as you like, Mr Box. Meanwhile, we have to ask ourselves the usual questions. Who did it, and why? Well, it might have been a ruined investor, though I doubt it. Or it might have been a private affair, in which someone took advantage of Peto's ruin to suggest that he'd committed suicide.'

Inspector,' said Box, as the two men walked out of the conservatory, 'this is an inside job. Avenging investors can't enter a gentleman's house, armed with a bottle of chloral, and lace his coffee and brandy with it. I don't believe it. I'd like to talk to that hysterical maid, Alice Parkes. Last time I talked to her, I thought she was a sensible, sober kind of girl, not given to making all that fuss I heard when I came in just now.'

'Yes, I think you're right. The girl's in a very peculiar state. There's more behind her mood than distress for a good master's death. She knows more than she'll tell. That's another reason why I sent for you to come.'

'Incidentally,' said Box, 'have you done anything yet with Snobby Quayle?'

'I have. He's been up before the magistrate, where he said nothing, and refused even to reserve his defence. He'll be found guilty of assisting at a burglary, and given three months.'

'That'll suit him down to the ground, Mr Price. He'll do his time, and then slimy Milton Fisher will peel twenty five-pound notes from a greasy wad, and give them to his faithful follower. Well, let's leave him with Croydon. He's small fry, as the saying goes.'

The two police officers emerged from a passage into the light, airy hall, with its delicate white panelling and curving art nouveau staircase. A man was sitting on an upright chair near the door, a tall, distinguished man sporting a waxed beard and moustaches. He started uneasily when he saw Box, and peered at him through tinted spectacles.

'Ah!' said Box, shaking the man's hand. 'Mr Paul Lombardo, the celebrated private detective. Someone posted a note at the Rents to say that you were on the prowl in Belsize Park. This is Inspector Price of the Croydon Police. I take it that your business is urgent? We're beginning a murder investigation here.'

Paul Lombardo whistled under his breath, and glanced nervously towards the closed door of the drawing-room.

'Murder! Do you mean Peto? Look, Mr Box, will you come out into the road with me for a moment? As a matter of fact, I didn't know you were here. I came by appointment to see someone in the house, and the butler told me that Lord Jocelyn had committed suicide. But if it's murder— Come outside. There's something I must tell you. It's for your ears alone.'

'I'll see about the mortuary van, Mr Box,' said Price, taking the hint. He turned back into the house, and closed the front door behind him. Box and Lombardo slipped out through the front garden and into the road.

'Listen, Mr Box,' said Lombardo, 'I came out here today to visit Lady Marion Peto by appointment. Lady Marion's been my client for the last three months. She hired me to find out whether or not her husband was being unfaithful to her.'

'And was he?'

'Yes. You'll understand that I wouldn't usually break a client's confidence, but if Lord Jocelyn's been murdered, than it's my duty to tell you what I know. You can draw whatever conclusions you like from what I'm going to tell you. Lord Jocelyn Peto was conducting what he imagined to be a clandestine affair with Madam Almena Sylvestris, the famous medium. He was a frequent and regular visitor to her at her house in Melbourne Avenue, Belsize Park. I expect you knew about that?'

'I didn't, Mr Lombardo. It's news to me, and very interesting news, too, though, as I said before, I knew you were watching her.'

'It was a full-blooded liaison, Mr Box,' Lombardo continued, 'and

I reported all the details to my client only last Saturday. She was obviously shocked, but you know what these society ladies are like. She made a valiant effort to show no emotion, but I thought to myself that Lord Jocelyn would be in for a bad time once his wife got her second wind, and decided to do something about his infidelities.'

'Did you find out anything else? You were always good at ferreting things out, Mr Lombardo.'

'I found out that the house in Belsize Park – 8 Melbourne Avenue – was wholly owned by Lord Jocelyn. He also bought his lady friend a new carriage, recently. He paid three hundred and fifty pounds for it.'

'You did right to tell me all this, Mr Lombardo. It certainly gives me food for thought. What will you do now?'

'I'll hover discreetly in the grounds, Mr Box. The butler told me that Lady Marion was indisposed, which is not surprising, but she may rally sufficiently to want to see me later. I wish you well in your search for Lord Jocelyn's killer.'

As the private detective walked towards the garden of Duppas Park House, he half turned to Box, and added, 'I don't think you'll have to look far.'

Alice Parkes sat on a chair in the drawing-room, and looked at Box fearfully. She was as pretty and smart as when he had last seen her, but the fear that had shone in her blue eyes then had been replaced by something more akin to terror. Once again, this young housemaid had been a witness to something frightful, and whatever it was, thought Box, it was something infinitely worse than the attack on the Reverend Mr Vickers.

'It was your day off, yesterday, Alice, and so you went to see Bert, didn't you?'

The girl nodded, and moistened her lips. She looked as white as her own starched apron.

'You returned to the house at about midnight. That's what you told Inspector Price. Now tell me, Alice, what happened after you came in. I can imagine why you're upset, but I don't see why you should be so frightened. What happened?'

'Sir, Bert saw me as far as Jubilee Road, and then I came through the wicket gate into the front gardens. I had my key, and entered the house through the front area door as usual. I went upstairs to the ground floor, lit one of the candles on the lamp table in the hall, and prepared to go upstairs to bed. At that time of night, sir, it's all right for servants to use the main staircase.' Again, the terrified girl moistened her lips. 'Well, as I began to climb the stairs I suddenly heard a shot. It was so loud, it seemed to echo through the whole house. It came from the other side of the passage—'

'What passage? Go on, Alice, you're doing very well.'

'I mean the long passage that runs right across the ground floor beyond the hall, the passage that leads to the library and the conservatory. I ran along the passage, and could see a light at the end. It was one of the gaslights in the conservatory. By then, I could hear the sound of voices as other people in the house came down to find out what had happened. I ran into the conservatory, and I saw—'

Alice suddenly began to scream. She writhed on her chair, and beat her head with her clenched fists. Box pulled her arms down to her lap, and shook her roughly until the screams changed to choking sobs. What ailed the girl? What had she seen?

'Now stop that, Alice, do you hear? You've done nothing wrong. Think of Bert, and the baby. That's better. You ran into the conservatory, Alice. What did you see? Just tell me briefly. There's no need to take on so.'

'Sir, I saw my master lying on the floor among the ferns. He'd been shot. . . . Oh, sir, there's a curse on this house. First my master was robbed, then poor Mr Vickers was murdered. And now, poor Lord Jocelyn! If my mother had kown that it would be like this, she'd never have let me work here.'

'Was there anyone else in the conservatory? Did you see anyone else?'

'No, no! It was empty. There was just Lord Jocelyn, lying there dead. There was nobody!'

'Then why are you so terrified? Lord Jocelyn was murdered. It's wasn't suicide. Who did you see, Alice Parkes? You saw somebody. If it was somebody you knew, and you won't tell me, you'll make yourself an accessory after the fact of murder, and you'll stand trial for your life. Think of Bert. Think of the baby.'

Alice began to cry, and her tears seemed to be those of hopeless despair.

'There was nobody. Nobody! Leave me alone. I've done nothing wrong.'

'Yes, leave her alone!'

The ringing, aristocratic tones of Lady Marion Peto made Box look up in surprise. Already dressed in deepest black, the widowed lady stood, upright and haughty, near the drawing-room door. Alice got hastily to her feet and curtsied.

'This poor, faithful girl, Inspector, did indeed see someone in the conservatory last night. She saw *me*! Alice, go to the servants' hall. I'll talk to this policeman alone. You've nothing to fear, girl. Go!'

Lady Marion stood on the threshold until Alice had gone, and then slowly closed the door. In her hour of distress she seemed to have regained some of the beauty for which she had been renowned in her youth. The almost wilful dowdiness of her middle years had disappeared. Box bowed gravely, and Lady Marion favoured him with a formal inclination of the head.

'Yes, Mr Box,' she said, in a high, clear voice, 'she saw *me*. Over the years I had come to accommodate myself to Lord Jocelyn's vile, low infidelities, his chorus girls and pretty shop assistants – yes, even this last dalliance, which was with a fraudulent medium! I swallowed my pride for the sake of our social position. But when he added total financial ruin to his catalogue of irresponsibilities, I sent him packing post haste out of this world. I rendered him senseless, and then I shot him. The gun was his own. There is, perhaps, a certain irony in that.'

Box had guessed as much from the heavy hints that Lombardo had dropped. Those hints had enabled him to interpret Alice Parkes's terror as something more than shock at finding her master dead. The girl had surprised her mistress, perhaps with the pistol still in her hand, but custom and habit had constrained her to hold her tongue.

Half an hour later, as Box led Lady Marion Peto away from the house through a crowd of weeping servants, he saw Inspector Price arriving at the end of Jubilee Road with the police hearse that would convey her murdered husband's body to the railway, and so to Horseferry Road mortuary.

From *The Morning Post*, Saturday, 5 August 1893

It is with the greatest satisfaction that we hear of the generous decision of Sir Hamo Strange to buy and operate Peto's Bank in the Strand. Readers will recall the distressing events of the week gone, in which hundreds of depositors feared that they had been ruined by the fall of the old-established banking house. We venture to reproduce the statement made to your Correspondent by Sir Hamo Strange:

Peto's Bank was never truly insolvent, and its demise was a great misfortune. I intend to open the bank for business this coming Monday, 7 August, and can assure all depositors that their funds will be made good immediately. Lord Jocelyn Peto, so tragically dead under circumstances that are not yet sufficiently clear, was a dear friend of long standing, and it is my wish that Peto's Bank should continue trading under his distinguished name.

In these self-seeking times, we venture to say that England is proud to have in its midst a man of the calibre of Sir Hamo Strange who, while ranging across the world in his pursuit of business, can yet turn a compassionate eye to the tragic events unfolded this week here in London, and apply his great charity to their alleviation. He is already a Knight Bachelor, and, we hear, a member of an Imperial Russian Order. Perhaps those advising the Queen will, in the near future, consider the conferring of a well-deserved barony upon Sir Hamo Strange.

The directors of Peto's Bank followed Sir Hamo Strange respectfully along the subterranean passage that gave access to their tiled bank vault. It was cold and cheerless under the pavement, and the bullion racks were still empty and forlorn. Later that day, they would be full again, as staunch allies of Sir Hamo in the banking world shored up Peto's credit by making loans of gold in considerable quantity to the stricken bank.

'And this, sir,' said Mr Robert Thorne, the Managing Director, a distinguished, grey-haired man in his sixties, 'is the late Lord Jocelyn's private deposit box.'

Sir Hamo Strange looked with kindly concern at the group of men whom, that very morning, he had newly confirmed as salaried directors. They returned his smile with deferential lowering of the eyes. Things, thought Strange, were going well.

'My dear Thorne,' he said, 'I have been greatly moved by your many years of loyalty to my late dear friend Jocelyn Peto, and I feel that a review of your remuneration should be my immediate concern. Further, I should like to make the link between Peto's and the Strange Foundation closer by appointing you as a voting member of the Board of Strange's.'

He held up a hand to stem the man's profuse flow of thanks.

'And this, you say, is the late Lord Jocelyn's private deposit box? Mine, now, I think?'

He smiled, and there was just a hint about the set of his right hand to suggest that he was holding it out as though expecting to receive something.

'Of course, sir,' Mr Robert Thorne replied. He placed a key in

Sir Hamo Strange's hand.

Strange listened to the retreating footsteps of the directors as they made their way along the dreary tiled tunnel to the stairs. It was nice to have got Peto's damned bank into his hands. It was even nicer to have got that million pounds insurance for the great and insoluble bullion robbery – the robbery that had never taken place. Then, of course, there'd be another million pounds coming in when the Swedish Loan was repaid. He'd have to do something about that fellow Box, though. A worthy young man, no doubt, but a considerable nuisance. Yes, he'd have to do something about Box.

Sir Hamo Strange inserted the key into Lord Jocelyn's deposit box, and pulled back the lid. There it was, still wrapped in its protective green baize, the Complutensian Polyglot Bible, the secret edition of 1519, and here, in this first of the six volumes – yes! There it was, in its cardboard pocket, the secret history of Charles the Fifth of Castile. It was his! Destiny had always designed it to be his.

The directors, huddled near the cobwebbed stairs that would take them up to the marbled banking hall in the Strand, froze as they heard the peals of laughter echoing through the vaults, laughter that seemed almost insane in its hooting triumph, and its air of abandoned gloating. The laughter died away at last, and the figure of their benefactor appeared, a bulky parcel in his arms, ready to join them in the banking adventure that lay so enticingly ahead of them all.

16

Winner Takes All

Arnold Box walked rapidly along the Strand. Monday, 7 August had dawned grey and rather chilly, and by seven o'clock steady summer rain was falling. He had chosen a devious route from Fleet Street to Great Scotland Yard in order to pass the premises of Peto's Bank. Would Sir Hamo Strange's promise to open it for business hold good? Yes. The 'Closed' placards had been taken down, the big double doors stood invitingly open, and the windows blazed with light. He turned off the rain-lashed Strand into Adelaide Street.

The murder of Lord Jocelyn Peto by his wife had come as a shock. Lady Marion had behaved impeccably, and had seemed calm and fully collected when he had handed her over into the custody of Inspector Price. Nevertheless, a strange, wild light had suddenly been kindled in her eyes, a light that Box had seen before in others. He thought it more than likely that Lady Marion Peto would be found unfit to plead.

Box turned out of Northumberland Street and into Great Scotland Yard. The granite pavements gleamed in the morning rain. Crossing the cobbles into King James's Rents, he hurried up the steps into Number 4. The floorboards in the entrance hall were already soaked by the passage of many wet boots, and the few offi-

210

cers assembled there waiting for orders smelt like wet sheep.

Box glimpsed the welcome fire burning in the grate of his office beyond the swing doors, but that Monday his priority was to call upon Superintendent Mackharness, and secure the warrant for Sir Hamo Strange's arrest on charges of embezzlement, fraudulent conversion, and conspiracy to defraud.

Superintendent Mackharness sat behind his big desk, a number of documents spread out in front of him. His face was stern, and there was a dangerous glint in his eye.

'Ah, Box! Sit down there, will you, and listen very carefully to what I am going to say— No, don't ask any questions, or make any requests. Just listen to me. I know how difficult you can be, how determined to thwart me whenever the fancy takes you.'

Mackharness fiddled restlessly with a paperknife, and Box saw the wariness which was always reserved for him alone flicker in his superior officer's eyes. Then he threw the knife down angrily on the table.

'Box,' said Mackharness, 'with effect from this moment, you are to drop all proceedings of any kind against Sir Hamo Strange. You will not seek to harass or question him about the events of these recent weeks. Your task now is to apprehend Francis Xavier Mahoney for the murders of the Reverend Mr Vickers and Police Constable Lane. I think that is all. Good morning.'

'But sir, those vaults at Carmelite Pavement were full of lead! There was no gold there. The man's a criminal fraud—'

Mackharness's face flushed red with anger. He banged his big right fist on the desk.

'Stop it, will you? I've told you that Sir Hamo Strange is not to be inconvenienced. If you think that you saw lead instead of gold, then you must persuade yourself that you were mistaken. I knew that you would forget yourself, and call my orders in question! The robbery at Carmelite Pavement will remain unsolved. There will be no warrant for Sir Hamo's arrest, either now, or subsequently. Do you hear? Do you understand me? That is all, Box. Good morning.'

Arnold Box flung out of his master's office, leaving the door ajar. It was clear what had happened. Mackharness had received orders from the top, and was content to thwart the demands of justice for the convenience of the established order. What was the point of continuing in the police?

Somebody asked him a question as he reached the hall floor, but he waved the man away, and hurried along the musty passage leading to the ablutions and the exercise yard. He would choke with rage and despair if he stayed any longer indoors, closeted with the stink of corruption.

The rain poured down relentlessly. Box crossed the secluded yard, and stood under the colonnade, looking back at the soot-blackened buildings of Number 4. He must control his rage! But one thing was certain: the time had come for him to quit the Metropolitan Police. It would be more wholesome to work with men like Paul Lombardo, men who could exercise their skills and talents free from political pressure. Yes; perhaps that was the way forward.

There was a noise behind him, and Superintendent Mackharness appeared from a door at the back of the colonnade. His face was no longer red with anger, but his wrath had not entirely abated. He seized Box by the arm, and shook him as though he were a recalcitrant little child.

'Do you think I like it?' he hissed. 'To have to stand there, saying nothing while I'm told that the Government has ordered me to drop a case? How do you think a man of my age and background feels? I have to swallow my rage and obey, because I'm there to obey orders as well as to give them to others. And the same applies to you. So get back in there, Box, and get on with your work.'

'I'm sorry, sir—'

'It makes me feel that I'm simply in charge of a box of marionettes,' Mackharness continued, looking not at Box but at the vertical summer rain washing across the yard. 'I'm allowed to pull the strings for a while, but when someone more important wants to take over, he pushes me aside. The commissioner himself is angry, and is going to storm the Foreign Office this very morning. That might afford us both a grain of comfort.'

'Sir Edward himself is going to complain? That certainly helps me, sir. Sir Edward Bradford is the best commissioner we've had for years.'

'He is, Box. Nobody would disagree with you on that. So, let us both move forward. I'll get over today's humiliation, Box, and so will you. Now, get back in there, do as you're told, and go after Mahoney. Leave Sir Hamo Strange alone.'

Sir Charles Napier sat sphinx-like behind his vast ornate desk in the Foreign Office, and listened gravely to the angry voice of Sir Edward Bradford, Commissioner of Police for the Metropolis. Few men had earned so much public and private respect, but his world was not the world of politics. It would be difficult, if not impossible, to give him a soothing answer to the question of Sir Hamo Strange.

'My officers had concluded a brilliant investigation,' Sir Edward was saying, 'in the course of which they had proved beyond doubt that Strange had engineered a fake robbery, and calmly pocketed the insurance paid to him for his non-existent loss. Inspector Box discovered that the man's vast bullion vaults were filled with nothing more precious than lead. It's just possible that he was on the periphery of the murder of one of my constables. And yet you tell me that I must drop all proceedings against Strange. Why?'

'Because, Commissioner,' said Sir Charles Napier, 'it is in the national interest to do so. The consequences of interfering with Sir Hamo Strange would be of the gravest import, doing enormous damage to Britain and her standing in the world.'

'Incalculable damage,' echoed the other man in the room.

Colonel Augustus Temperley, strategic adviser to the China Desk, felt the same distaste as Napier at the prospect of fencing with Sir Edward Bradford. He looked at him now, his empty left sleeve pinned to the lapel of his frock coat, his firm features adorned by a white cavalryman's moustache. He was the very portrait of integrity. He and Napier must tell him the truth. But would he ever understand?

'You see, Commissioner,' said Temperley, 'Sir Hamo Strange has only recently co-operated with us in a special act of secret diplomacy which has triumphantly strengthened our unwritten agreements with the Russian Empire. You know all about India. You served in the Madras Cavalry, and you understand the situation on the Sino-Indian border—'

'Colonel Temperley is referring to our attempts to keep Russia's eyes away from Afghanistan,' said Napier. 'Last time they crossed the border it cost us eleven million pounds to repel them. This time, Sir Hamo Strange raised private money to render Russian interest in the area quiescent. His power and influence stretches far beyond the United Kingdom.'

'Some parts of Britain's foreign policy, Sir Edward, are carved in letters of stone,' Temperley continued. 'One such part is, that the borders of India are inviolable, and not open to negotiation. Any violation of those borders will lead to war. Sir Hamo Strange has helped us to avert any such possibility.'

'How did he do that?' asked Sir Edward Bradford. Despite himself, he was becoming absorbed by the way in which these two men thought.

'He did it, Commissioner,' said Napier, 'by raising an enormous sum of money at practically no notice to buy a railway for the Tsar of Russia, which will carry him – and his subjects – away from India and towards China. Hamo Strange does things like that. He never says "No", and his word is as good as his bond. He's vital to Britain's interests, both at home and in the Empire.'

Sir Edward remained silent for a long while, mulling over what the two professional diplomats had told him. Napier and Temperley waited.

'Very well,' said Sir Edward at length in a tired voice. 'I can see your point of view – no, I'm sorry, it's more than that, isn't it? You have a long view of Britain's vital interests denied to the layman. But you can't get away from the fact that my officer, Inspector Box, was not exaggerating when he said that Strange's vaults were filled with worthless lead. You may know all about India and China, but I'm quite sure that you didn't know *that*.'

Sir Charles Napier blushed scarlet. For once, his diplomatic mask failed to conceal his embarrassment. He glanced briefly at Bradford, and then looked away.

'Of course I knew,' he said in a low voice. 'Everybody here knows about Strange's disappearing gold. And nobody *cares*, I tell you! Perhaps he arranged a fictitious raid on his own empty vaults, and perhaps he claimed the insurance – and perhaps Her Majesty's Government quietly made good the loss! It's because he knows that we will turn a blind eye to some of his peculiar habits, that he is able to organize these instantaneous loans of unimaginable sums to the Government.'

'You *knew* his vaults were empty?'

'Yes. They frequently are. And then, as year succeeds to year, the gold comes in again, the lead disappears, and the vaults beneath Carmelite Pavement are once more as fabulously rich as the mines of Southern Africa. Meanwhile, Sir Hamo Strange continues to be of national and international value. Leave him alone. Mr Gladstone wishes it, and so does Lord Salisbury. I know Inspector Box quite well. Let him pursue the murderers who were peripheral to this business, and bring them to justice. But once again let me repeat my injunction: leave Sir Hamo Strange alone.'

'It's high time, Mahoney,' said the urbane Mr Curteis, 'that you quit these shores for foreign climes. Or, to put it in words that you'll understand, it's time for you to cross the Channel, where friends of ours will see that you come to no harm.'

Francis Xavier Mahoney looked at the man who was both his friend and tormentor, and felt as grateful as such a man could be

215

for the chance he was being given to escape the gallows. What cursed luck! Dead men told no tales, which is why he'd finished off that old clergyman and the dangerous PC Lane. He'd made a mistake, though, with Knollys. He'd crossed his path, but had lived to tell the tale. Curse him! There was unfinished business there.

Curteis had found a set of rooms on the third floor of one of a number of tumbledown tenements in Garlick Hill, and here he had installed the fugitive Mahoney.

'Let me tell you what you must do,' said Curteis. 'At the bottom of this street, and on the far side of Upper Thames Street, you'll find a place called Syria Wharf. There are a lot of tall warehouses there, and beyond them you'll find a private landing-place called Stew Lane Steps. On this coming Friday, the eleventh, make sure that you are there, on the steps, at seven o'clock in the morning. A tug boat, the *Mary Barton*, on its way out for duty at Sheerness, will pick you up and take you out to a French freighter lying off the Isle of Grain. It will convey you to Boulogne, where friends will be waiting for you.'

'Thanks, Mr Curteis. I'll be there, never fear. How are things with old Strange? Has he managed to throw the vultures off his back?'

'He has. Everybody's praising him to the skies for rescuing Peto's Bank. He and I went there on Tuesday, the day after they'd reopened for business. A crowd of customers caught sight of him, and gave a rousing cheer.' Curteis laughed. 'Sir Hamo actually blushed, and made them a little speech there and then. "This is my confidential secretary, Mr Curteis", he said, realizing that I was standing there, smiling like an idiot. So I got a rousing cheer as well!'

'So you should, so you should. And Spooky Portman? What's happened to him?'

'Mr Arthur Portman's been transferred to Sir Hamo's central business room at Medici House, on three times his former salary.

He's to be in charge of day-to-day administration. I believe he's going to drop spiritualism, and join the Church of England. Very wise of him.'

'Some people have all the luck.'

'Well, you won't do so badly. When you get to Boulogne, you'll find a bank account opened in your name, with a thousand pounds in it. Well, I must be on my way. Goodbye, Mahoney. Perhaps we'll meet again. Meanwhile, let's shake hands.'

Mahoney grasped the secretary's hand, and a moment later found himself lying in a crumpled heap across the ash-strewn hearth.

'A letter for you, sir. With an Austrian stamp.'

'Thank you, Portman,' said Sir Hamo Strange. 'Are you enjoying your work here at Medici House?'

'I am, sir. I can hardly believe my good fortune. You have been very kind.'

'Not at all. Curteis tells me that you have already improved some of the daily procedures here in the business room.'

Mr Arthur Portman placed the letter on Sir Hamo Strange's desk, and returned to his own business table, which stood like an altar on a dais surrounded by wooden rails. What wonderful luck! It was fascinating to work in this long Renaissance room, with its ancient frescoes and painted ceilings, and the battery of telegraph machines and telephones at the far end, bringing financial news from the four corners of the world!

It was time, he thought, to dismiss his inventive treacheries concerning Peto's Bank from his mind, and give his whole attention to the present. He had already persuaded the badly shaken committee of the Temple of Light to wind the business up, and sell the premises to the highest bidder. Mrs Pennymint would continue to be a good friend, but he and his wife would return to the bosom of the Established Church.

Sir Hamo Strange slit open the letter from Austria with a silver-bladed paper knife, reputed to have belonged once to Pope Pius V. He extracted a banker's draft for £5000 made payable to him, and a brief note, written in a spiky German hand.

Count Fuentes proved to have been a rogue. He sold the authentic work to Lord Jocelyn Peto, and fobbed me off with his impudent falsification. May bad luck dog his heels! I thus failed to comply with the bargain struck between you and me, and I accordingly return your £5000. The foundation of successful business is trust. I had rather lose this money than forfeit your esteem.

The note was signed by Aaron Sudermann.

Well, well, thought Sir Hamo Strange. It was refreshing to see that there was at least one honest businessman in the world! He put the letter and its enclosed draft aside, and picked up a document, sent to him by an agent in Lima, which suggested that a substantial loan would be required later in the year by the Government of Peru.

On the bright, hot Thursday morning, Francis Xavier Mahoney glanced out of the single grimy window of his third-floor hideaway, and saw the massively unmistakable figure of Detective Sergeant Knollys striding purposefully along the dingy and arid canyon of Garlick Hill. Curse him! What was he doing there?

Mahoney watched him. As he passed the towering church of St James, Garlickhythe, he glanced up at the great clock suspended over the road, and then walked rapidly down the hill towards Upper Thames Street.

He thought he'd left him for dead when he'd attacked him in the lodge at Carmelite Pavement, but there'd been no time to make sure. The other policeman – PC Lane – had been an easy job, and in a quiet moment when all the staff at the vaults had been busy below, he'd carried his body down to the launch, where it had been taken aboard by Sir Hamo Strange's mysterious gang of mariners.

Count on it, that hulking bobby had found out where he was hiding. He'd pretend to hurry past the house, and then he'd double back, and come creeping up the stairs to take him into custody. Well, Knollys' number was up. Better safe than sorry.

Mahoney dragged on the dark pea jacket and nautical cap with a glazed peak that Mr Curteis had given him for disguise. Seizing a stout walking stick fitted with a heavy ball of lead as a handle, he clattered down the three flights of stairs and out into the heat and bustle of Garlick Hill.

Jack Knollys had been out all night, engaged on a case which had ended very satisfactorily with the arrest of three coiners in their cellar headquarters out at Bethnal Green Road. He and the three constables assisting him had travelled through the dawn in the police van, sitting opposite their mournful and manacled prisoners on their way to New Street Police Station.

He had allowed himself the luxury of a cab as far as the Mansion House, and had then struck out through the sunny streets that would take him into Garlick Hill, and so down to his lodgings on the sixth floor of a tall warehouse belonging to Anton Berg, an importer of silk, at Syria Wharf. From the many windows of his sixth-floor eyrie he could enjoy panoramic views of London, and the sense of airiness and light denied to most dwellers below him in the crowded city.

Soon after he had passed the church of St James, Garlickhythe, Jack Knollys realized that he was being followed. He glanced very briefly over his shoulder, and his trained eye, passing over the people walking just behind him, saw the ungainly bulk of Francis Xavier Mahoney, walking at a swift pace, clutching a dangerous-looking weighted stick, and making a clumsy attempt to hide his face in the upturned collar of his jacket.

Jack Knollys felt a sudden surge of excitement. He was no stranger to men of Mahoney's ilk. Mahoney would have regarded

219

the man whom he had stunned but not killed at Carmelite Pavement as a piece of unfinished business.

Knollys would lead his opponent into a trap from which there would be no escape. He slowed down his pace, in order to give his pursuer the chance to catch him up. He crossed Upper Thames Street, weaving his way through the traffic, and hurried down the lane that took him out on to the stone flags of Syria Wharf. He glanced up at the looming bulk of the great warehouse, with its stark inscription in huge white letters above the upper ranks of windows: A. BERG. IMPORTER.

Mahoney was still following him, blundering along the lane. Knollys allowed himself to be seen for a moment, and then stepped into the dark vestibule housing the building's hydraulic lift. There was a staircase at the other end of the warehouse, but access to Knollys' apartment was gained from the lift.

He pulled both pairs of lattice gates closed, and waited until he saw Mahoney enter the vestibule. The man saw him, and rushed forward with a bellow of rage. Knollys pulled the lever that started the mechanism, and the lift began its creaking ascent through the brick shaft. He saw the killer's wrathful face looking up at him, and when he had passed from sight, he heard the man rattle the outer gates in frustrated anger.

What should he do? It would be a mistake to let the man gain entry to his own quarters. If there was to be another fight, then it needed to be in the open. He would take the lift up into its weathered cage on the roof, directly under the steel structure that housed the winding-cable and other mechanisms of the lift machinery. An iron arrow in a half-circle of numbers above the lift gates told to what floor the lift had climbed. Whatever the danger, Mahoney, he knew, would come after him.

The flat roof of Berg's warehouse held no convenient hiding places. Apart from the structures connected with the lift, it was innocent of any other buildings. It stretched from the river on one side to the crowded thoroughfare of Upper Thames Street on the other, flat and without parapets, lead-covered, and swept by a strong humming wind. Knollys stood at a point midway between river and road, and waited.

Presently, the winding-wheel and cable began to turn in their housing, and the lift moved down out of its cage to the floors below. The minutes following seemed like hours. All that could be heard was the humming of the aerial wind high above Syria Wharf.

Then the lift appeared in the cage, and before Knollys could act, Mahoney had ripped open the gates and was charging towards him, his weighted stick flailing through the air. Knollys could hear his heavy breathing, and saw the settled determination in the man's brutal face. Thr flailing stick struck him a stinging blow across the arm, and he fell down on to the roof.

Mahoney flung the stick aside, and hurled himself on to Knollys, pinning him to the leads with his bulk, his murderous hands seeking for his throat. Knollys waited for the fumbling fingers to find their mark, and then suddenly jabbed his raised knees into Mahoney's stomach. At the same time he brought up his massive forearms crosswise over the killer's chest, and flung him aside like a rag doll.

Knollys scrambled to his feet, and fumbled for his handcuffs, but in seconds Mahoney had rolled sideways and up on to his feet in a single movement. Evidently, he was far more nimble than his lumbering gait suggested. But Knollys' action reminded him too closely of Curteis' physical teasing. Roaring with blind rage, he charged towards Knollys, arms outstretched like the claws of a pair of pincers, only to reel under a sudden and quite unexpected straight left from his opponent.

Mahoney lurched backwards, his eyes temporarily glazed. Seizing his chance, Knollys rushed to where the weighted stick lay on the roof and, as Mahoney was still trying to recover his senses, he threw the stick between the thug's unsteady legs. Once he was down on the roof, he could be secured and taken into custody.

Mahoney seemed unable to steady himself. He staggered backwards towards the perilous edge of the roof, his eyes still glazed, and his arms flailing in the air. Very few men could have withstood a straight blow from one of Knollys' deadly fists, and Mahoney was no exception. Jack Knollys suddenly realized what was going to happen. Forgetful of his own safety, he darted forward, intending to pull the man away from the edge.

Mahoney interpreted the move as a further deadly attack, and instinctively retreated. He uttered a kind of strangled bleat of fear, and toppled backwards, arms flailing, off the roof. His shocked opponent waited for the high scream of a doomed man, but no such harrowing sound came to his ears.

Knollys stood in stunned silence for a while, listening to the high wind moaning across the rooftops. Above him, a few small white clouds scudded across the tranquil blue sky. Not trusting his own legs to do his bidding, he fell to his knees, crawled towards the edge of the roof, and looked down. Far below, a shapeless figure lay on the flags of the wharf, and a stream of men was running towards it, like a column of ants drawn to one of their number that had been crushed and killed.

The convalescent home in the pleasant little Surrey town of Esher was a long, two-storeyed mansion in five acres of wooded grounds. Mr Toby Box, Arnold Box's 73-year-old father, sat in his wooden wheeled chair under the shade of a stately oak tree, talking to his son, and his son's lady friend, Miss Louise Whittaker. A rustic table near his right hand held a number of letters and a few books. It was the hot and hazy twelfth of August.

'I don't know how this Mrs Pennymint of yours found out about it, Arnold,' said Toby Box, 'but it's quite true. They're coming to measure me for a false leg next Wednesday. I thought it was going to be a timber toe, like Long John Silver's got in Mr Stevenson's tale. But no, it's a proper leg, with a real shoe at the end. Wonderful what they can do, these days.'

He turned an appraising eye to Louise, who was looking very

cool in a long linen dress and matching white, wide-brimmed hat.

'So everything turned out well for you in the end, didn't it, Miss Whittaker? Arnold was telling me that Peto's Bank was taken over by Sir Hamo Strange. So you'll be spared the workhouse, God be praised!'

Louise Whittaker laughed, and glanced at her friend Arnold Box. He had blushed to the ears at his old father's quaint way of putting things. This was her second visit to Esher. On the first occasion, she and the old retired police sergeant had taken to each other immediately.

'I'll leave you two together,' she said, rising from the basket chair in which she had been sitting. 'I want to examine that fine herbaceous border across the lawn.'

When Louise had gone, old Toby Box fixed a quizzical eye on his only son.

'Arnold,' he said, 'are your intentions to that young woman honourable?'

'Certainly not!' cried Box confusedly, blushing again. 'At least— Well, you know what I mean. Really, Pa, the things you say! And she's not a young woman. Well, she is in one way, of course, but she's a friend, that's all. She's far too good for me—'

'Dear me, Arnold, if you blush any more like that, you'll make me think you've swallowed a beetroot! Of course she's too good for you, but that shouldn't stop you proposing when the time's right. She likes you, you know. She's told me so. And she admires you, too, which is understandable—'

'Have you finished, Pa? All this is very embarrassing.'

'Yes, I've finished. Now, here's something that will interest you.' Toby picked up an envelope from the table, and extracted a letter. 'This came only yesterday from Australia, Arnold. It's from a parson in Adelaide to say that your Uncle Cuthbert's dead.'

'Cuthbert?' said Box faintly, recalling Mrs Pennymint's revelation. 'I haven't got an Uncle Cuthbert.'

'We never mentioned him in the family, Arnold. Your poor

mother would never allow his name to be spoken in the house. Bless the boy, he's gone *pale*, now! First red, then white. What's the matter with you? You'd better get back to London: I don't think the air here agrees with you. Here's Miss Whittaker now. Go on, take her back with you to London. And remember what I said. When the time comes, pop the question. I think you'll be very surprised at the answer.'

Louise Whittaker came smiling to him across the grass, and when they had said farewell to Toby Box, they passed through the gate and into the winding country lane that would take them to the station of the London and South Western Railway.